WELCOME TO

The Abyss line of cutting-edge psychological horror is committed to publishing the best, most innovative works of dark fiction available. Abyss is horror unlike anything you've ever read before. It's not about haunted houses or evil children or ancient Indian burial grounds. We've all read those books, and we all know their plots by heart.

Abyss is for the seeker of truth, no matter how disturbing or twisted it may be. It's about people, and the darkness we all carry within us. Abyss is the new horror from the dark frontier. And in that place, where we come face-to-face with terror, what we find is ourselves.

"Thank you for introducing me to the remarkable line of novels currently being issued under Dell's Abyss imprint. I have given a great many blurbs over the last twelve years or so, but this one marks two firsts: first *unsolicited* blurb (*I* called *you*) and the first time I have blurbed a whole *line* of books. In terms of quality, production, and plain old story-telling reliability (that's the bottom line, isn't it?), Dell's new line is amazingly satisfying . . . a rare and wonderful bargain for readers. I hope to be looking into the Abyss for a long time to come."

—Stephen King

TURN THE PAGE FOR MORE EXTRAORDINARY ACCLAIM

PRAISE FOR *ABYSS*

"What *The Twilight Zone* was to TV in 1959, what *Night of the Living Dead* was to horror films in 1968, what Stephen King was to dark fiction in the mid-70s—Abyss books will be to horror in the 1990s."

—Mark Hurst, editor of *The Golden Man*

"Gorgeously macabre eye-catching packages . . . I don't think Abyss could have picked a weirder, more accomplished novel [than *The Cipher*] to demonstrate by example what the tone and level of ambition of the new line might be."

—*Locus*

"A splendid debut."

—*Rave Reviews*

"Dell is leading the way."

—*Writer's Digest*

"They are exploring new themes and dimensions in the horror field. My hat's off to Koja, Hodge, Dee and Dillard, as the others forthcoming! And hats off to Dell Abyss!"

—Gary S. Potter, *The Point Beyond*

FACADE

KRISTINE
KATHRYN
RUSCH

A DELL BOOK

Published by
Dell Publishing
a division of
Bantam Doubleday Dell Publishing Group, Inc.
666 Fifth Avenue
New York, New York 10103

ISBN: 0-440-21290-1

Printed in the United States of America

Published simultaneously in Canada

March 1993

10 9 8 7 6 5 4 3 2 1

OPM

To Dean for introducing me to the sea,
among other things

And in memory of Buglet,
who was always there,
always opinionated,
and always loved.

ACKNOWLEDGMENTS

I owe a large debt on this book to Jeanne Cavelos, for providing me with her insightful comments which helped in the revision; to Alan Brennert for letting me see his little corner of Hollywood; to Harlan and Susan Ellison for the fun, and the great conversations; and to Richard Curtis for all his support and good advice.

OPENING
SCENE

Take One

(Now)

FADE IN:
EXT. VILLAGE STREET ALONG ROCKY SEASHORE. OPEN with water breaking along the rocks, surf splashing over the edges of the cliff, spraying bypassers on this street in a small seaside town. In the distance, a lighthouse looms. Gray clouds overhead, old gray buildings weathered by the ocean—even the bypassers are gray. The entire area evokes a mood of gloomy darkness. Shoot almost FILM NOIR, gritty and shadowy, à la 1930s B movies.

ANTHONY SHORT and his cat, RUMBLES, stroll across the road. Rumbles is half Siamese, half everything else, all mouth and no substance. Short is tall, lanky, and very impressive. His rain cape billows out behind him, making him look as if he is flying.

"Cut! Cut! Dash it, Thomas, the coat is supposed to billow out behind you. You're supposed to look important, not like the Wicked Witch of the West after she's met with a bucket of water."

Thomas shakes the moisture out of his black hair. Skizits, the cat, easily drops her Rumbles role and runs for a drier section of road. "Sorry," he says.

The camera crew relaxes. One of the grips reaches beside his chair for a thermos. The assistant director checks the script as if it is at fault for the flub instead of Thomas.

"Sorry? Sorry?" Michael takes a step closer to him. "We only have the morning to do the damn opening scene, and all you can say is sorry?"

Fifteen people wait for him. The cameras and equipment hide the road. Thomas turns away from them, and gazes at the lighthouse, half lost in the morning mist. "I'm not much for grimy sea-scapes," he says.

(Then)

The house had a heavy, wet look. Ocean-logged, as Heather would have called it. A shutter banged against the frame. The wind off the sea rose bitter here; its cold bit into his unprotected skin. Thomas climbed onto the porch without grabbing the rail. The wood groaned beneath his feet.

"Twenty-five thousand?" he asked the realtor.

She nodded. The wind whipped her brown hair against her face. She looked reluctant to enter the house. He had been the one who suggested it. The place looked perfect, off on a side road, near the ocean, private and cheap. Too cheap to trust.

He waited for her to open the door. She shrugged. "It's not locked," she said, hanging back.

The shutter banged again. The wind gave this

old house life. He grabbed the brass knob, twisted it, and shoved the door open. No one had entered for a long time. A thin layer of dirt carpeted the floor. The air smelled musty, damp, closed in. He glanced back at the realtor. She huddled against the house, her arms crossed in front of her chest as a protection against the wind. He could see the ocean behind her, waves wild, foaming, crashing on the beach. "You coming in?"

For a minute, he thought she was going to say no. Then she smiled tightly and pushed past him. He watched her walk into the empty, open living room as if she had never seen it before. Slowly, he let the door slide closed. It slammed, making him jump even though he expected the sound.

"Tell me what is going on." His voice echoed in the room.

Her hands clutched at her sweater and a slow flush rose in her cheeks. She looked like Heather at three—trapped and unable to lie. "A woman was murdered here. Awful thing. Her blood painted across the walls—" The realtor laughed nervously. "Here I am trying to sell you the house and I tell you something like that."

"At least you're honest." Thomas took a step inward. A large brick fireplace dwarfed the room. The walls were white, the paint carrying an unused, new look. The kitchen stood off to the right. Thomas walked into it. Under the dust, the cabinets wore a fresh coat of varnish. The appliances were about three years old—he recognized the make and model from his year as Mr. Appliance—and still bore a local store's stickers. No-wax tile, obviously not original to the house, covered the floor.

"The kitchen is big enough for a table and a china hutch. The appliances are new, never been—"

"Yes, I see that." Thomas didn't care if he sounded harsh. He had given her a chance to do her job earlier. Trying to sell the house now only irritated him. "She died down here?"

"No." The realtor's voice had become small. "Upstairs. But then he dragged her down the steps—"

"He? They caught the guy?"

"No, but he was sighted, running from here, his cape billowing out behind him in the fog."

Thomas smiled. It sounded like a gothic. Something in black and white. Not film noir, but using shadows like poetry used words, to obscure and enlighten at the same time. "Enough to know he wasn't local, huh?"

"It was three years ago."

"Then why are you so frightened?"

"Steve usually shows this place. He's on vacation." She rubbed her hands against her upper arms. "I've never been here before."

Thomas nodded. "I'll look at the upstairs by myself," he said. The stairs ran off a small hallway opposite the kitchen. He climbed the steps slowly, noting the high polish and the nail holes in the wood. The stairs opened into an attic room with no hallway. The ceiling was low; he had to walk in the middle so that he could stand upright. The faint scent of fresh paint still lingered, but the window was covered with three years' growth of spiderwebs and grime. He cleared the dirt away.

The ocean roared below him, in constant motion. Waves broke against the rocks off to his left. The waves pulled at the beach, as if trying to drag it back into the ocean—recapture it, reclaim it. Thomas watched, finding the water's violence both soothing and disturbing.

The room felt cozy. He could imagine himself, lying on his bed, staring at the ocean in the dark.

He gave the rest of the house a cursory look, noting the bathroom's old paint and rusty shower, the tiny laundry room, and the dank, dark basement. Then he stopped beside the realtor. She was standing in front of the large picture window, still hugging herself as she stared at the sea.

"Steve picked a bad time to go on vacation."

She jumped. One hand covered her mouth as if to block a scream. When she saw him, she relaxed slightly.

Thomas smiled. "I'm going to buy it."

Take Two

(Now)

FADE IN:
EXT. LIGHTHOUSE, tall and imposing against the broad expanse of sky. The white paint has turned gray from years of standing so close to the ocean. A railing runs about the base of the house, though no one stands be-

fore it. Waves hit the cliffs below, spraying the area with water as dark as the clouds.

ANTHONY SHORT and his cat, RUMBLES, walk to the edge. Short grabs the railing and leans into the spray. Rumbles stands at his feet, ignoring the water as it pours over her.

"Cut! Cut!" Michael stands up. His rain slicker is dry. "Thomas, we'll never finish this bit if you don't follow the bloody script."

Thomas nods and picks up Skizits who is rooted to her spot. "I don't understand why standing at the railing is necessary. It looks slippery and dangerous there."

The members of the crew get up and move away. These conversations have become commonplace, and the crew uses them as breaks.

"It's an establishing shot." Michael takes a deep breath and then releases it, as if he is trying to calm himself. "You're the first actor I know who can handle the interior dialogue but mucks up the establishing shots. They're the bloody easy ones, Thomas."

Water splashes against Thomas. He turns, protecting the cat from the droplets, but she shudders anyway. The sea froths below them, laughing at Thomas for cringing.

"I don't know what's so easy about them," Thomas murmurs.

(Then)

He found her sitting on the doorstep his third day in the house. She had her jacket wrapped tightly about her body, her hands stuck in the pockets. She didn't say hello as he approached, but stood, sniffled, and wiped her nose with her sleeve.

He didn't say hello either. He shifted the grocery bags slightly so that he could extend the hand holding his keys. She grabbed them and opened the door as if she had been doing so for years. He hurried into the kitchen, set the bags down on the counter, and turned to see if she had followed him.

She hadn't. She was standing in the living room, staring at the poster for his latest film. Finally, she looked at him. Her cheeks were ruddy with the cold and there were deep shadows under her brown eyes.

"You're taller," he said, knowing that he had to make an obligatory remark about her appearance.

"Thinner," she corrected. She shoved her hands back into her pockets, uncertain about her welcome. "And no. Mother doesn't know that I'm here."

He reached into the grocery bag and pulled out food for his single lifestyle: TV dinners, hamburger, boxed meals, and four six-packs of diet Coke. "You want something?"

"Coffee." She sniffled again. He dug further in the bag, brought out a box of Kleenex, and handed it to her. His mother would never have allowed him to drink coffee at thirteen, but he didn't say anything.

"All I got is instant."

"Fine." Heather opened the box, tossed the oval-shaped cardboard onto the counter, and pulled out a tissue. She blew her nose loudly, then set the used Kleenex beside the cardboard.

"Garbage is under the sink." The first fatherly thing he had said. He didn't feel like much of a father—it was a role he played for one week annually, a part in summer stock forgotten as quickly as it had been learned.

Heather grabbed her garbage, opened the door under the sink, and tossed everything away. Then she closed the door and leaned against the basin, still hugging her coat to her chest.

Thomas handed her the kettle. "Take off your coat and stay awhile," he said.

She took the kettle from him. He turned his attention back to the groceries. The bag rattled against his arm as he pulled out lettuce, cucumbers, and some Ivory soap. He glanced over at Heather; she was struggling to turn on the faucet. He reached over and yanked it for her. With a squeal of rusted metal, the handle turned. Water splooshed out of the pipe and sprayed against the top of the kettle. Heather wiped her face with her free hand, then shut the faucet off.

"What the hell are you doing on the Oregon coast?" She didn't look at him. Her tone was not conversational. It had an element of blame.

He watched her set the kettle on the front burner and turn on the stove. "Hell" was a new word. The attitude was new too. He pictured three scenarios: in the first, he took his father's tactic and yelled about Heather's vocabulary and immediately alienated her; in the second, he answered her question, ignoring all the complexities; and in the third—

"How did you find me?" he asked.

"Connie."

His agent. She was probably wondering why *she* hadn't heard from him. "I've got to let your mom know you're here."

Heather sighed. Beside her the kettle rattled. "I know. Connie explained it to me. 'He's famous, you know' "—Heather mimicked Connie's nasal Brooklyn tones perfectly—" 'We can't have some kidnapping scandal hit him now.' "

Not exactly the most tactful woman. But then that was Connie's strength in Hollywood. Thomas reached up and took a mug from the cupboard. It was tall and had a lighthouse painted on the front. He had picked it up the morning before in one of the little touristy shops that lined Highway 101. "I was actually thinking she might be worried," he said.

"Mom? She doesn't worry." Heather pulled open a cupboard door. "Where's the—oh." She took the coffee off the shelf, twisted off the top, and poured the freeze-dried granules into the mug. "Can we at least wait until tomorrow to call her?"

"No," Thomas said. He folded up the grocery bag and put it next to the garbage under the sink. The kettle made a slow whine. "You'll call her tonight, tell her you're with me, and you don't know when you're coming home. Tell her I'll talk to her later."

The kettle screamed. Heather shut off the burner and poured the hot water into the mug. "I suppose you want me to do that now."

He handed her a spoon. She took it, swirled it in the mug, then wrapped her hands around the lighthouse.

"It would probably be a good idea," he said. "The phone's in the living room."

She sighed, took her mug with her, and headed out of the kitchen. She had gotten thinner. Much thinner. Her legs were like sticks. "And take off your coat," he said.

Heather didn't seem to hear him or, if she had, she didn't want to obey. She sat in the big green armchair by the picture window and cradled the phone's receiver between her ear and shoulder as she dialed.

Thomas watched her, wondering what role to slide into—father or friend. He decided not to decide, to wait and see what she needed most.

Take Three

(Now)

FADE IN:
EXT. HOUSE ON DESERTED BEACH-FRONT. OPEN with wild sea. Waves compress into the rock crevices, then spout into the air as they break, sending spray to the

edge of the lawn. The empty house stares at the sea. No one has lived here in decades.

ANTHONY SHORT walks purposefully up the porch steps. His cat, RUMBLES, follows, but stops on the second step to lick her paws. Short approaches the door and Rumbles screams.

"Cut! Cut!" Michael's voice follows Thomas across the beach. Thomas runs in sand, his feet sinking, his legs aching. The wind whips across his face and he can taste sea salt in the air. Spray washes his face. The ocean pounds with his footsteps. "Will someone stop that lunatic?"

Thomas stops running on his own. He can't see the man anymore—hasn't seen him since leaping off the porch. Two grips run up alongside him, tall men, big, like bouncers in a single's bar. One puts his hand on Thomas's arm. "You okay, Mr. Stanton?"

Thomas wipes the sweat off his forehead. "Did you see him? The man in the cape?"

The grip looks at his companion, then frowns. "That was you, sir. They caught your reflection in the glass they were moving for the next scene."

"Are you ready to work?" Michael yells. He is still standing by the house, the cameras crowded behind him like bodyguards. He looks tiny, ineffectual, D.W. Griffith beside a director's chair, clutching a bullhorn.

"Not here," Thomas whispers. "Not ever."

(Then)

He bobbed into wakefulness, narrowly missing the low ceiling as he sat up. His throat was dry, his heart pounding. Moonlight streamed across the bed. Downstairs, a shutter banged.

He threw back the covers, grabbed a robe, and started toward the stairs. Then he stopped. Heather was thirteen. If she was frightened, she would come for him. The creaking stairs would probably wake her and she would resent him for interrupting her sleep to calm his own fears.

He never worried about her when she was with Marge. Strange that he would worry now.

The shutter banged again. In the morning he would have to fix it so that he could sleep on windy nights. He tossed his robe on the bed and walked over to the window. The moonlight trimmed fifteen pounds off his naked body, hiding the paunch he was gaining, making him look twenty-five again. He ran his hands down his sides, feeling the layer of skin that was still there. In the morning, too, he would start running and maybe ask Heather to join him.

She had changed, his daughter, become tight, suspicious, too thin and cold, always cold. She had picked at dinner and said nothing. He wasn't the enemy, but he was little better since he had made her make the phone call. He hated the anger he felt wave off her, never permitted it in himself. Perhaps, in time, she would tell him why she had run away. Or maybe she wouldn't. He still hadn't decided what role to play.

A final bang—loud, sharp, like a pistol shooting blanks. Thomas leaned out the window in time to see a figure running down the beach. The water foamed and once Thomas thought the figure would get dragged in. The moonlight reflecting off the sand sharpened the world's edges with the clarity of day. Thomas stared at the runner—a man, his cloak billowing out behind him—and then remembered the realtor's words about the three-year-old murder.

His fear was back, strong, rising in his throat like bile. He grabbed his robe and shoved his arms in its sleeves as he ran down the stairs. His feet thudded against the wood—Heather would hear the panic in all of his movements. He ran across the hardwood floor and into the living room.

Covers trailed off the couch. The pillow was crumpled between the back and the armrest, and the bottom sheet had been scrunched. The kitchen door stood open, the room dark and empty.

"Heather?" His voice echoed in the still house. "Sweetheart?"

Nothing. No reply. Her clothes were piled beside the couch, where she had left them, her coat tossed casually over the armchair by the phone. The screen door was open. As he watched, it banged against the frame, and slowly eased open again.

"Heather?"

He went to the door, pushed it open, and stepped out on the porch. The weathered wood was cold against his bare feet. He traced the length of the porch, shivering in the damp, looking across the sand and seeing nothing but the ocean, frothing ghostly white in the moonlight. Finally he went in the back door—unlocked, damn his absentmindedness—and through the foyer.

"Heather?"

She wasn't upstairs or down. He checked the basement, turning on the light so that he could see past the cobwebs, afraid he might find her, crumpled like her bedclothes at the bottom of the stairs. Nothing. No one.

He walked to the living room, feeling shell-shocked, trying to ignore the fright. He turned his back on the empty couch as he picked up the phone to tell the authorities that his daughter had disappeared.

Take Four

(Now)

FADE IN:
EXT. RUGGED CLIFF-FACE SHROUDED IN FOG. The sea has receded—the tide is out. The sand below looks black and wet. An occasional gull cries, but the land is deserted.

ANTHONY SHORT stands on the edge, dangerously close—is he going to jump?—and stares wistfully at the sea. His cat, RUMBLES, sits beside him. She wails. Short leans—

Thomas falls. Rocks scraping his legs, his back. He brings up his arms to protect his head. All around him he hears the slither of falling rocks, the screams from above—Michael—"Cut! Cut! Stop the goddamn cameras. Catch him, someone, and move that blooming cat!"

Thomas clutches at the rock face, but it is slippery, wet. He can feel the skin along his palms tear. Something pops as his shoulder rips, and the pain of bumping, slipping, falling against hard pointed stone takes his breath away.

He can hear the roar of the sea, and he wishes it were there to catch him as the sand looms toward him, damp, and cold, and flat. They make concrete from sand, he thinks, then tucks himself into a ball. Balls bounce. Thomas doesn't.

ACT ONE

1

Marge called it morbid, and perhaps it was—returning to the sight of his daughter's disappearance and death—but Thomas thought it fitting somehow. He leaned on his crutches and stared at the ocean. The sun sparkled off the waves as they tumbled their way to shore. The smell of salt and moisture was strong here, natural, not cloying, almost soothing. A group of tourists—a mother, father, and two daughters—bumped him in their haste to get to the beach. He watched them, feeling wistful.

He had never had a traditional family. His parents divorced when he was twelve, and he had been shuttled back and forth between his mother's house and foster homes. He had married Marge, dreaming of a ranch house with a two-car garage, but somewhere that dream had been lost in casting calls and bit parts. By the time Heather was born, he spent more than half the year away from home, working, and sleeping with women not his wife. When Heather turned five, he left home for good and thought he had no regrets.

The mother spread a blanket on the beach. The father helped his daughters take off their shoes. Then they walked along the sandy edge, tracing the morning's water line and examining stones half buried in the wet. The sea slid up the shore, tickling their feet. The girls giggled and ran, and their father watched, smiling.

Thomas's leg ached. He turned away from the lookout point and crossed the parking lot. A young couple necked in the front seat of the first car he passed. The second car, a dark blue station wagon with California plates, was filled with toys, pillows, and luggage. It probably belonged to the family.

He walked across the street to a large bakery. A bell tinkled as he pulled the door open. The bakery smelled of fresh dough and chocolate. Three families still crowded the tables, but a chair near the window was open. He hung a crutch on it and limped toward the counter. The woman behind it flashed him a smile—the one she gave all the tourists—as she grabbed the bismarck he ordered from the two remaining on the tray. He paid her for the food and a cup of coffee that he had to pour himself from a side table. The coffeepots were full, but the table bore the marks of heavy usage—spilled creamer, cup rings, crumpled napkins, and used swizzle sticks. He hadn't been on the coast in the summer, hadn't realized what the locals had complained about, how the tourists took over everything. But Seavy Village, although it was sprawled along the coast, had a population of ten thousand and even a handful of people would have been noticed. The tourists arrived by the dozens, filling every restaurant, hotel, and sidewalk to capacity.

He moved his crutch and sat down, watching the people through the window. The ones who wore shorts and tank tops were tourists; the natives had enough sense to wear jeans and summer sweaters. The temperature hovered around fifty-five here, although on some sunny summer days it might rise as high as seventy-five.

All of the people worried him. He kept expecting to hear the familiar squeal, followed by "Thomas Stanton! Are you Thomas Stanton?" or even more likely, "Jason Michaels! My God, it's Jason Michaels!" the soap character he hadn't portrayed in nearly five years. Only a few—the semicultured ones—would call "Anthony Short! Jesus, honey, look. It's that detective!" But so far, no one had recognized him.

Not that he blamed them. His bruises were fading—the left side of his face was a dull yellow now instead of deep purple—but he still had thirty pounds to lose from his hospital stay. Thomas Stanton was a slender, darkly handsome man who played the melancholy detective Anthony Short for public television. The man sitting in Seavy Village's only bakery was pudgy and unshaven, with a cast that ran up his entire left leg and eyes gray with pain.

He bit into the bismarck, relishing the doughy chocolate taste, and then took a sip of his coffee. A few people had recognized him, locals, people he had met in the few short weeks he had lived here before. A girl at the grocery checkout the night before asked him if he had really tried to commit suicide in Depoe Bay. He smiled at her, shook his head, and reassured her that it had been an accident, he had slipped on a rock during filming. If he was going to commit suicide, he almost added, he would do something surer, like a gun to the head.

The Short series was in hiatus, perhaps permanent hiatus, while he got his health back. He could have started shooting last week when they let him out of the hospital, but he refused. Marge's visit had thrown him. He needed time to think.

Superficially, Marge had looked lovely: she was still slender, and her brown hair had silver-gray highlights. But the circles beneath her eyes and the long, deeply etched lines in her face showed him that Heather's disappearance had weighed as much on her as it had on him.

Thomas took a sip of his coffee and pushed the half-eaten bismarck away. Two years. Heather had been missing for two years and finally they found her body, her skeleton actually, in one of the sea caves a mile from his house. "Sometimes the sea gives things back," the detective had said. But Thomas didn't believe it. He knew that nothing had been given back, only taken. Bones and dental records were not Heather—they were symbols of Heather's loss.

Marge thought him ridiculous, returning to Seavy Village once Heather's death had been confirmed. But it wasn't ridiculous; it was something he should have done earlier, but had lacked the courage. He had known two years ago that Heather was dead. She wouldn't have run away, not without her coat or the fifty dollars he had found in her pockets. They hadn't had a fight, and even though things were strained, they were getting along. She had come to see him, to talk to him, and in the middle of the night, while he slept, something had happened to her.

Now that he knew she was dead, he could find out what killed her. And, he suspected, it was something that the bevy of detectives he had hired wouldn't find. The secret was in the house, in the moonlight, locked in the confines of what the tourists saw as Seavy Village.

Thomas drank the last of his coffee and sighed. The time had finally come to move his things from the overpriced hotel room with a view of the highway to his house by the sea. The tiny, windswept house on a deserted stretch of beachfront road where he had last seen his daughter alive.

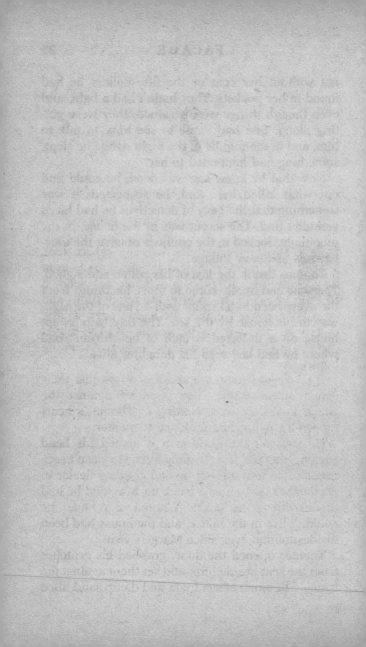

2

The house had the barren, forlorn look that most abandoned houses had, even though he paid a woman to clean it weekly. The house attracted him, and even after losing Heather, he hadn't been willing to give it up. Now, as he pulled into the gravel driveway, he had the strange feeling of coming home.

The sea was louder here. The waves lost their gentle shush-shush. They pounded against the beach as if they were beating it. Thomas's heart tapped a rhythm that matched the water.

He shut off the ignition and leaned his head back against the seat. Driving hurt. He wasn't supposed to do it at all, but he had gotten a dealer in Portland to customize a truck for him, and he had driven down the coast. Without a vehicle, he couldn't live in the house, and the house had been his destination ever since Marge's visit.

Thomas opened the door, grabbed his crutches from the seat beside him, and set them against the frame. The smell of sea foam and damp sand filled the cab. He pivoted his body, swung his legs out, and eased himself onto the ground. Pain shot up his leg, sending tears to his eyes. He would have to find a doctor near Seavy Village, someone to look at his leg and make sure that he hadn't done any serious damage to it in his travels.

A trail of fear settled in his stomach. The house's windows caught the light, reflecting it like the fathomless eyes of a cat. He half expected to see Heather sitting on the porch stairs, huddled in her coat, waiting for him.

Marge had never told him why Heather ran away. He suspected that there wasn't any one reason. Heather seemed to have left because she didn't like life with Marge—and she had come to him expecting something better.

He slipped the crutches under his arms. Something better from a man who bounced from project to project, whose entire experience of fatherhood was a series of strained "special" evenings in which the two of them stared at each other and tried to pretend they had something in common. Thirteen-year-olds were idealistic, Heather more than others.

The crutches leaned awkwardly in the gravel. He felt unsteady, uncertain, doubting his decision. The house had stood empty for two years. It held very few memories for him, but it held some: Heather spraying herself with water; the cloaked figure running in the moonlight. The Short filming in Depoe Bay had been the first time Thomas had returned to the Oregon coast. Heather had haunted him there in the grayness and the wet.

What would happen here, where she had actually stayed? Where she had died.

He leaned his weight on the crutches and pulled himself forward, careful to move only when he was certain that the crutches were securely placed. He would bring his luggage in later, when he was less tired, or maybe see if he could get someone out here to help him with the groceries and the other chores. He was supposed to be off his leg as much as possible. He knew that the doctor had meant bed rest, but Thomas wasn't the type to lie down. Especially when something bothered him.

The stairs were unevenly spaced and difficult to climb. He lifted himself carefully, knowing that if he fell it might be days before someone found him. The thought of falling made his heart ache. He got dizzy from standing up too fast, leaning over any edge. He had developed vertigo—and he had an irrational fear of the fear. Fear of falling reminded him of Jimmy Stewart and Hitchcockian camera angles spinning, spinning, creating a slightly sick feeling in the stomach—a feeling that he had too often lately, whenever his balance slipped slightly.

At the top of the porch, he stopped to catch his breath. The sea edged toward the beach, the white waves rolling in at irregular intervals. Living here would be like living next to a wild animal, unpredictable and lovely. He remembered the dreams he had had in the hospital—memory dreams of falling, landing on the sand, and then being eaten by the salt water seeping into his wounds. He shuddered. The sea didn't frighten him, but the sand did. He remembered its gritty taste against his teeth, the doctor saying that he had cleaned sand out of every wound in Thomas's body.

Thomas looked away and hobbled the last few feet to the front door, then fished for his keys in the front pockets of his pants. Nothing but some change and a few loose dollar bills. He had forgotten the keys in the ignition. A tiredness, deeper than any he had felt in days, swept over him. He would have to go back to the truck. Down the stairs and back.

Then he heard a smacking as the door opened. He took one quick step backward and nearly lost his balance. Fear jolted through him as, in his memory, sand rushed up to greet him. He leaned on the crutches, taking the weight off of his bad leg, his breath coming in heavy bursts. A girl stood behind the screen and, for a moment, he thought it was Heather.

"Mr. Stanton?" she asked. Her question snapped him to himself and he realized that she wasn't a ghost, but a girl, a real, live girl, a woman actually, the woman he had hired to clean the house.

"You startled me," he said.

She smiled and swung the screen door open. "I heard you were in town. I was getting it ready for you."

She stepped back so that he could go through the door. The house had a musty, unused odor. The furniture, the movie posters, everything looked as if it had been waiting for him, as if he had been gone only a few hours. He could almost see Heather's coat tossed across one of the chairs.

"Thank you, Mrs.—" Damn. He had forgotten her name.

Her smile grew wider, cracking lines in her face and revealing one missing tooth. "Carolyn." She closed the door behind him, then walked back to the kitchen. "I opened the windows to air out the place. And I put some fresh flowers in every room to lighten things up. My boy is going to bring over some groceries if you want and can help with anything you need." She shook her head. "Looks like we have to rig you up some kind of downstairs bed."

Her effervescence startled him, this woman with skin the texture of weathered wood. He remembered hiring her, remembered how quiet she had seemed, how serious. He had gotten used to that kind of treatment—his fame had given him a curious type of power—and he had almost forgotten how people acted when they were simply being themselves. In all the years of caring for his house, and of receiving his short notes along with the check, Carolyn must have felt as if she had gotten to know him.

"I was sorry to hear about the accident, sir," she said. "If there's something we can do. . . ."

"You're doing plenty. The place looks wonderful." And it did. The gray light from the picture window bathed the furniture. The wild roses on the end tables made the living room look like something out of *House Beautiful*. He got the sense, as he had on that strange, windblown afternoon with the realtor, that he could be happy in this house.

"That fall crippled you up pretty bad."

He looked back at her. Her gray eyes were filled with warmth. It tugged at a loneliness in him. "I'm doing a lot better than I was."

"Not good enough to be living way out here alone." She picked a dust rag off the arm of the couch. He hadn't even seen the cloth until she touched it. "If you want, me or my boy could check up on you every day, see if you need something."

Their presence would intrude on his solitude, bring something to the house that didn't really belong, but he knew that in a day or so, he wouldn't want to be so solitary. And she was right, in his condition, he needed someone to check up on him.

"I would like that," he said. "I'll pay you extra, of course."

"Do that, and I'll have to see to it that you get one good meal every day." Carolyn leaned against the couch. A slight blush touched her cheeks. "I got to say I was awful worried when I read about your accident. They weren't real sure there for a time what was going to happen to you, and, well, I did my talking to the Lord. Then when they found your little girl—" Carolyn shook her head. "You've had your share of burdens, Mr. Stanton."

The crunch of gravel echoed in the room as a car pulled into the driveway. Thomas welcomed the sound to free him from Carolyn's good wishes.

"That must be my boy," she said as she walked

to the door. "That's who I thought you were 'til I saw you trying the stairs."

The ache in Thomas's leg had grown fiery. He limped to the couch, set his crutches against the coffee table, and propped his leg up. Sitting down felt good. He watched as Carolyn opened the door to admit a man in his early twenties. Thomas had been expecting a boy; Carolyn hardly seemed old enough, despite her tough skin and bad teeth, to have borne the young man who towered over her.

"This is Ken," Carolyn said as if they were at some important social function. "Ken, say 'hi' to Mr. Stanton."

Ken nodded through the groceries. He hurried into the kitchen to set his burden down. Thomas could hear bags rattling, cans clinking, and cupboards closing, as Ken put the groceries away. Carolyn brought Thomas a pillow, and he leaned back, savoring the exhaustion in his body. The home sounds drifted around him as he sank into sleep.

Thomas awoke to the sound of children screaming. The light had moved out of the window; it was near dusk and the house was empty. Carolyn and Ken had left, but not before they set up a cot on the far side of the fireplace, and left his keys on the end table beside the couch. Thomas smiled, wondering what he had done to deserve such good treatment, and then decided not to reflect on it, uncertain about whether he would like the answer.

The scream came again, long and cold. Not the scream of a child having fun, but the cry of someone in pain.

He bolted upright, his mind already racing on how he could help, how he could move fast if someone needed him. He grabbed his crutches and made himself stand up carefully—he couldn't do much if he hurt himself again.

He hobbled over to the window. The beach was empty. A gull eased down onto the shore, picked in the sand, then flew off again. The ocean whispered to him, but the sound was more a part of the house than the outdoors. He saw no children, heard no more screams.

His heart pounded. Thomas limped toward the door, let himself out, and stood on the porch. The evening air was cool and he could feel the spray in it. The beach was empty for what seemed like miles. He shook his head. He must have dreamed the sound.

His heart was still pounding. He took several deep breaths to calm himself. Everything would not be peaceful here. He shivered in the cold and went back into the house.

The semidarkness made the place look foreign, grainy, like the stuff of a dream. He flicked on the light by the sofa and bathed everything in softness. It felt as if no time had passed since the evening Heather came to visit, as if he had just found the house and moved in.

He went into the kitchen, took out some hamburger, and made patties. He fried one and froze the others, relishing the simple tasks that no one had let him do in months. Maybe he wouldn't take Carolyn up on her cooking offer. Maybe he would do that himself.

He set the burger on the table, then pulled the thick file of detective reports out of his duffel. He had read the reports before, but now, living here, he hoped he would find a clue, something different, something he hadn't seen before.

The first file came from a reputable firm out of Portland. Of course, the reputation had come from successful divorce cases, but at the time, Thomas hadn't known that. Inside the file, he had stashed the report, police papers, and pictures.

Thomas put the papers aside and stared at the pictures. There it was again, that horrible evening, captured in black-and-white glossy. Heather's makeshift bed, with its crumpled bedclothes, dominated the living room. A footprint in the sand, a footprint that later turned out to belong to a careless sheriff's deputy. And finally, Heather herself. The photo had been taken three months before she had come to see Thomas. She had applied at a modeling agency—and a friend had taken enough pictures to fill a portfolio. Marge had brought the pictures with her. This one was the best of the lot, but the least like Heather.

Expertly applied makeup had leveled out the planes and hollows in her face, making them look like the caress of years rather than the results of excessive dieting. Her eyes were large, luminous, and dark—the eyes he had seen on Anthony Short, the detective—their expression alluring, mysterious. Her lips were parted slightly and an unseen wind blew her long hair behind her.

He stared at her hair for a moment, wishing the picture wasn't in black and white. He couldn't remember what color her hair had been. Not really. If pressed, he would have said brown, but whether it had been sandy brown or dark brown, with copper highlights or blond streaks, he couldn't say. The tragedy wasn't that he couldn't remember his daughter's hair color. The tragedy was that he had probably never even noticed.

He set the picture aside and took a bite out of

the burger. The meat was cool and raw inside, but he ate it anyway. He grabbed the stack of reports and thumbed through them, stopping occasionally as something caught his attention.

Heather had arrived on one of those buses tour groups chartered. She had booked at the last minute, taking a bus that was doing a quick tour of the coast, and she had asked to get off in Seavy Village. No one had talked to her on the trip except an elderly man, traveling alone, who later said that she had reminded him of his granddaughter. Then she had asked directions from the clerk in a local gift shop and had walked the three-plus miles to Thomas's house where, presumably, she had waited until he had arrived an hour or so later.

The detectives found nothing in the house. All the fingerprints belonged to Thomas and Heather. No footprints led to the beach or down the road. No one had seen her leave Seavy Village, and no one saw her in the surrounding area.

Thomas turned another page and found an analysis of his lie detector test. He stared at the document for a moment, the undigested hamburger twisting in his stomach. For three days, they had questioned him over and over, and his attorney had let them.

"You have nothing to hide, Thomas," he had said. "The worst they can decide is that you let her go for a midnight stroll and the sea took her."

They made him take the test twice. The first time, he had sat in the tiny room, listening to the scritch of needles behind him, his heart pounding against his chest. He had been so nervous that he had choked on his own name. He remembered everything he had read about the test—how it recorded differences in pulse rate and breathing—and he grew angry at his own nervous reaction. Still, somehow, he had passed. The little machine had claimed that Thomas had not killed his own daughter.

But a few items had made the tester curious and so they tested Thomas again. This time, he resisted. He had not been the perfect father to Heather, he knew that, acknowledged it, but that didn't mean that he had killed her. His attorney maintained they were doing it strictly for the publicity value, but he knew they actually believed he had gotten up in the middle of the night, strangled his daughter, given her to the sea, and then crept back into the house to call the police.

He had gone into that test upset at the police. So upset that he had called up his own shell, his acting shell, the one that protected him against stage fright, and answered each of the questions. Twice he had lied *on purpose* and neither time the machine caught it.

They had left him alone after that. The final verdict was that Heather had taken a midnight stroll and had lost a battle with the ocean. The cloaked figure Thomas had seen must have been Heather herself, running across the beach, pursued by her own demons.

The Portland detectives had concurred with that verdict. Thomas stuffed their report, along with the police reports back into the file. He left Heather's picture out.

He picked up his dishes, rinsed them, and set them in the sink. The next firm he had hired had specialized in criminal investigations. They had been from San Francisco. He could almost quote their report from memory. They had cited Thomas's knowledge of the house's history, the lack of footprints, fingerprints and other evidence, and had implied that Thomas made up the entire story. They hadn't gone far enough to suggest that he had killed Heather—after all, he was paying their fees—but the accusation was buried in the pages of the report.

Thomas had paid them, denying any requests for additional expenses, and immediately turned around and hired their rivals.

DeFreeze and Garity had spent nearly a year investigating the matter. They would send him tiny, updating reports with expense vouchers clipped to the paperwork, telling him nothing. The actual report, a tome the size of a script for a feature film, had arrived at his home in Hollywood while he was in Depoe Bay, filming Anthony Short. His agent had forwarded the report while he was in the hospital, but he had never read it. He could not face the thick pages after he had seen Margery.

Thomas sat back down at the table and pulled the report from its manila envelope. AN INVESTIGATION INTO THE DISAPPEARANCE OF HEATHER STANTON was emblazoned across the top. They had used a MacIntosh computer and the report almost appeared professionally published.

Heather's photo stared at Thomas. His eyes burned. He was getting tired again. For some rea-

son, this report frightened him. It was the last one
written before they discovered Heather's body, the
last one to have any hope that Heather was still
alive. By reading it, the fact of her death might
come clear to him, and he would know with a cer-
tainty, without that startled pain running up his
belly into his heart, that his daughter was truly
dead.

The scream echoed again outside. Thomas froze,
his hand on the clear plastic cover of the report.
He turned and looked out the kitchen window. A
gull flew by, its cry whipped and molded by the sea
wind until the thick, throaty bird-sound had human qualities.

He stuffed the reports back into his duffel. He
had had enough for one night. The final report
could wait for morning.

4

The air in Seavy Village always smelled like fall. Cool, crisp, with a tang of salt. Thomas kept his windows up, but the smell seeped into the pickup, rich and strong. Highway 101 was filled with campers and RVs, fast cars with out-of-state plates and drivers who shook their fists at anyone who got in their way. The pace made him think of California where everyone was late, late, running late, and he sighed. One of the things he had loved about the coast was its relaxed atmosphere.

He turned on Rhododendron Drive and immediately left the tourists behind. The town became sleepy again. An old man wearing loose trousers and a flannel shirt walked toward the lake. Seavy Village was sprawled between the beach and a small natural lake. Although the population was small, the town appeared twice as large as it was. And in the illogic of town planning, the ideal home sites were along the dying lake shore, near the thick weeds and algae, instead of the sand and expanse of the Pacific Ocean. The old man tipped his pipe at Thomas in greeting, and Thomas waved back. He followed the narrow, winding road around the rows of ranch houses half-hidden by rhododendron bushes, flowers, and thick pine-shaped shrubs until he saw the small sign. THE SEAVY VILLAGE GAZETTE. He stopped the pickup, swung himself out, and grabbed his crutches.

The building was an old white house, built in the late twenties, with wild roses climbing a trellis outside. The lawn was neatly mowed, and a red brick sidewalk led up to the door. If Thomas squinted slightly, he could imagine it as a single-family dwelling instead of an office. But the clack of typewriters, the open screen door, and the blinds on the picture window ruined the family effect.

He yanked the screen door open and hurried inside before it had a chance to close on his back. The door banged shut. The young man sitting at the desk looked up with a startled expression. His hair was red, he had a sprinkling of freckles across his cheeks and, if it weren't for the scruffy blue jeans and the Def Leppard T-shirt, he would have looked just like Jimmy Olsen out of the old Superman comic books.

"Hi," Thomas said.

The boy scrambled out of his seat, nearly knocking over the stack of papers near his typewriter. "Jillian!" he called, an edge of panic in his voice. "Jillian!"

A woman came around the beige office dividers. She too was wearing jeans, and a stylish white sweatshirt with the sleeves pushed up past her elbows. Wide glasses hid her nose and accented her eyes. Her hair, cropped short, looked as if she constantly ran her fingers through it.

"Can I help you, Mr. Stanton?" she asked and he blinked twice, not because she knew his name, but because such a cool, professional voice emerged from a woman who looked like she had been cleaning the garage. He was used to city women, Hollywood women, who felt naked without makeup and the latest Bill Blass.

"I, um, I would like to look in your archives." His voice sounded nervous, and he recognized the tingling in his stomach. Normally he would have been calm in a situation like this—he was Thomas Stanton, after all—but lately he thought that he had scraped off his self-confidence along with his skin as he slipped down that rock face.

The woman smiled. "We're just a weekly, Mr. Stanton. We don't have much. If you want information, you should drive up to the Newport library and dig through the *Oregonian*."

"I want to look up something local."

She pushed her glasses up with one finger. They slid back down to the edge of her snub nose. She glanced at the boy who hovered near the typewriter, eyeing Thomas nervously. "I suppose you can at least get a start here," she said. Then she extended her hand. "I'm Jillian Maxwell."

He had to lean forward and let his crutches dig into his armpits in order to shake her hand. Her palm was warm and dry, her bones delicate beneath his. "Thomas Stanton," he said unnecessarily.

"Let me take you into the morgue, such as it is."
She turned around and headed for the back of
the house. Thomas started at the ghoulish word,
then remembered that "morgue" was a newspaper term for file room. He got a good grip on his
crutches and followed her.

Three empty desks sat near the picture window.
Another, its top covered with papers, coffee cups,
and half-eaten pieces of fudge, dominated the center of the room. A hand-painted sign, with letters
like little quill pens, read JILLIAN MAXWELL. Jillian
stopped at the desk, opened a top drawer, and
pushed the contents around. Pens rolled against
the metal. Thomas looked at the pictures hanging
around the desk. One showed a long-haired Jillian
standing with President Carter in front of Air
Force One. Another was of Jillian bent over her
desk, head in her arms, asleep. A framed quote
written in black calligraphy—*God May Be the Su-
preme Being, But Even the Bible Had an Editor*—
hung above a newspaper clipping bearing Jillian's
picture and a headline—FIRST WOMAN NAMED EDITOR
OF GAZETTE.

"Found 'em!" she said. She clutched a ring of
keys in her hand. "We were vandalized in June
and since then we've been keeping most of the office locked. I'll be glad when the damn tourists
leave."

Thomas nodded. He was too busy watching Jillian. She was built small and slender and she
moved like a girl fresh out of college. But the pictures and the responsibility she had put her in her
thirties, at the youngest.

She unlocked a door, flicked on a light, and walked down two small steps. The musty, metallic scent of old books, ink, and file cabinets wafted up at him. "You be okay on the stairs?" she asked.

His answer was to take them, carefully, and stop in front of her. She smiled. Laugh lines were forming in the corners of her eyes. "Guess so," she said.

Then, as quickly as it appeared, the smile was gone. Jillian turned to the first file cabinet and touched the label. "Nineteen-eighty-six to the present," she said, "and it goes down from here. Sorry we're not real modern and don't have things on microfiche. You're going to have to be careful with the old clippings. We just don't have the money."

"I understand," he said.

The cool contempt in her gaze told him that he didn't. He found himself wondering what she made every year. Thirty thousand? Twenty? Ten? How could anyone live on sums that low?

"I'll come get you around quarter to twelve. We lock up for lunch."

"Thanks," he said. He watched her go back up the stairs and close the door. Then he headed for the drawer labeled 1982–'85.He had to use the cabinet itself for support to pull the drawer open.

It took nearly a half an hour of leaning on his good foot before he found the stories on the murder. He pulled the papers surrounding the incident, set them on the desk, then sat down. His entire lower body ached, his head throbbed, and tears lined his eyes. He pushed himself too hard.

He should have waited another month, until his body had had a chance to recover.

He didn't know how long he sat with his eyes closed, willing the pain to go away. Finally, it subsided enough for him to take a deep breath and thumb through the paper.

Her name had been Lisa Wilson. She had lived alone in the house, purchasing it after her husband had died. She had moved to Seavy Village from Seattle, and some of the locals speculated that she was running from something, although that had never been proven. What people did know was that she moved to Seavy Village in September and had made few friends by the time of her death in April.

The moon had been full that night. A young couple, newlyweds, were strolling along the road that ran parallel to the beach when they saw a figure in a cape running near the water's edge. The husband shouted to the figure, trying to warn him that the sea, tricky in the daylight, could be deadly at night. But at the sound of the man's voice, the figure ran harder and disappeared near the sea caves where Heather's body had been found.

The next morning, the mailman discovered Lisa Wilson's naked body sprawled on the porch. She had been stabbed nearly fifty times. Apparently, she had been attacked in her bedroom, then dragged down the stairs into the living room and left on the porch.

Grainy black and white photographs illustrated the articles. The pictures made his stomach turn. He lived in that house, had walked across the porch where a woman had died, had slept in the same room where she had first been stabbed. His movie posters covered the spot where her blood had decorated the walls and his daughter had disappeared through the same door as Lisa Wilson's murderer.

"That wasn't the first murder on that stretch of beach, you know."

Thomas jumped, his heart leaping into his throat. Newspapers scattered across the desk and his crutches clattered to the floor.

"Sorry." Jillian leaned over to pick up the crutches. "I didn't mean to startle you."

"That's all right," Thomas said, taking deep breaths to slow his pulse. "I've been nervous ever since the fall."

Jillian set the crutches against the desk and helped him gather up the papers. "What are you trying to do?"

He didn't know quite what he was trying to do. Saying he was looking for Heather's killer sounded too melodramatic, like the TV movies he had starred in around the time Jillian was posing with Jimmy Carter. Yet that was what Thomas was doing, searching for the way Heather had died, so that he could vindicate himself and move forward.

Jillian sat on the edge of the desk and studied him. He watched her look through him, into him, as if she were trying to see past the bruises, bit parts, and starring roles to Thomas Stanton. "Your daughter's death is part of a pattern," Jillian said. "She isn't the first woman to die on that stretch of beach, and I don't think she'll be the last."

"Why?" he asked.

She looked up at him, her eyes big through her glasses. He realized that she wasn't used to being questioned; she was used to asking the questions herself.

"Two years before Lisa Wilson died, a little girl was playing on the beach with her brother and her dog. The girl was about nine. It was the middle of the afternoon, dark—the clouds were thick. The children shouldn't have been outside, but their mother was sick and asleep in the house. She didn't even know they were gone until the boy came running in, saying a ghost had stolen his sister."

"In a cape?"

Jillian nodded. "Before that, it was a teenage girl whose boyfriend had left her after a fight. He felt bad leaving her there and drove back in time to see someone running. She had been stabbed too. There are more, scattered over the years. I've only been here since '80. When the little girl died, I wanted to trace the other murders and disappearances. I did a lot of research before the story was killed. It has all the makings of some kind of serial killing centered on that stretch of beach. An artist living near the beach was a suspect for a while, but then he was ruled out."

"No one told me when I bought the house."

She pushed her glasses up with the middle finger of her right hand. "And lose all the potential profit a celebrity would bring to Seavy Village? No one thought you were in danger. You're a man."

Thomas pushed the papers aside. This talk was making him dizzy. "I'm not convinced, Jillian."

"People around here like to believe the killings were random. They don't want to see any pattern." She took the clippings and refiled them, careful not to rip the paper. "But no one goes down to that stretch of beach either."

The room felt tight, closed in. Morgue was a good name for the place. "What do you think it is?"

"I don't know." She sighed. "If it was some maniac, he'd be doing other killings around town. No one lived in the house until Lisa Wilson. And I don't believe in ghosts. Sometimes I'd like to believe the killings are random too, but they aren't. I think someone is protecting something."

"From a little girl, two teenagers, and a sleeping woman?"

"I don't know, Thomas. Your daughter is dead. Why don't you leave it go?"

He stood up, proud that he didn't slip. Jillian gripped the file cabinet, her expression serious, as if she wanted to retract what she had just said. *No, wait, Mr. Stanton. I meant to say, "No comment." You aren't going to use that, are you?*

"Who took your picture with Jimmy Carter?" he asked.

Jillian frowned, unable to follow his mental leap. She looked wary. "A friend."

"Here in Seavy Village?"

"No." She ran her hand through her hair. Her fingers were shaking. He had succeeded. She was as off-balance as he was. There was something painful behind that Carter picture, something that Jillian didn't want to examine.

And he had poked at it. Purposely. Thomas, at his cruel best.

"I'm sorry," he said.

She shook her head. "I shouldn't have said that about your daughter."

He shrugged. "It's probably true."

They stared at each other for a moment, the thin threads of an understanding between them. She was the first person that he had met in almost a year that he wanted to see again.

Perhaps it was because she had information about Heather.

"I would like to talk with you some more," he said.

She nodded. "I have an interview to do and then some work to finish."

"Tomorrow? I'll make you lunch."

Her expression was tentative. "I would like that."

"Good." Thomas felt his pulse pounding against his throat. He hadn't been this nervous with a woman since college. "You know where to find me?"

She smiled. He liked the way it softened her face. "Of course I do, silly. The house on the beach. I have wanted to go inside there for a long, long time."

5

 He was upstairs, lying on his bed, his arms behind his head. His leg was throbbing, but whole; with its cast gone, it looked smaller than its fellow—a stick leg, like Heather's.

Moonlight carved a hole in the darkness. Outside, the surf sounded wild, crashing and booming below. The wind echoed in the room, rattling the windows, like it used to during thunderstorms in the Midwest. Something banged downstairs. He sat up—and found he was on the couch in the semilit living room, his coat tossed casually across a chair. He threw the covers back and stood. Another bang, sharp and commanding, came from the front porch. He rubbed his arms against the chill—the fire had died—and hurried to the door.

A scream, female and piercing, echoed from upstairs. Footsteps slapped against the floorboards above him, and he turned in time to see Heather, her hair trailing behind her—windblown like the photo—running down the stairs. She was naked, and he wanted to turn his head away, but he couldn't. When she reached the bottom of the stairs, she slipped and crumpled against the floor like used linen. A hand reached down and grabbed her hair—

Thomas forced himself awake. He lay on the cot, his heart pounding. His entire body ached from lying in one position too long. The fire had died in the fireplace; the glowing embers illuminated a room made too dark by the absence of the moon. He groped for his crutches, afraid to go back to sleep, afraid to see another hand reach down and slice Heather's throat.

The thought sent a shudder through him. He hadn't had a dream that vivid since—when? Since they had started shooting at Depoe Bay.

He found the crutches. They felt warm and solid against his fingertips. He picked the crutches up and stood, easing the crutches into position. They tugged at the hair in his armpits. His body, overweight and lumpy with fading bruises, embarrassed him. An actor's body was his instrument and, with the exception of the year Heather had died, Thomas had worked hard to keep his instrument in perfect condition. If he went back to work now, he would be suited only to character roles and bit parts, not the leading roles he had had so long.

Back to work. He hobbled along the living room floor until he reached the kitchen. Work felt alien to him, another world, one he had dreamed like that dream of Heather, filled with thought images and half-remembered pictures. He flicked on the light and the kitchen leapt to sharp life around him. The cabinets hung half-open, almost threatening him, and the shine of the appliances hurt his eyes. He blinked away the brightness, and then focused on the mess he had left on the table. Detective reports covered the surface and, in the center, the thick tome waited for his perusal. Heather's photo sat by itself on the table's edge. Beside it sat a mug half filled with diet Coke and a plate dotted with crumbs and the unchewable crust of an overcooked frozen pizza.

If Jillian saw this place now, she would be appalled. Or maybe not. He remembered her desk with its dirty coffee cups and half-eaten pieces of fudge. She had intrigued him. Perhaps he was getting better, to finally notice a woman with interest. He hadn't had a lover since Heather died. Every time he thought of taking a woman to bed, Marge rose in his mind—the young Marge, her stomach bulging with a half-formed child. He had thought it almost sick, his way of keeping Heather alive. But perhaps it had been an unconscious warning. He had been in a state of stasis, like a man wrapped in a cocoon. If a woman had broken through that shell, she would have found a nearly dead caterpillar or an unfinished butterfly, something she would have had to take care of for the rest of her life.

He slipped on the robe he had flung over his chair on the way to bed. The velvet felt good against his skin. He filled the tea kettle, holding it properly so that it didn't spray him, and set it on the stove. Diet Coke was the wrong thing for the middle of the night. It was a daytime drink, filled with sparkle and energy. He would make hot chocolate and savor it until he felt sleepy again.

He took out a mug, one that Carolyn had bought him, with a picture of the coast and the words SEAVY VILLAGE written beneath the dark brown lines. He put three scoops of cocoa mix in the cup and set it by the kettle. The burner was glowing red; he would have his drink soon. He sat down at the table and stared at the tome.

INVESTIGATION INTO THE DISAPPEARANCE OF HEATHER STANTON. He ran his fingers along the words. Amazing that a man could reach thirty-seven years of age, be a success in a profession that had too many failures, and still feel empty inside. He'd had a wife once, and a daughter, a daughter who had said to him when he arrived late for her fifth birthday party, "Mister? Do you know where my daddy is? He said he'd come."

He opened the book and flipped past the introductory pages, the table of contents, and the acknowledgments. He half expected to find a dedication ("to my loving wife") but knew that the detectives had been too professional for that. He rested his chin against his palm, and read.

The report started with Heather's life history. She had been born in Eisenhower Memorial Hospital in Palm Springs. He had not been present because, according to the detectives, Marge was leaving him. He hadn't known that; he had simply thought she had decided to stay with her parents until the baby was born. It did explain, though, Marge's coolness when he arrived two days later, typical movie-hero father, with an unlit cigar stuck between his lips and a large overstuffed panda bear in his arms.

He skimmed over the intervening years, the accounts of scrapes and bruises, grades, teachers, and childhood friends, stopping only at the divorce ("the little girl didn't speak to her mother for days when she learned that her father was never coming back"). The tea kettle's whistle brought him out of the document. He reached over, shut off the burner, and poured the water. Then he took the mug, careful not to spill it, and set it beside the report. He remembered Heather, clutching his lighthouse mug as if it could warm some cold spot inside, and he resisted an urge to do the same.

He started reading seriously the last year of Heather's life. She had returned from her final visit with him determined to be a model, someone beautiful, someone her father could respect. She stopped eating regularly and began to exercise, whittling her already slender body down to its finely etched bones. Marge sent Heather to a state hospital but she ran away, disappearing for nearly a week before the police found her and brought her home. Marge managed to enroll her for a second time late in the spring. Heather stayed long enough for the diagnosis to be confirmed: anorexia nervosa—severe and chronic.

He rubbed his eyes. The hot chocolate had cooled beside him, but he sipped it anyway. He had done an after-school special about anorexia, playing the overbearing, unseeing father, whose preoccupation with his work had driven his daughter to starve herself so that she could be beautiful for him.

"You're taller," he said.

"Thinner," she corrected.

He picked up the photo and stared at it for a moment. The hollows in her cheeks, the camera angle, the sharp edge to her nose gave her face an all-American beauty. He set the photo down, closed the report, poured his cocoa in the sink, and went back to bed.

6

He adjusted the paper napkin on the plate for the fourth time when a knock echoed through the house. The sound was sharp, intrusive, even though he had been expecting it. He took one final glance around the kitchen—dishes done and hidden, two simple place settings minus a candle (a candle seemed out of place somehow), and a trivet waiting for the main course—and hobbled to the door.

Jillian was looking across the porch at the ocean. The waves were calmer, rolling against the beach instead of pounding as they had in his dreams. He stared at her for a moment, smiling appreciatively as she ran a slender hand through her short-cropped hair. He took a deep breath and yanked the door open. The smacking sound made her turn, and he caught a glimpse of panic before her face slid into an insincere smile.

"Hi," she said.

"Hi." Thomas stepped away from the door. She came inside, her reporter's eyes taking in every detail. She probably expected blood on the walls, his daughter's clothes still huddling in their corner, but the room looked simple and elegant. Carolyn had kept the place spotless and the flowers fresh. He had built a fire in the grate.

"This is nice," she said. He could hear the surprise in her voice.

"I like it." He felt awkward, like a fifteen-year-old on his first date. "You want something to drink?"

She had gone over to the picture window. Sunlight filtered through the clouds, giving the ocean and the beach a light, almost wintry air. "A beer would be nice."

He hesitated too long, because she looked over her shoulder at him. Her glasses had slid down her nose. "Should I get it?"

"Oh, no." He scrambled toward the kitchen, feeling a blush rise in his cheeks. Somehow he thought that only Hollywood types drank during lunch. He never expected someone in the real world to touch alcohol before the end of the work day. He opened the refrigerator door, grabbed a beer for her and a diet Coke for himself—he needed to stay fresh, alert. Alcohol hit him much harder these days.

Thomas set the Coke on the counter and took the beer to Jillian. She eased the bottle out of his hand, took a long sip out of it, and sighed. "I never expected it to be lovely here," she said.

"You thought I was strange, living here, among all the cobwebs and death." His words sounded bitter; he winced inwardly.

But Jillian smiled. "Maybe. Heathcliff wandering the moors."

"Sounds romantic," he said.

"It's not." She took another sip of her beer. "*Wuthering Heights* is dreadfully morbid."

"I played Heathcliff once." He had almost forgotten that play, done years ago, when he was sitting next to Marge in English Literature.

Jillian was studying him. It seemed as if her cool gray eyes could see every memory he had stored, every thought he had hidden away. "You would have made a good Heathcliff."

He shrugged. "It was college."

A silence followed his remark and he felt awkward. Damn the woman for making him so uncomfortable. He never had this trouble, could always make conversation—and appropriate conversation at that.

Jillian held her bottle between two fingers. She looked as uncomfortable as he felt. "What's for lunch?"

"Oh!" Lunch. He had forgotten the casserole that Carolyn had left for him. He had been planning to cook himself, but then decided to ask for help at the last minute. This lunch with Jillian was important somehow, important because he wanted to make up for the day before. He felt as if it were his fault that it had gone so badly.

Jillian turned her head quizzically at him. "Did you forget to make it?"

"Damn near," he said. He went into the kitchen and opened the oven. The casserole was bubbling and dark brown. Saved—barely. He slipped a potholder glove over one hand and grabbed another potholder with the other. Then he steadied himself, and reached into the intense dry heat of the oven. The casserole was heavy, but didn't hurt his balance. He was getting used to standing on the mountain of plaster. He would probably be very uncomfortable when the cast came off.

"Smells good," Jillian said.

He set the casserole on the trivet, then smiled at her. Her cheeks had flushed in the heat rising from the open oven door. She shut off the oven and closed the door.

"I have a confession to make," he said. "I didn't cook it."

"I didn't expect that you did," she said.

Her remark, so casually made, so diffident, struck something inside him. "I was planning to," he heard himself say. The tone sounded defensive. "But I—I wanted it to be nice."

Jillian relaxed. She touched his arm. Her fingers were calloused on the edges. "It is nice, Thomas."

Her words pleased him more than a good review ever had. He indicated a place for her, then sat across from her and dished out the food. He didn't know how to swing the conversation to Heather and the murders. Maybe he didn't want to.

"Is it different here?" Jillian asked as she salted her food.

"Different?" For a moment his hand froze. Of course it was different. He was different. Heather's death had sobered him, destroyed a part of him that he hadn't known existed.

"Seavy Village," Jillian said. Her cheeks were flushed and he realized that it wasn't the heat, but an actual blush that had been building. "Weren't you filming here in '79?"

He frowned. 1979. Heather had been seven. What had he been doing that year?

"The articles said that Heather was with you. They had trouble getting her out of Seavy Village when she wanted to go home."

"That was here?" He had forgotten. No wonder this place felt like home. He had spent two weeks here, filming a stylish gothic horror film that had enough mystery to get him cast as Anthony Short years later. He had loved the beach and walked it a lot with that starlet—what was her name? Suzanne? "It was so long ago, I barely remember."

"That was the first incident that I could find," Jillian said. "That extra."

She had been eighteen. She hadn't shown up for work one afternoon and the director grabbed someone else from the pool of eager townies. That night, one of the cameramen discovered the girl's blood-soaked body on the beach. And that was when Thomas sent Heather home.

"There were a lot of strange things about that filming." He took a bite of the casserole. The combination of tuna and cream of mushroom soup made him think of his mother. She always made nice, wholesome one-dish meals to fatten him up. "Some of the crew found things in their rooms, bloated fish, dead gulls. Someone even found a finger on the beach."

And he and Suzanne had seen something one

night, something near the ocean front, by the house, something—

"Thomas?"

Jillian was looking at him expectantly. "You really didn't remember that when you bought the house?"

She asked the question in a way that made him realize she had asked him before. He had to keep paying attention.

"I remembered that we shot in Oregon. I didn't remember where." Even though a part of him had. Enough so that he had bought the house.

Jillian looked down at her plate. "Not the best conversation for lunch, is it?"

"It's what I wanted to talk about." Thomas scraped the last bits of casserole off his plate. "You have a theory."

"Not really," she said. "I just noticed how many people have died on this stretch of beach. I think there is something going on here and that no one wants to talk about it."

"You're in the position to get it talked about."

The smile on Jillian's lips didn't reach her eyes. "I already explained that one to you."

Thomas took another helping from the bowl. "You strike me as the kind of woman who could change that if she wanted to."

"I don't fight those kind of battles."

"Not anymore," he said.

She stopped eating. The expression on her face was surprise.

"I can see details too," he said. "That Carter picture. It takes a special person to be the White

House Correspondent for a major newspaper at what? Twenty-two?"

"Twenty-five," she said. "I wasn't White House Correspondent. And I was working for National Public Radio."

"And one year later," he said, "You came to the Oregon Coast where things are slow and decisions are focused on a local stretch of beach."

She laughed, but it sounded hollow. "More beer?" she said, holding up the bottle.

"In the fridge."

She got up. He shoved his plate away. The casserole looked runny and unappetizing. Famous actor realizes woman isn't impressed by home-cooked meal. He probably looked ridiculous to her. His conversation certainly was.

Bottles clanged together as Jillian closed the refrigerator door. She used the bottle opener to pry the top off, then took another long swig.

"I'm sorry," Thomas said.

She turned. Her eyes were wide and dark, her hair mussed. She pushed her glasses against her forehead. "I'm the one that's sorry. I come over here and drink like I can't keep my hands off the stuff."

She sat back down and spooned out more casserole. "Camp David was my first big story," she said. "The takeover of the embassy in Tehran was my last. I've been hiding out longer than I was actually working."

Her fork clinked against her plate. She pushed the food around. He gripped the warm Coke can.

"Jillian, you don't have to say anything. I shouldn't have pushed—"

"No." She set her fork down. "I want to tell you. It'll be the short version. I promise."

She ran her hand through her hair and set her plate next to his. Her fingers were shaking. He longed to reach out and hold them.

"I started out as a volunteer for a public radio station in Wisconsin my first year in college. By my sophomore year, I was covering local stories with national angles and reporting them for NPR. I decided to take my junior year off, and went to Washington, interned at *All Things Considered*. They hired me, shit jobs at first, but it didn't take long. I moved fast. And I got to know people. They trusted me. I seemed so young and innocent."

Thomas smiled. She still seemed that way to him. The brittleness felt like a patina that would disappear with a good polish.

Jillian sighed and took another sip of beer. "Nothing really went wrong. I was just doing news all the time. I worked constantly. Sometimes I would get so wrapped up in a story that I didn't even make it home to sleep. And when I did, my phone would ring at all hours. I kind of fell into the White House job—the regular reporter was sick, I took it, and the people there liked me. I made more than enough contacts. NPR had two White House Correspondents for a while. And Carter always liked talking to me."

She was toying with the edge of the trivet the casserole dish sat on. Thomas placed his hand over hers. Her fingers were surprisingly warm. "Burnout?"

"I don't know," she said. "I just woke up one morning and found I hated it. All of it. I just stacked everything in my car and drove. Ended up here on the coast, and somehow got this job. I never even called to say I had quit."

He waited for her to say more, but she didn't. Her thumb twitched nervously. "Reader's Digest Condensed version," he said.

She smiled. "Yeah. You know. They always leave out the good parts."

He nodded, squeezed her hand, and picked up the plates. Then, without leaving his chair, he set the dishes by the sink. White House Correspondent. That explained her ease with him. She was used to meeting famous people.

"You're good at that," she said.

"Have to be." He slid his chair back and got up. "Let's go into the living room. Would you mind bringing my Coke?"

"Sure," she said. He led them to the porch window and sat so that they could look out over the sea.

Large white-topped waves rolled in, pushing at the sand. The water had a life of its own, a feeling that he had never encountered anywhere else in nature. He wanted to ask about Heather, about the stretch of beach. But he also wanted to charm Jillian, to enjoy the afternoon. All they had to talk about was past pain.

"You miss her, don't you?" Jillian asked as she sat beside him.

He almost asked her who, even though he knew she was referring to Heather. "In a strange way," he said. "Sometimes I think I concentrate more on her now than I did when she was alive."

He could feel Jillian's surprise rather than see it. Casual acquaintances weren't supposed to make that sort of comment.

"I rarely saw her. She lived with Marge." Thomas leaned back and added, "My ex-wife."

He glanced at Jillian. She was listening intently, her gaze fixed on him. Maybe that was why she had become White House Correspondent so young. That solid, intense look had a feel of compassion to it.

"I'm trying to find out how she died," he found himself saying. "That's become really important to me. And I'd like your help."

"My help?" Jillian was leaning sideways in her chair, her fist tucked under her chin and her elbow resting on the armrest. She was very close to him.

He was surprised that the words had come out. But once he said them, he found that he really meant it. "Would you mind looking up those articles again? Reading the detective reports? Seeing if you can find anything, anything that those detectives might have missed?"

"No," she said. He felt disappointment slide to the base of his stomach. Then she smiled. "I don't mind at all."

He grinned back at her, feeling like a kid who had just gotten a date to the senior prom. He got up and grabbed the detective reports off the table, leaving Heather's picture and the tome. "I haven't finished this one yet," he said, "But I'd like you to take the other two. I'll bring the other one to you as soon as I'm done."

"Okay." She set her beer bottle down, took the reports, and hugged them to her chest. They stared at the ocean for a moment, then she made the slight, almost imperceptible motions signifying that she was going to leave. Disappointment slid through him again, but he couldn't think of any way to keep her there. He wanted to take her hand and sit by the window, staring at the gray ocean, enjoying the solitude together. But she had a job to go back to and a life that didn't include playing nurse to an ailing actor.

She gazed at him, her smile tentative. He knew then that she couldn't leave until he touched her. He leaned forward on his crutches, then took her elbow in his hand and pulled her toward him. She tilted her face toward his and he kissed her, letting his lips brush hers lightly.

She pulled back and he stood, feeling awkward. He had never been with a woman like her before. All the other women seemed to expect him to be attracted and he had responded to their bodies and little else. Jillian was more. Jillian was someone that he wanted to get to know.

Suddenly she put her hand on his cheek, stood on her toes, and kissed him quickly, her tongue just tasting his upper lip. "Thanks for lunch, Thomas," she said and half-ran, half-walked out the door.

7

The fire cast dancing shadows around the room. Thomas huddled on the couch, his right elbow leaning on the armrest, and the last detective report open across his lap. The room felt cold, even though Thomas had stoked the fire twice.

DeFreeze and Garity were the only ones who mentioned his previous visit to Seavy Village. They devoted an entire section to it. They described the filming, the people in the production, and even had an interview with Suzette. He had smiled when he came to her name. It had been Suzette, not Suzanne. Perhaps he had to rethink his lifestyle if he couldn't even remember the names of the women he slept with.

She had described, in embarrassing detail, the night they had spent on the beach. He did remember making love to her, with the waves crashing in the background, but he didn't remember leaving her alone on that beach as she claimed he had. That night, the extra had been murdered, and

Heather, not Suzette, had provided Thomas's alibi.

He sighed and turned the page. His memories were so fuzzy during that period. He had been running on no sleep and very little food. Heather hardly saw him, although it was their summer stay together. But another actress had introduced him to cocaine and he loved how it allowed him to run, to keep moving, stay awake and keep functioning without collapsing. The collapse came a month later, after Heather had left, and the filming had moved back to the studios. He had passed out one evening and it took the emergency room nearly an hour to revive him, and two weeks of bed rest before he recovered. He didn't touch another drug again, except alcohol, and even that he wondered if he had used to excess.

Heather. She had hardly seen him, and when she did, he was hurrying from one place to another, with barely time for hello. Then, after the murder, the police interrogated her until she burst into tears and Thomas sent her home. To Marge. Without contacting her again until Christmas.

He sighed and ran his hand over his face. If he had been reading a script instead of his daughter's life, he would have demanded that the director lighten up on the father character. He could imagine himself pacing in the director's office. *The man has to have some redeeming qualities. He has to at least like his daughter, for crissake.*

"He didn't even know his daughter," Thomas whispered. And it wasn't her fault. It was his. The report said that she was running away from home to move in with him. She had told friends that she finally had enough nerve to do what was right, to go live with her father, where everything would be better.

Better. Yeah.

He closed the report and listened to the wood snap in the fireplace. Outside, the constant rush of the ocean sounded like traffic noise. Someone had snuck in the house through a door he had left unlocked, and taken his daughter. Maybe she had escaped and run across the sand. Maybe the cloaked figure he had seen had been chasing Heather. Maybe, if he had gone down the stairs when he first heard a noise, he could have saved her.

The shrill ring of the phone made him jump. He stared at it, his heart pounding. The only person who'd called him had been his agent, and that had been to nag him about Anthony Short. The phone rang again. He picked up the receiver and kept his voice neutral as he answered, so that he could slide into annoyed if he had to.

"Thomas?" The voice was rich, full, and feminine, with no trace of a Brooklyn accent. It took him a minute to realize he was speaking with Jillian.

"Hi," he said, sounding as relieved as he felt. He had been too tense.

"You okay?" He liked the level of concern that had crept into her voice.

"Yeah," he said. "Just tired." As soon as the words left his mouth, he regretted them. Tired meant that he couldn't spend time with her that evening, if that was what she wanted. Tired meant he wasn't interested in seeing her.

"I think I found something," she said.

He sat upright and clenched the phone so tightly that his fingers hurt. "What?"

"I went to the sheriff's office and checked his records. They do think all the deaths are linked. The cause of death in almost all of the cases is similar."

"Except Heather's."

"Even Heather's. One of her bones had been struck by a sharp object. It could have been a knife. It could also have occurred after death. They don't know."

Thomas shivered. He remembered the cloaked figure running down the beach. If only he had—

"Thomas? You there?"

"Yes."

"The interesting thing about this is that they're not investigating it as a serial killing."

He made himself concentrate on her words. "Why not?"

"I don't know," she said. "I couldn't get a straight answer. And when I can't get a straight answer, I start to worry."

"What do you think is going on?"

"I have no idea." Her voice sounded harsh. "But I would like to keep digging into this, if you'll let me."

He nodded, then realized that she couldn't hear him. "I'd like your help," he said.

"Good. When can I have that other detective's report?"

He looked down at the open pages, the words blurring and running together. Something was in his eyes. He wiped at them and his hands came away wet. Heather. Stabbed to death like the woman who had lived in this house. And he had done nothing. "Tomorrow," he said.

"Okay, I'll talk to you then." He waited for her to hang up, but she didn't. "Thomas?"

"Yes?"

"Are you really all right?"

"I'm fine, thanks, Jillian. I'll talk to you later." He hung up the phone and stared into the fire. A serial killer. In a cloak. Starting in 1979, when he was doing a gothic horror movie. In a cloak.

8

Thomas pulled up outside the newspaper office. Rain slapped against the windshield, a hard, coastal rain that reminded him the ocean was right nearby. He took a deep breath and shut off the ignition. The truck rumbled, then became silent. The rain beating against the metal was the only sound he heard.

He eased the door open and slid his crutches out. Then he climbed down, careful not to slip on the wet, and grabbed the remaining detective's report. He hadn't finished reading it, but he had promised it to Jillian. The rain was cold, biting—a winter rain, Carolyn had said. He wondered how she could tell the difference since the temperature on the coast always stayed the same.

He slid the report under his jacket, and tucked his jacket in so that the report wouldn't fall. Then he slogged his way to the door.

The lights through the window gave him a good view of the front office. All the desks were clean and no one sat in any of the chairs. He felt a sudden stab of worry that Jillian was out. Even though it was only five, he had no idea how late she worked.

He opened the door and shook the rain off his coat. The office was warm and smelled faintly of ink. "Hello?" he called. A radio blared in the background, but he could hear no movement.

"Hello?" he called as he threaded his way to the back. Finally he saw Jillian.

She was sprawled on her desk, her hands flung forward, and her head turned toward the wall. A steaming coffee cup sat on top of a pile of papers. Near her fingers, a crumpled fudge wrapper rested.

He touched her back. "Jillian?"

"Jesus!" She sat straight up, hitting her coffee with one hand and catching the cup with the other. He smiled. She probably did that often. She looked up at him. Her glasses were missing, giving her face a half-dressed look. Her face looked good half-dressed. "God, Thomas," she said. "You could have called."

"I did. I said I'd be in this afternoon."

"Oh." She ran a hand through her hair, then found her glasses and put them back on. With her glasses, her competent personality returned. "Did you bring the report?"

He pulled it out of his jacket. She took it from him, hefted it like it was a weight, and then smiled at him. "I'm getting really intrigued by this," she said. "The locals know more than they're letting on. People aren't telling me things that they would normally talk about. I always thought I had to get off that story because it would hurt business, you know—"

"The motels and restaurants and California tourists," he said, more to protect himself from the torrent of words than to display his knowledge. "Yeah, I know."

She nodded. "But I don't think so. I think something else is going on here. I think I might call Portland, see why the *Oregonian* hasn't picked up this serial killer thing."

Thomas hunched over protectively. The "serial killer thing" had killed his daughter. Sometimes he felt so stupid, as if it were all his fault. If Seavy Village had a serial killer, why hadn't he done more to protect Heather? Leaving the door unlocked, letting her sleep downstairs in a house where a woman had been murdered. He had been so—

"I'm sorry." Jillian put her hand on his arm.

Thomas made himself smile. Had he done that to her yesterday when he had so casually asked her about her past? Had he taken her breath away, made her ache as she sat across from him in his comfortable kitchen? "I didn't finish the report," he said. "Let me know if you find anything in it."

"I will," she said. She licked her upper lip and he watched her small tongue move. He remembered its soft feel against his mouth. So silly.

He walked past the beige office dividers.

"Thomas?"

He stopped. She was half-standing, her coffee cup balanced precariously on the edge of a group of papers. "How about dinner? I've got some soup in the crockpot."

The invitation eased the discomfort he was feeling. "Soup sounds good," he said.

"Great." She took a rain slicker off the coatrack. "Follow me."

Hers was the only other car parked in front of the building. Thomas waited for her in his truck, watching as she shut off the remaining lights and locked the front door. Then she got into her car, and pulled out onto the street.

The traffic was light, but Thomas still had trouble keeping up as Jillian weaved in and out of the lanes. She led him to a small house on top of a steep hill. He suspected that, on clear nights, the view of the ocean was spectacular.

The lights were on and the curtains drawn. Jillian pulled up in front of the two-car garage. Thomas pulled in next to her. She waited as he got out of the truck.

"Bet you'll be happy when that comes off," she said.

He looked down at the cast. "I don't know. I'm afraid I'm getting used to it."

She smiled and hugged the report to her chest. "I hope you like split pea."

"One of my favorites," he lied. Maybe he would find something else for them to do. But in a small town, the only places to go were restaurants. The movie theater was playing a feature film he had seen at a screening over a year ago.

He waited while she unlocked the door. Then she stepped inside, placed the report on an overloaded end table near the entrance, threw her slicker across the back of the chair, and called, "Hello?"

Thomas froze at the doorway. He hadn't expected her to live with anyone. Maybe there was a husband lurking in the back room or a boyfriend. That would explain her strange behavior with him the day before.

Jillian saw his hesitation. She grabbed his arm, pulled him closer, and closed the door. "It's okay," she said. Then, in a louder tone, "Come on. We have company."

Thomas peered into the side hallway. A figure came out one of the bedroom doors. Too small to be a man, the woman was lithe, slender, too slender, almost birdlike. She stepped into the light and he had to lean on his crutches to keep from falling.

"Heather?" he whispered.

The girl stepped into the light. She had legs like sticks. Her face was gaunt, hollow, with a faint dusting of makeup. She had pulled her hair back so that he couldn't see its color, accenting her large, dark eyes. Instead of a jacket, she had wrapped herself in a car-coat sweater. Narrow wrists peeked out of the cable pockets.

At some point, Jillian had grabbed his arm. Her fingers dug between the flesh and bone, pinching him. He stared at his daughter and waited for her to speak.

"This is my sister, Alicia," Jillian said. "Allie, this is Thomas Stanton."

"Pleasure." The voice was laconic, deep, with the long vowels of a midwesterner. Not Heather's quick, breathless voice at all. Thomas pulled himself out of the vision.

She did look like Heather, the same thin appearance, and defiant stance. But her features were wrong. She looked like a too-slim, angry version of Jillian.

"What's with him?"

Thomas shook his head. "You startled me," he said. "You bear an uncanny resemblance to my daughter."

"The dead one?"

Jillian's hand tightened on Thomas's arm. "Allie—"

"It's okay, Jillian." Thomas took his arm out of Jillian's grasp. He could feel the indentations left by her fingers. "I only had one child, Allie."

"Alicia." She pulled her slender, bony hand out of her pocket and pushed a strand of hair out of her face. "I suppose he's having dinner here."

Jillian nodded. Thomas noticed thin lines running from her eyes that he had never seen before.

"I ate."

"When, Allie?"

Alicia shrugged. "A while ago. It was in the crockpot. I just helped myself. I'll have some more when I feel like it."

"Alicia—"

"Oh, for crissake. You do that mom stuff so badly. I'll eat when I want to, Jillian."

The girl turned around and stalked back down the hall, closing the door behind her. Jillian took a deep breath. "I'm sorry, Thomas."

"I didn't know you lived with your family," he said.

"Just Alicia. My brother sent her here six months ago. He couldn't do anything with her."

"And your parents?"

"They died about three months after she was born. Car accident. Our grandmother raised her until two years ago when she couldn't care for her anymore. Then Grayson took her."

Jillian walked into the kitchen. She took the lid off the soup and a pea-scented steam wafted into the air. Thomas's stomach rumbled.

"Has she always been this thin?"

Jillian shook her head. She grabbed two hand-made bowls from the cupboard, took two spoons out of the drawer, and stuck a ladle in the soup. "That started when Grammie died. Before that, Allie and I could polish off one of Grammie's chocolate marshmallow fudge cakes in an afternoon. Before she got here, I was telling everybody my sister was coming and I was going to get fat."

She looked up and seemed to notice Thomas's crutches for the first time. "Why don't you go sit? I'll bring it to you."

She indicated a table covered with magazines, newspapers, and books lying open facedown. He glanced at the material as he pushed it aside: a two-day-old *New York Times*, the Sunday *Oregonian*, a *Ms. Magazine* half covering a *Mother Jones* that lay on top of a *National Review*, two romance novels, a horror novel, three science fiction novels, an award-winning collection of short stories, and a novelization of the latest *Star Trek* movie.

"You and your sister have diverse tastes," he said as she set a bowl of soup down in front of him.

Jillian blushed. "Allie doesn't read," she said.

Thomas smiled. He took a spoonful of the soup. It was rich, thick, and surprisingly good. He was about to say so when a door in the back slammed. Jillian's entire body became rigid as Alicia sauntered into the dining room.

"Guess I'll try some after all," she said. She took a bowl from the cupboard, filled it with soup, pulled a diet 7-Up from the refrigerator, and sat down with them.

Thomas could see the bones in her hand, how they attached to her wrist and led to her fingers. He could remember staring at the delicate bones in Heather's hand.

Alicia took a spoonful of the soup and grimaced. "This stuff sucks." She got up, dumped the soup in the sink, and leaned against the doorway as she sipped her soda. "So you're here with my sister. What do you plan to do to her? I would hope that—"

"Allie." Jillian slid her chair back. "Knock it off."

"I think she doesn't like me, Jillian," Thomas said. "And that's okay. I didn't come here to see her." He ate his soup slowly, feeling the girl glare at him. She was jealous. He recognized all of the signs. Only he had seen them before with old girlfriends, not with younger sisters.

"Why don't you sit down and try talking to Thomas, Allie. You might enjoy yourself."

Alicia shook her head. "I got stuff to do. Nice meeting you, I think."

Thomas took a final sip of the soup. "You too," he said, wishing he hadn't met her at all. Jillian was proving herself different from the other women he had known. This sister was going to be trouble, and he wasn't sure he had energy for trouble.

The girl sauntered off to her room. Jillian watched her go. "I have tried to do things with her, but she's been like that since she got here."

Thomas glanced down the hallway. He couldn't imagine living with that. He couldn't imagine living with anyone. "It must be tough," he said. He was feeling antsy. He wasn't ready for this type of conversation—one that demanded advice and answers.

Jillian nodded. She sensed his restlessness. "Allie can be nice sometimes."

He smiled, not willing to say anything. He pushed the soup bowl away. "I should be going."

Jillian looked at him as if she had expected him to say that. "Okay."

He stood up and carefully put the crutches back under his arm. "Thanks for the soup." He touched Jillian's shoulder. "I'll call you."

He hurried out the front door, into the cold, driving rain. One crutch slipped as he went down the walk—and he nearly lost his balance. His breath was coming rapidly. He hadn't realized how uncomfortable he was feeling until he got outside. Damn that little girl. He kept seeing Heather before him, hating him as clearly as Jillian's sister did.

And with more of a reason.

9

Moonlight streamed across his bed, making him cold. The covers held him, twisted around his throat and shoulders, binding him as effectively as a straightjacket.

"Daddy!"

He tried to sit up, but couldn't. Each movement pulled the sheet-noose tighter around his neck.

"Daddy, help!"

A shutter banged downstairs. Bile rose strong and bitter in the back of his mouth. He groped for the edge of the covers, trying to untangle himself.

"Daddy!"

Finally he pulled the sheet free. He sat up, naked and shivering in the moonlight.

"Dad—"

The cry ended. Thomas flung himself out of bed. As his cast hit the floor, the plaster shattered. He stumbled, then collapsed, pain shooting through him, pain so intense that he—

—screamed. He sat up. His breathing was shallow. The living room was dark except for a few small embers still glowing in the fireplace. He rubbed a hand over his face. The third nightmare so far that night. And he knew what had caused it. Jillian's sister. Alicia looked too much like Heather. The ages and builds were so similar.

His leg throbbed. He was on it too much. He had to make an appointment for himself in Newport. The last thing he needed was a permanent disfigurement, yet he was heading toward it, as mindlessly as he had headed toward a separation from his daughter.

He got up, ignored the pain in his leg, and stoked the fire. Then he hobbled into the kitchen and put on some water for tea. As he waited for the water to boil, he rested his forehead on his palms. He had to do something. This lack of sleep would catch up to him. It probably already was. And the brooding was doing no good either. He had come to Seavy Village to exorcise his demons. Instead, he seemed to be making them worse.

He had to become active. Jillian had given him a number of leads to follow on Heather's death. Yet he hadn't followed up on a single one of them. He couldn't even finish reading the reports—probably because they made him look so bad. Because he had been so bad. That was the real problem. Facing up to Heather's death meant facing up to his failure as a parent.

The shrill of the tea kettle made him jump. He reached over and poured the water into the lighthouse mug, the same one Heather had used. Then he set the mug in front of himself and watched the tea bag stain the water brown.

He felt as if he were acting alone, doing his first

soliloquy without the benefit of a director or even a scriptwriter. Ad libbing everything from the first sentence to the last. His ultimate nightmare.

He brought his tea into the living room and watched as the first rays of the dawn edged across the beach. The water reached toward the sunlight, pushing the sand forward. The ocean controlled the sand, but the sand dominated everything. The waves, as they splashed against the rocks, were almost unreal—a simulation created by a computer, stored on tape, and replayed for an indifferent audience.

Thomas leaned his head back. He had watched ocean sunrises in California, but never had he seen the sun steal across a cold, gray Pacific. He stared for what seemed like hours, trying to think of nothing as he watched the gulls dive in low, land, and dig in the sand. Medium-size waves, perhaps as tall as he was, sprayed droplets into the air and the sun caught them, making them sparkle.

The phone rang. Thomas spilled some cold tea in his lap. His heart was pounding. Who would call so early in the morning? Jillian?

As the phone rang again, he slid his chair to the end table. Then he picked up the receiver and cradled the cold plastic against his ear. "Yes?" he said, keeping his tone neutral to discourage the caller from making other early morning calls.

"I knew you'd be home at this ungodly hour." The strong Brooklyn accent cleared the static from the phone line. His agent, Connie.

"I'm home a lot."

"Bullshit," Connie said good-naturedly. "I've been trying to reach you for days. Recuperated yet?"

"I'm still wearing my cast."

"That's fine. They got your fall on tape and Michael wants to use it. That way, Anthony Short will have a cast and a limp and whatnot. He wants to start filming again—soon."

"When is soon?"

"Yesterday."

"Connie, I'm not ready to go back."

He heard an exasperated snort on the other end. "You continue this Connie-I'm-not-ready-to-go-back shit and that's the end of Thomas Stanton aka Anthony Short. Actors aren't in charge of production. You're good, Thomas, but not that good."

Thomas sighed and brushed at the wet spot the tea had left on his robe. "I really don't care," he said.

"Well, I do. I happen to like those lovely commission checks your work garners for me."

"You've got other clients," Thomas snapped. He was hanging up the phone when he heard a screech from the other end.

"Thomas? You there?"

He put the receiver back to his ear. "Yeah."

"Look, Thomas." Connie's voice was warmer, richer. She had used that voice only two or three times with him—when he lost that big contract with Universal, when he split up with Marge, and when Heather disappeared. "I'm really worried about you. I talked to Marge after she saw you in the hospital and she says you're really obsessed with Heather."

Obsessed is a good word, Thomas thought. *Leave it to Marge the English major.* "So?"

"So let it rest. There's nothing you can do."

"I'm not doing this for Heather," he said, and as he spoke, he realized it was the truth. "I'm doing it for me. I'm sorry if that hurts your commissions, Connie, but frankly, work is the farthest thing from my mind."

"Do me a favor, Thomas? See somebody?"

"You mean somebody professional, like for my head?"

"Yeah."

"Sure," he said, not meaning it.

"Thomas?"

"Yes?"

"I'm trying to help."

He nodded. A gull perched on his porch railing. "I know."

"I'm going to call again in a couple of days, see how you're doing. Then—"

"I'll be doing fine, Connie. I'll call you."

"Thomas—"

He hung up. The gull half turned and stared at him. Its white feathers were streaked with sand and grit. Its eyes glittered, accusing him. Maybe he should go back to work and forget this whole thing. Return to the Thomas he had always been, the man with no ties and no cares, who made love to women whose names he couldn't even remember (although they could remember everything and could tell private detectives in exacting detail), who had a family more for its résumé value than for its emotional one. He could be Anthony Short with a limp, Anthony Short without a limp, Anthony Short for the rest of his life—or at least until the end of the season—and then he could become someone else until he died or his dick gave out, whichever came first.

But he couldn't do that. Maybe for the first time in years, he wasn't playing a role, and that was why he was so tired and things didn't work out like he had planned.

He ran his hand along the top of the phone. He could call Connie back, tell her to let him go, he was done acting. But he couldn't do that either. If he didn't find what he needed in Seavy Village, then he needed something to go back to. And acting, at least, was something.

Finally, he picked up the receiver and placed it against his ear. The dial tone hummed loudly, insistently. He reached into his back pocket and pulled out his wallet. In there, he found a scrap of paper with the phone number for the doctor in Newport. He dialed and the phone rang until a sleepy, disinterested male voice answered. "Doctor's offices."

Thomas had heard enough answering services to know when he was in the presence of yet another one. "What time is it?" he asked.

"Ah—seven. Can I help you?"

"I didn't realize it was so early," Thomas said and hung up.

He would call later. His leg could wait. Suddenly he felt overwhelmed with a tiredness that seemed more than physical. He closed the curtains, put a few more logs on the fire, took off his robe, and went back to bed.

10

She sat on the steps of the newspaper office, sipping a diet Coke and wrapped in a heavy jacket. Thomas stopped the truck. If he squinted just so, she looked exactly like Heather. Alicia looked up and grimaced at him. He smiled back.

He hadn't really planned to stop at the newspaper, but he found he couldn't just drive by. He told himself he needed to pick up the reports, and tried to ignore the thoughts of Jillian—eating fudge, slumped over her desk, standing in the doorway to the file room—that overwhelmed him at the strangest moments.

Thomas opened the truck door. The air was cold, damp. A fog had risen off the sea that hovered over the town. The chill stung his cheeks. He didn't feel good, but he didn't feel particularly bad either. He was a man without a purpose, and sometimes he wondered if he even existed.

He slid the crutches under his arms and swung around to the front of the truck.

"She's not here," Alicia said. Her breath seemed to intensify the fog.

"I didn't really come to see her."

"Oh, really?"

He placed his crutches on the curb and hoisted himself up. He was getting tired of this fast. "What's your problem?" he asked.

Alicia wiped her nose with the back of her hand. Her fingers were as red as her cheeks. She had been outside a long time. "I don't like people who think they're important."

"Or maybe you're just jealous of people who have made a name for themselves."

"You're a son of a bitch," Allie said. "You're not like that detective at all."

Thomas made his way up the sidewalk. The cold had seeped into his lungs. "Of course I'm not," he said. "That's why they call it acting."

Alicia slid over on the steps, but said nothing else. She wrapped her coat tighter and shivered against the damp. He didn't remember Heather ever looking so pathetic, but then, he had never looked at her with the kind of detachment he felt for Alicia. Detachment that could easily slide into something nasty, like hatred.

He opened the door and walked inside. The front office was warm, almost stifling. The boy who looked like Jimmy Olsen was sitting behind the desk reading a novel. He jumped when he saw Thomas.

"M-M-Mr. St-St-Stanton. I d-d-didn't hear you come in."

At least the boy wasn't running in fright this time. "You seemed pretty engrossed in that book."

Jimmy Olsen smiled and shrugged. A blush rose from the base of his throat to his chin and up his cheekbones.

Thomas shifted slightly. The boy made him as uncomfortable as he made the boy. "Do you know where Jillian is?"

The boy looked confused. "She's in back—or she should be. Sh-Sh-Should I tell her you're here?"

"No," Thomas said. "I'll just go see if I can find her."

He walked slowly back to the main offices. Jillian sat at a different desk, her head bowed in concentration, her fingers dancing across the keys of an electric typewriter. He watched her for a moment, marveling at how different she was from her sister. Alicia huddled on the front steps, her attitude sour and bitter even though she was only sixteen. Jillian, who had suffered a clear number of disappointments, worked as hard as she could to keep a little weekly afloat.

"Hi," he said.

Jillian continued typing. She stopped for a moment, checked her notes, then shoved a pencil in her mouth. The clatter of the keys began again.

"Jillian?" Thomas said.

The words kept appearing on the page, each letter accompanied by a corresponding clack. Thomas touched her shoulder. Jillian jumped.

"Jesus, Thomas," she said around the pencil. "Don't do that to me."

He held out his hand in supplication. "Sorry," he said.

"Give me a minute," she said and turned her attention back to the page in front of her. Her hair stood out at an odd angle and a streak of soot ran down the back of her baseball jersey.

Finally she pulled the page out of the typewriter, took the pencil out of her mouth, and made a few corrections. Then she set the page in a wire basket and ran her fingers through her bangs. "Fire down at the bakery on 101. I wanted to get the details down before I forgot them."

He nodded, although he really didn't understand. She got up and filled her coffee mug. "You want one?" she asked.

"No, thanks."

"I know," she said. "You're here to pick up the reports. But, Thomas, I've been too busy to really give them the attention they deserve. If you could—"

"No, actually," he said. "I'm here to see if you think this thing is worth pursuing."

"Worth pursuing? Jesus, Thomas, we have a major cover-up here. It would be a crime not to—"

"No." His voice sounded harsh. He leaned against the desk and took the weight off his leg. "I mean for me."

"Oh." She sat down and put her feet up on the desk. "You're the only one who can answer that."

"My agent called this morning. She wants me to go back to work."

"Mmm-hmm." Jillian buried her face in the steam rising from her coffee mug.

"I'm not sure I want to work anymore, Jillian."

"That's—"

"Up to me, I know." He watched her for a minute. She continued to look in her coffee. He sighed. "I should go."

She looked up. "You just got here."

"I came for some advice. Not for a few nods and a 'that's-up-to-you-Thomas.' I know it's up to me. I just wanted to talk about it."

Jillian's eyes seemed to grow bigger. "I'm sorry."

His back felt stiff. His entire body felt stiff. He had expected too much without even realizing he was expecting anything. "I'll talk to you later, okay?"

He stood up.

"I really don't know what's best for you," Jillian said. "I don't know you that well. But . . ." She stopped. Thomas found himself leaning into the silence.

"But what?"

She took a deep breath. "I would kind of like it if you stayed."

He smiled. He leaned down, bracing his right hand against her desk, and kissed the top of her head. Jillian turned so that her lips brushed his chin.

"I was hoping you'd say that," he said.

Jillian touched him briefly and then let go. She picked up her coffee and blew on it, even though no steam was rising from the top. "I suppose you want the reports back."

Thomas frowned at the change of subject. He

glanced down at Jillian. She was shuffling papers on her desk, apparently looking for the reports. He felt as if he had missed something—an opportunity, a moment to hold her, something that might never come again.

"Jillian . . ."

She looked up, her expression businesslike once more.

"I—" He cast in his mind for Thomas Stanton, the man who was at ease with everyone. That Thomas was gone. "—I, um, haven't done anything on Heather's case."

As soon as he spoke, he felt stupid, vulnerable. He pulled over a chair and took the weight off his leg. "I haven't finished reading the reports, I haven't looked at any records. I don't know what I'm doing, Jillian."

Jillian stopped rustling papers. She swung her chair over toward him, her eyes sparkling with something like compassion. Maybe that was what he had failed to do. He had thought about himself and how he felt instead of listening to Jillian.

"Do you want help?" she asked. "Or do you want to figure this out on your own?"

He paused for a split second, amazed that she had given him the choice. "Help," he said.

"Then, the first thing you do is forget the reports. They're someone else's opinion of what happened. You have to form your own opinion from your own evidence. You start this investigation as if no one has done it before."

"But," he said, "if someone else has done the work . . ."

Jillian was shaking her head as he spoke. "They have their own agendas which lead them to come to their own conclusions, make them ignore certain facts and pay attention to others. You have your own agenda too, Thomas. That's what you have to pursue."

"I don't know how to even start," he said, feeling tired.

"I do." Jillian's cheeks were flushed. Her entire body seemed animated. "Let me help you, Thomas."

"I get the sense that I should be doing this on my own."

"Oh, for crissake." She pushed her chair back on its heels. The chair squeaked. "Every cub reporter has an ace who adopts him. Every police detective works with a partner. Why the hell not use expertise that you have available? It'll probably take you one year instead of four."

"One year?"

Jillian shrugged. "A figure of speech." She stood up and extended her hand. "Come on."

"Where're we going?"

"First we're going to find out what has become of my sister, then we're going to start at the very beginning."

"Alicia was sitting out front when I came."

Jillian frowned. "She was?"

"And, from the looks of her, she'd been sitting there for a while. She told me that you weren't here."

Jillian made an exasperated sound in the back of her throat. She handed him his crutches and waited as he got to his feet. Then she walked out of the office. "Take messages," she said to Jimmy Olsen. Thomas half expected the boy to salute.

They didn't have to go far to find Alicia. She was huddled next to Thomas's truck, smoking a cigarette. "That's new," Jillian said.

"Cuts my appetite," Alicia said.

"Your life span too." Jillian took the cigarette from Alicia, dropped it on the sidewalk, and stomped the butt out.

"There are faster ways to kill yourself," Thomas said.

"I don't need any lip from you." Alicia drew her coat tighter around her small frame.

"Slashed wrists, a gun to the head, an overdose of pills—"

"A jump off a cliff into the sea."

Thomas felt as if he had been punched. Alicia's eyes were bright. "You're very good," he said. Not many people could compete in a verbal argument with him. He would have to pay attention with Alicia.

She nodded, acknowledging him as a worthy person for perhaps the first time.

"I'm taking you home," Jillian said. "Thomas, why don't you follow me? I'll—"

"No," Thomas said. "I'll drive." He went to the driver's side of the truck and opened the door. The door opened on the other side and Jillian got in, followed by Alicia. He felt strange, taking such forceful control, but he needed to. The search for the reasons behind Heather's death was his search, and the more he abdicated to Jillian, the less he felt was his.

Jillian fiddled with the radio as they drove to her house. The radio station in Seavy Village faded on one side of the lake, only to return too strong on the other. Sometimes he could pick up Portland or Eugene, and once, on a strange half-cloudy night, he got L.A. It had sent him back to that other life, the one Connie wanted him to go back to now.

Static echoed in the silent truck. Alicia reached over and clicked the radio off. Jillian reached over to turn it back on.

"Leave it off," Thomas said.

He could feel the tension, thick and ugly in the car, and he thought of Jillian and Alicia, laughing as they ate cake at their grandmother's.

"Stop here, Thomas," Jillian said. "Thomas!"

He had almost passed the house. He turned into the driveway, and Alicia opened the door before the truck stopped.

"What do you want me to do?" she asked Jillian.

"Stay out of trouble," Jillian said tightly. "I'll be home later."

She reached over and closed the door. Alicia watched them for a moment, then turned and let herself into the house. Jillian let out a long sigh and put her head back against the seat. Thomas took her hand. Her fingers were warm and dry. She didn't move for a long time.

"Where are we going?" he asked.

She put on a persona. He had watched actresses do it all the time, but he never expected to see someone like Jillian suddenly snap into character.

She smiled at him, but her eyes remained full of anger.

"We start at the beginning," she said. "The place I always start when I'm working on a Seavy Village story."

"Great," he said. "You're being cryptic."

She nodded, smile still in place. Only now, laugh lines were forming around her eyes. She instructed him to drive to Highway 101. They weaved in and out of the traffic, past the burned-out bakery, and finally she made him pull into a Safeway parking lot. Jillian opened the door and hurried into the store before Thomas could get his crutches outside the vehicle. He waited, watching her disappear behind the glass windows.

The night was damp and his hands were getting cold. He felt as if he were on the edge of something, about to slide into a place he would never be able to leave. Maybe he could turn around, climb out, and head back to L.A. as if nothing had happened. But he knew he couldn't.

Jillian walked through the automatic doors. Her step was lively, her movements graceful. If he hadn't seen her fade for that moment in the truck, he would have thought she was in high spirits. As she got closer, he realized that she was carrying a bouquet in one hand and a six-pack of beer in the other.

"I thought we were going to work," he said as she opened the door.

She set the beer beside him and climbed in. The door slammed with a metallic bang. "These aren't for you."

"Curiouser and curiouser," he said.

She shot him a quizzical glance. "So who were you in *Alice in Wonderland*?"

"I wasn't." His turn to smile. "I just like the book."

He didn't say any more about the flowers and the beer. Instead he said nothing as he followed Jillian's instructions to the edge of town. She had him turn down an unmarked road running through a small wood. The trees were ocean-swept; all of their branches bent as if they had been frozen during a gale. She pointed and he turned the truck onto a narrow, muddy driveway. To his left, peeking through the trees, he could see the ocean, spitting and foaming at the shore. Two large, barking dogs ran in front of the headlights.

"They'll move," she said.

Finally, he reached the end of the driveway and stopped in front of what he thought of as a typical coastal house. The sea wind had long stripped the paint from the building. The wood looked weatherbeaten and tired. The lawn, though neat and trim, contained oddly shaped bits of drift-wood. The impression was not so much that of poverty as of a different aesthetic, one that had long ago stopped fighting nature and had given in to the changes the sea made in the landscape.

Jillian got out her side of the truck and was fending off the dogs by waving the six-pack before her as if it were a shield. Thomas got out his crutches and eased himself down into the mud. One of the dogs, a huge collie bitch, ran over to him and rubbed her head against his cast. He petted her, grimacing as he felt thick, matted grime in her fur.

"Who did you bring?" The voice was querulous and loud.

Thomas swung himself around the truck. An old man stood beside Jillian, his hand on the other dog's back.

"Hargrave," she said, "This is Thomas. Thomas, Hargrave Lester."

"You're that actor."

Thomas nodded.

"I watched your program once. Fell asleep."

"I do that too," Thomas said. "Not enough action."

Hargrave nodded. "Too damn much talking for me," he said. "Which is I suppose what you want. Jillie brought me my flowers and my beer and she always wants stories in return."

"Not always," Jillian chided.

Hargrave smiled at her and put his arm around her shoulder. "No, not always."

He led her inside. Thomas followed, studying the old man from the back. Hargrave had once been a large man—he still had the big bones and long limbs. But his muscles seemed to have shrunk, bending him into a shape that vaguely resembled a question mark. He pulled open the door to his house and led them inside.

The living room was warm, almost excessively so, and smelled like wet dogs. Plants hung from every corner, off ceilings, on shelves, draped over cabinets. Half-read books sat, spine bent, on each chair. Hargrave moved one so that he could sit down. Jillian wandered in the back, toward the kitchen, Thomas assumed. He heard the pneumatic sound of a refrigerator door opening.

"Sit," Hargrave commanded.

Thomas moved two books—one high-class pornography and the other a Stephen King novel—leaned his crutches against a table, and sat on the sofa. Hargrave was watching closely.

"I had three daughters," he said. "Lost the first in 1925. She was six. The second died in 1945. She was an AWAC. Army never did tell me what happened. The last died last year. Cancer. Never had one disappear, though. I always knew where they were, even up to the end."

Thomas took a deep breath. The old man's sympathy made his stomach grow tight.

"You get old," Hargrave said and closed the book beside him with a resounding snap. "And it don't get easier. Sometimes I think it gets worse."

Thomas nodded. But he'd only had one daughter to lose, and he'd lost her years before she died.

"You were right," Jillian said. She handed him a beer and then set the bouquet, which she had arranged in a vase, down on one of his end tables. "We did come here to ask questions."

"You don't got your tape recorder," Hargrave said.

"Nope." Jillian smiled and reached into the long pocket of her coat. "This time I have a steno pad."

She pulled out a notebook, flipped it open, and poised a pen over its pages.

"You got to ask me a question first." Hargrave's expression was serious, but his voice held laughter. Thomas got the sense that he was watching an old, long-established routine.

"All right," Jillian said. "I want stories. Stories about the beach where Thomas lives."

Hargrave took a sip of his beer. "It's a beach. A few miles of sea and sand. Nothing special."

Jillian frowned and leaned forward. "But people have died there."

"People have died all over this countryside. I bet you can't walk on a patch of land without touching a place where someone died."

"Hargrave." Jillian's voice held a bit of warning. "People died violently on that stretch of beach."

"Since sometime in the late seventies. I know, Jilly." Hargrave looked down at his beer can, then back at her. "What do you want me to tell you? That there's old Indian legends about the place? There's old legends about the entire state. They called the Willamette Valley 'the valley of sickness' because so many people died there—took science to discover the inversions and the marsh-bred disease. The spouting horns in Depoe Bay were sacred to some tribes, and it took the first settlers to name the Devil's Churn near Yachats, not because that treacherous bit of rock looked like a butter churn, like the papers say now, but because so many people died in those early years."

"What about this stretch of beach?"

He shrugged. "Maybe it's got a bit of magic, is all. I've heard folks say that they've felt as if that beach took the bad away." He looked at Thomas. "Did it make you feel better?"

Thomas didn't like the mumbo jumbo, but Jillian thought this old man could lead them somewhere. "Maybe that's why I bought a house there."

Hargrave squeezed his beer can. A bit of foam eased out the top. "No. I mean the first time you were there."

Thomas sat up straighter. Did everyone remember he had been to Seavy Village before but him?

Hargrave set his beer down and studied Thomas. "You famous people have short memories, don't you?"

The muscles in Thomas's back and shoulders were tight. He had to fight to keep the expression on his face neutral. "What do you mean?"

"I met you years ago. I was one of the extras on that detective film. I saw your little girl. She had the look of you in her face, only her eyes were wide and sad. Don't think I had ever seen eyes like that on a well-to-do child before. Saw it in the Depression now and again. On orphans. But not on a little rich kid."

Jillian glanced back and forth between them. She set her pen and notebook aside. "Hargrave—"

"But I didn't really watch her. I watched you. You were skinnier then, and you jittered like you couldn't hold still. You touched the women as if they were as disposable to you as the stuff you were shoveling up your nose. You got mad at me one afternoon for cutting in front of you during a take. 'Follow the blocking, you old fuck!' you said, even though I had been following, and you were the one who was improvising. When those cameras went on, though, you were good. You were damn good. And the director said once to one of the producers that if you could get yourself under control, you'd be one of the greats. The producer laughed and said that the greats never let their personal junk interfere with their work."

Thomas was shaking. He had no memory of that at all. Connie had told him, though, just after that film, that the coke would kill his career if he didn't control it.

Hargrave took a sip of beer. "And I kept thinking that little girl deserved better. Only I didn't blame you. Anyone who watched could see some demon was eating you from the inside out. And someday it would chew you up and spit you out, leaving only a husk."

Thomas didn't move. If he groped for his crutches, he would be acknowledging that the old man had gotten to him.

Jillian had clasped her hands tightly together. "Hargrave, why are you doing this?"

"Because the beach isn't evil, Jilly. Nothing in nature is, no matter what it does. When a storm blows off that ocean and knocks down trees and power lines, we don't call that storm evil. We call it the force of nature. Only people can be evil, Jilly."

Thomas felt the old man's gaze on him. The look sent a chill through him that reached all the way down to his toes.

"You're saying a person did all that?"

"I'm not saying that either." Hargrave stood up.

"I'm going to bed. You can let yourselves out. And Jilly?"

"Yes?"

"Next time, don't take so long between visits. You can come even if you don't have questions."

Jillian smiled. She got up and hugged Hargrave. The old man closed his eyes and slid his hand into her short-cropped hair. Thomas felt as if he were watching something private. He grabbed his crutches and made his way out the door. Jittery. Some great demon. The little girl deserved better. Well, so did he. He and Jilly had come to the old man for help, and had gotten an analysis of Thomas's character based on something that had happened over ten years before.

When he got outside, the dogs came over to him, sniffing and shuffling. He looked away from them, at the bit of ocean foaming on the horizon. He made himself breathe as he had been taught. Slowly. In. Out. Calm. Remain calm. And centered. The words didn't affect him. They were only words.

The door closed behind him, and Jillian touched his arm. "What was the purpose behind that?" The question came out sharper than he intended.

She opened the truck door and climbed into the cab. "Hargrave knows the lore of Seavy Village. He's always the best place to start."

Thomas tossed his crutches behind the seat. They clattered against the metal back. "Felt like a waste of time to me, Jillian."

"It's not," she said. She closed her door and rolled down the window to get the moisture off.

Thomas closed his door, started the engine, turned on the lights and the wipers. The dogs had disappeared.

"I use Hargrave as a barometer," Jillian said into the silence. "I always check on what he says. And he always leads me in a direction I never would go, but should probably look at."

Thomas backed the truck into the lawn and turned around. Then he drove down the narrow driveway to the road. "So you're going to look at me. At what a horror I was."

"He was talking about the power of the beach," Jillian said.

"Mystical magical mumbo jumbo."

"Maybe," she said. "Or maybe there's something to it. We have to examine it as if it's real. It's called having an open mind, Thomas."

"He knows about all the deaths. He as good as said someone did it. How do you know it wasn't him?" Thomas's hands were tight on the wheel.

Jillian's eyes glittered in the dark. "He can barely walk, Thomas."

"Now," Thomas said. "But what about before?"

She exhaled loudly, hands clasped in her lap. "He wouldn't kill people."

"You can't know that. You can't know that about anyone."

Thomas's words hung in the chill air. Jillian didn't move. He wished he could take the words back. As he turned the truck onto Highway 101, he said, "Does this make you not want to come to my house?"

The look she gave him was appraising, as if she

were trying to figure out what he meant by the question. "Not yet," she said. "Everything he said was in the reports."

"Except the mystical stuff."

"Except that."

"If that beach is magic, I wonder what kind of spell it casts during sex." As soon as the words left his mouth, he couldn't believe he'd said them. That sounded like the old Thomas, the callous Thomas, the one who'd once been thrown out of a woman's bedroom for calling her by the wrong name—twice.

Her laugh sounded forced. They drove along in silence for a moment. The bright streetlights reflected the fog, making it seem as if they drove inside a large poorly lit warehouse. Thomas glanced at Jillian. She had moved farther away from him.

"So what's the next step, coach?" he asked.

She smiled at him, apparently relieved to be on familiar territory. "Research. Digging through old newspapers and old files to see if anything confirms Hargrave's theory. I thought I would do it and then report back to you."

"I thought I was supposed to look at these things." He sounded petulant. He didn't care. "You said I had to follow my own agenda."

"It's going to be a lot of work, Thomas, and I thought it would be easier—"

"But what about the details? What about the things I'm supposed to see?"

Jillian glanced out the window. Her entire body

looked more rigid than it had before. "I could copy the articles for you. Let you look at them."

"Maybe I should do the digging myself." He was pushing the point too far. He could feel it.

Jillian sighed. "I know how to manipulate those files and find things quickly. To be frank, Thomas, you would just get in the way."

"Maybe if you showed me how, I wouldn't get in the way." He turned on the hill leading up to her house.

She spun sharply in her seat. He had finally pushed too far. "Dammit, Thomas, you're being ridiculous. Do you want my help or not?"

"Yes, but—"

"Then use it in the spirit it's being offered. I will give you photocopies of the articles I find, okay?"

He felt bad, almost sick to his stomach. He didn't know what he had been thinking; the old man had him so upset. Demons inside him. Indeed.

"Okay?" Her repeated question was soft.

"Yeah." He stopped the truck in front of her driveway. Jillian pulled the door handle. As she stepped out, he said, "Jillian?"

She looked at him. He couldn't see her face in the fog. "What, Thomas?"

"I'm sorry. I do appreciate all that you're doing."

She reached out and touched his hand ever so lightly. "I know you do," she said, and gently closed the door.

He waited until she got into the house, then he backed out of the driveway and drove down the hill to 101. The highway was deserted, but he sat at the stop sign anyway and leaned his forehead against the steering wheel. He wasn't acting like himself—or he was acting too much like himself— or he was acting half like himself and half not. He couldn't really tell, except that he was uncomfortable.

The whole night had a surrealistic aspect. The old man's story had a certain veracity, an emotional strength that the best theater had. Thomas's old drama instructor used to call it the intangibles, the part of theater that changed from night to night. The old man's obvious upset, the mention of his daughters, his rough affection for Jillian almost seemed staged. And then, Thomas, slipping back into his old self, what he had begun to think of as his Hollywood self, making that comment about getting Jillian into the house after he had been so careful to treat her with respect. She made it clear that she would continue to help him, but that warmth between them might disappear—had already disappeared because of his carelessness.

A honk behind him made him sit up. He glanced in the rearview mirror. A Datsun sat behind him, its lights illuminating the back end of the truck. He slid guiltily into the intersection without looking and narrowly missed a BMW speeding in the right-hand lane.

His heart was pounding. *Stupid, Thomas. Stupid.* He forced himself to continue even though he was shaking. A few cars passed him, appearing and disappearing in the fog like fireflies. The fog grew thicker as he approached the house. He had to turn on the wipers to clear the moisture off his windshield.

As he pulled in the driveway, he could see the ocean tossing wildly. Water boomed against the rocks, sending shoots of spray into the nooks. Funny how the ocean sounded louder at times than it did at others. He noted that the lights were on in the kitchen. Through the window, he could see Carolyn wipe her hands on a towel. Somehow her presence reassured him. The old man's story had spooked him more than he thought.

Thomas got out of the truck and carefully made his way up the stairs. He had learned a few days ago that the stairs got slick during damp weather, and he was deathly afraid of falling again. In the hospital, his nightmares had all been of falling. Sometimes he would relive the original fall and sometimes the feeling of sliding would return, his body completely out of control. His leg was aching and he wondered how much of it was fatigue, how much the dampness, and how much his emotional condition. He didn't want to spend too much time finding out.

Carolyn opened the door for him. Her cheeks were flushed and her eyes sparkled. As she smiled, she held her lips down to cover her bad teeth. "I hope you don't mind, sir," she said. "I just got to thinking that you haven't eaten everything I left for you and I wanted to make sure that you actually downed a meal."

"That's very considerate of you, Carolyn." His words sounded insincere. The Hollywood Thomas was peeking through more than usual tonight. She stood back so that he could get in the door.

The house was warm and smelled of turkey and woodsmoke. A fire burned in the fireplace, sending shadows dancing around the living room. Carolyn had replaced the flowers and straightened. On the stove, two pots steamed and the oven light glowed red, indicating that something was cooking inside.

Thomas went into the kitchen. "What are you making?"

"Safeway had a special on turkey," she said, "and I got a small one. I figure you could piece on it when I'm not here."

"You're a wonder, Carolyn," he said.

She smiled and ducked away. He had seen fans act like that, the women who used to daydream about his soap character, Jason Michaels, and expect Thomas to be as virile and as confused. He wondered if Carolyn spent part of her afternoons watching *Restless Heart* and decided that she probably did.

He left the kitchen and went to his favorite spot near the large picture window. He could see the light from the porch reflecting on the sand. Carolyn handed him a glass of wine and for the first time in nearly a year, he didn't refuse the alcohol. He leaned back in the chair, sipped the wine, and stared.

The beach looked the same as it had the night he and Suzette had gone for their midnight stroll. The night had had an air of unreality to it, as if they were walking inside, on a movie set. The sea was glassy, the fog thick, and the air was heavy with ghosts. Thomas had felt the presence of others but, paradoxically, he had also known that he and Suzette were alone.

They had walked in the sand, arm in arm. The damp air was chilling, but the feel of Suzette's breasts against his arm kept him warm. The ocean shushed against the shore, and Thomas could feel it there, beside them, accompanying them on their silent trek across the sand. The walk had been Suzette's idea and soon he understood why. She got more aroused the farther they walked. She reached down and rubbed her fingers along his zipper. Finally he slid his arm around her back and held her right breast. She stopped walking and kissed him, a heady, passionate kiss full of lipstick and perfume. Almost before he knew it, she had pulled him down onto the sand. She unbuckled her jeans and wriggled out of them, then undid his. He hadn't been that aroused in days, maybe months. With one hand, she grabbed him, spread her legs and slipped him inside her. She was already very wet. He moved back and forth, reveling in the friction, the warmth of her body against the chill of the night, the silent threat of the ocean, shushing near them, the movement as she writhed and he rubbed, and suddenly—too suddenly—he came and she must have come too because he was forced out of her body before he was done. He collapsed on her and she laughed. She pushed him away. "Cold," she had said by way of explanation, but he had known, even then, that she had been disappointed in him. The studio's grand lover who couldn't last more than five minutes on an Oregon beach with the surf pounding the same rhythm his body had.

A small wet spot formed a hole where they had been lying and sand stuck to his penis. He tried to wipe it off, but felt embarrassed as Suzette laughed at him. Finally he stuck it back inside his underwear and felt the scratch of the little granules all the way back. By the time they reached the set, Suzette looked as clean and fresh as she always did, but he felt grimy. He begged off and went to his room where Heather (Heather!) had been sleeping.

A hand touched his shoulder. He jumped.

"I said, Mr. Stanton, dinner's done. Would you like to eat now?"

He took a deep breath to still his heart, then turned, the Hollywood smile already planted on his lips. "That sounds good, Carolyn."

He got up. She hurried into the kitchen ahead of him to shut off the stove. "If you don't mind," she said, "I'll just do the dishes tomorrow and leave you to yourself."

"Thank you," he said. She grabbed her coat and scurried out the door. When he turned and looked at the table, he wished he had said more. She had set his place with the good dishes. The food looked like something out of a restaurant commercial and she had lit two candles in the center of the table. Beautiful. He wished Jillian had joined him, then sighed. He was on his own, and he usually didn't mind that. But tonight he would have liked to spend the night with someone witty, someone caring, someone warm. And the only person in Seavy Village who was even close was Jillian.

Although Carolyn was giving him a home. Quietly, unobtrusively, she was making him feel welcome. But he couldn't warm to her. He didn't dare.

He sat down, served himself dinner, and tried to think of anything but Jillian, Heather, and the old man's conversation. He wasn't very successful.

11

For two days, he stayed in the house, waiting. He felt as if he couldn't call Jillian, that she had to call him, and yet, he also felt as if he couldn't work on anything else without Jillian's help. He had never been this passive before and he wasn't sure he liked it.

He told himself that his leg was part of the problem. It had begun to ache the night he and Jillian went to see Hargrave, and the ache continued. Three or four times, he picked up the phone to call the doctor in Newport and then hung up, afraid of what the doctor would say.

On the third morning, he drank tea in front of the picture window and realized how silly he was being. He didn't need Jillian and he did need the doctor. No one cared for him but himself. It was time that he started treating himself well again.

Thomas called the doctor and set up an appointment for as soon as possible—sometime the following week. Then he gathered up his things and sat at the kitchen table, meaning to make a game plan. But when Carolyn arrived, she brought in a package that had been sitting on the porch—three Anthony Short scripts that Connie had sent him.

Thomas took the scripts to his chair by the window and read them while Carolyn cleaned and cooked dinner. He was so engrossed in the second script that he didn't hear when she left. These scripts were richer, fuller, with less humor and more atmosphere. Anthony Short had nearly died in his fall, and come back a little stronger and a lot more melancholy. Connie had been right; Thomas could play the role now and do it well.

The wind came up, and a shutter banged against the side of the house. Thomas sat up, a chill running through him. It had gotten dark. The ocean was ferocious. Large waves boomed against the beach, sending spray and foam toward the house. The darkness was thick, no light coming through the heavy cloud cover. Drops of rain slashed against the window as if they were trying to break it. Thomas slid his chair back. The fire was low and the entire room had grown cold.

He got up, opened the grate, and stoked the fire. As he tossed on logs, sparks flew, circling up the chimney and then landing on the flagstone. He watched the sparks glow red, then die, leaving black ash on the stones. He closed the grate, then hobbled back to his chair. A wild night. It seemed as if he was on the only island of sanity in the midst of something frightening and too natural.

The shutter banged again. The sound made his skin crawl, sent memories of that night when he had listened to a shutter bang as Heather ran for her life across the beach.

Finally the living room door opened. Thomas whirled in the chair, his heart pounding.

"Jesus," Jillian said. "Don't you ever answer your door?"

Water ran down her face. Her glasses had steamed up and her short hair was plastered against her skull. Her jacket clung to her slender frame, and she clutched a plastic bag against her chest.

"Do you mind if I come in?"

"No." Thomas found his voice. He stood up. "I'm sorry. I didn't hear you."

"I thought I was going to break the door down." She set the plastic bag near the door, took off her glasses, and tried to rub them on the edge of her jacket. "God, I'm soaked."

He hobbled over to her. Her teeth were chattering and her lips were blue. "You've got to get out of those clothes," he said. "The bathroom is just down the hall. I've got a few things you could probably wear—"

"I can't stay," she said. "I just wanted to drop off the photocopies you wanted and then I was planning to go. I didn't think the rain would hit so fast."

He reached over and wiped her wet hair from her face. "Carolyn made me a good dinner that I haven't even started yet. I want to talk to you. Stay, all right?"

"I am drenched," she said. "Where's the bathroom?"

"Just down that hall," he said. "There's a clean towel on the rack. Hang up your clothes and I'll bring you some of mine. They'll be too big, but they should do."

She took off her shoes and walked stocking-footed to the bathroom, leaving little wet foot-prints on the hardwood floor. Thomas smiled at her back, feeling a relief greater than he expected at the sight of her. He wasn't just attracted to her. He felt something more. The realization frightened him. He remembered Marge, looking so pretty and fresh that day in English Lit, and then as she became toward the end, her face screwed up in anger, screaming that he didn't love her, that he had never loved her, that he only loved himself. For years he wondered if she had been right.

He hobbled over to the makeshift dresser that Carolyn and her son had rigged up for him. He leaned over the crutches and pulled open a drawer, removing a flannel shirt, underwear, and a pair of jeans that had shrunk. Then he closed the drawer and wrapped the items around his hand-holds, and walked toward the bathroom.

Jillian had left the door ajar. The shower was running and warm steam bathed the room. The shower curtain was a heavy blue—not see-through at all. He set the clothes on the toilet seat and toyed with staying until Jillian shoved the curtain back. But that was the old Thomas, the one who had gotten him into trouble two nights ago. He would wait until she appeared, warmer, drier, and wrapped in his clothes.

He felt a tightening in his groin. For the first time since the accident, his body was responding. He caught a glimpse of Jillian's arm as it brushed the shower curtain and he tried to imagine her in there. She would be small, with a narrow waist, small breasts and good-sized hips. Her legs would be well-formed and where they met her hips—his imagination stopped.

Thomas took a deep breath to calm himself, then headed out of the bathroom. She had come to discuss Heather with him, not to make love in front of the fireplace. Maybe his injury was causing the passiveness. He would never have taken so long with any other woman. And now, even though Jillian was nude and showering in his home, he still didn't take advantage of her.

The shower shut off.

Thomas hovered near the fireplace. His palms were sweaty, but not from the heat. The rain slashed against the windows and he could hear the waves crash along the shore. The bathroom door opened and closed. Thomas tightened his grip on the crutches.

Jillian appeared in the doorway. She had rolled up the sleeves of his shirt and let it hang. The jeans needed to be rolled up too. But despite the looseness of the clothing, the faint contours of her body were clearly visible.

"The underwear doesn't fit," she said and tossed the pair at him. He let go of his right crutch and caught the underwear. He looked at the pair, then at Jillian, realizing that beneath his clothing, she wore nothing.

"Jillian," he said, "I'm sorry about the other night."

"You should be." She didn't smile as she spoke, but she took a step closer.

The underwear made his hand tingle and the tingle traveled from his palm to his groin. "I really care about you," he said.

She pushed her glasses up. "Is that a line?"

He shook his head.

"Good," she said and took another step forward. "You didn't wait for me in the bathroom."

The open door was an invitation, then. So unlike him to miss the cues. She was standing right next to him. He let the underwear fall to the floor. She looked up at him, her lips quirking into a half-smile. He leaned over to kiss her and then stopped. "May I?" he asked.

"Certainly," she said and rose up on her toes. Her mouth met his faster than he expected and he nearly lost his balance. Jillian touched his shoulder lightly, stabilizing him. Her lips were warm, soft, and she smelled of Ivory Soap. He wished he wasn't on the damn crutches. He wanted to take her in his arms, hold her against his chest, and kiss her long, hard, and full, until their lips were sore and they needed air. But he had to content himself with this ever-so-light touching, feather kissing. He could feel the fire's heat scorching his side.

He lifted his mouth from hers. "You'd better call Alicia," he said.

"Yeah, I better." She kissed his nose, then walked over to the phone and dialed. She tucked the receiver between her ear and her shoulder, grabbed the cord with her left hand and leaned against the wall. The shirt gaped slightly in front, revealing rounded flesh with a touch of pink.

"Allie? It's me. I'm going to be here for a while."

Thomas braced himself against the couch, then grabbed two large pillows and threw them in front of the fireplace.

"What are you worried about dinner for?" Jillian's voice rose a notch. "You never eat it."

Thomas glanced at her. She was standing up now, the phone cord wrapped around her fingers.

"Maybe. Or maybe I'll be home in a couple of hours. I don't know. I'm not making any promises, Allie. You know where I am if you need me." Jillian hung up, stared at the phone for a moment, and then sighed.

Thomas eased himself onto the pillows then set the crutches aside. "Join me?" he asked.

Jillian came over and sat beside him, but the mood had left her. She sat stiffly, her fingers clasped tightly around her knee. "I suppose I should go right after dinner."

He put his hands on her shoulders and massaged the clenched muscles. "We'll see," he said.

"Feels good." She turned her head, first one way and then the other. The soft skin yielded beneath his fingers and he slid his hands down her back, rubbing the muscles along her shoulder blades and occasionally brushing her breasts.

She leaned against him and he ran his hands along her sides, feeling her warmth through the flannel. Her hair was damp and smelled slightly herbal. He reached the end of the flannel and stuck his fingers underneath it and into the top of her jeans.

Her skin was hot from the shower. She snuggled up closer and he could feel the curves of her body against his chest. Her breath felt warm in the hollow between his neck and his shoulders. He leaned down and found her mouth.

She wrapped her arms around him and pulled him tightly to her. He had to slide his hands out of her pants to keep from losing his balance. He gripped her tightly too, holding her small frame against him. Her hands were in his hair, forcing him closer, her mouth all over his, inside it, outside it, dotting small kisses on the sides of his face. She kissed each of his bruises and murmured over them, then kissed his chin and down his neck. When she reached his shirt, her hands unbuttoned while her mouth touched every bare patch of skin. He moaned, reached for the buttons on her shirt, but she pushed his hands away, and leaned him down on the pillows. As she reached the final button, she pulled his shirt open and hooked it over his shoulders, trapping his arms. Then she looked up at him with a mischievous smile and reached for the buckle on his pants.

"Jillian, I can't reach you."

"I know," she said and then followed the same pattern with his jeans. First her hands, then her mouth. His jeans had been split along the inside seam to fit over his cast and so slid down his legs easily. Outside, he could hear the ocean booming and for a moment, he remembered Suzette.

Then Jillian sat up, and in agonizingly slow motion, unbuttoned each button on her flannel shirt. It fell open, revealing soft, white skin and a small navel. He pulled himself up on his elbows and fought his way out of his own shirt. Jillian smiled, waited until he was done, and then eased the flannel shirt off her shoulders.

Her breasts were small and pointed upward. He had seen women with breasts like those in a Della Costa painting, but never in real life. They entranced him. He reached up with his left hand and touched her nipple with his thumb. Then he cupped the heavy bottom side of the breast, feeling its weight resting against his palm.

"You're beautiful," he said, and she simply smiled at him. Then she kissed his wrist, pulled away, and undid her jeans.

They were so large that they slipped off her waist and pooled around her knees. Her waist was small, her hips just wide enough, and the bones were slightly visible, tapering into the dark, almost black hair. She forced him back until he lay flat against the pillow, then she straddled him and eased herself over him.

She felt warm and wet and good. He heard a small sound and then realized that it had come from the back of his throat. His heart was thudding against his chest. He rested his hands on her hips and guided her as she moved up and down against him. He hadn't felt anything that good in so long.

Each time she moved, he had to grit back an orgasm. He wanted it to be good for her, so good that whenever her body shuddered, he wanted it to shudder again.

"Don't wait anymore," she whispered and he let free, flowing into her, his body shuddering in an almost painful exquisiteness. She tightened, grabbed him, and dug her face into his neck and they rocked for what seemed like forever, holding each other like that, close and warm and covered with sweat.

Then the spasms stopped, but his heart kept beating, loudly, in time with hers. A log fell in the fire, sending sparks fluttering up the chimney, and outside, the wind swept the rain into the windows. The surf pounded against the shore and Jillian's breathing was soft in his ear.

She sat up and touched his cast with her right hand. "I didn't hurt you, did I?"

He smiled. "If you did, I didn't notice."

She smoothed his hair away from his forehead. Her fingers slid over his skin. Rain slapped against the glass. "Wild night."

"Inside and out."

Her face softened and a small worry line he hadn't even realized was there smoothed off her brow. "We on talking terms again, Mr. Stanton?"

"I hope so," he said, touching those small, fascinating breasts. "I find talking almost as stimulating as this."

"Almost?"

"Almost." He wrapped his arms around her and brought her back down beside him. He wanted to hold her against him as long as he could.

"You tired?" she whispered.

"Am I supposed to be?"

She laughed and huddled against him, her body leaning feather-light on his, her head tucked in the hollow of his neck. He put his hand in her short, soft hair and listened to her breathe. The sound became regular, even, soothing. He had missed listening to another person's rhythm, feeling another person's warmth.

His pulse was slowing and he felt warm and comfortable. The fire still burned steadily, cackling above the constant pounding of the ocean. Gradually, his breathing echoed hers and he felt himself easing into sleep.

A bang startled him. Jillian stirred against him, then remained asleep. He lay there, his heart pounding, listening for the sound again. But the wind had died down and the rain had stopped. He listened for what seemed like forever and so listening, gradually slipped into a deep, contented sleep.

12

A fierce, rhythmic pounding awoke him. Thomas opened his eyes. He was cold. The fire had died and Jillian huddled against his side, taking the remaining warmth from the ashes. He listened and the pounding came again, harsh, firm, a repeating rat-a-tat that sounded human.

Jillian stirred. "Wha—?"

"I don't know," he whispered. He reached for his shirt. The ocean boomed against the beach, but the outdoors seemed quieter somehow.

Jillian blinked herself awake. "You're frightened," she said.

He was amazed at how quickly she had come to herself. He slipped the shirt over his shoulders and silently cursed at the thought of putting on his pants. It was hard enough to do alone, but he dreaded doing it now, with Jillian beside him.

The pounding started one final time. He recognized the rat-a-tat sound. It was—

"Someone is hitting a window," Jillian said. She

sat up, slipped on the large jeans and the flannel shirt before Thomas could find his underwear.

"You stay with me."

"Christ, Thomas, I've been in worse situations than this—"

"I'm not being macho, Jillian, I'm being worried."

She reached over and helped him ease the pants over his cast. The pounding continued, a counterpoint to their movements.

"It's coming from the kitchen," Jillian said. She let him lean on her as he stood, then she handed him his crutches.

The pounding stopped.

He pushed his way into the kitchen and looked out the window over the sink. The night had cleared. Rich moonlight danced across the waves, giving him a strong view of the beach. No one. He couldn't really see the porch, but—

Suddenly the front door slammed. He whirled, nearly lost his balance, and leaned against the counter for support. He couldn't see Jillian.

His breath was coming rapidly and he still wasn't getting enough oxygen. He placed his crutches before him as he started to walk, but all of his movements seemed to be in slow motion. Where would he find her? On the porch? Or would she disappear like Heather?

He bumped a kitchen chair as he moved. It hurt his rhythm, nearly knocking him over. He kept going, though, hurrying across the hardwood floor toward the door. The big door was open and the screen closed, although in his mind's eye, he could see it banging with the wind, as it had the night Heather disappeared.

God, he wished he had two good legs and the ability to run. His mind was running, seeing Jillian in the arms of a cloaked figure, being dragged across the beach, himself helpless to stop it. He pushed the screen door open. It swung back and slammed against the outside wall. He hurried across the porch, the rubber tips of his crutches sliding along the wet wood.

As he turned the corner, he saw Jillian standing near the kitchen window and he took a deep breath in relief.

She looked back at him. Her expression was flat, what she probably used as her reporter's face. "Thomas."

She wanted him to come over there. A fear rose hard within him and he wanted to remain where he was. But he made himself take the last few steps to Jillian.

The porch was empty.

She touched his arm and pointed. A rose had been taped to a beam, wedged against the wood. Its fragile petals moved with the slight breeze. It couldn't have been there long or the storm would have destroyed it. He leaned over. Something white—a card—had been attached to the stem.

"Can you get it?" he asked.

Jillian reached over and removed both the card and the rose. She glanced at the card, her lower lip tightening ever so slightly, and then handed everything to him.

The rose was fresh, hothouse grown, almost

scentless. He had seen so many like them on movie sets and he used to bring them home or to the women he was seeing. Marge called them his "token displays of affection" long after they had split up.

Finally he let his gaze drop to the card. It wasn't a card really, more a piece of paper attached to the stem and wrapped around two thorns. In the faint light, he could barely make out what it said. *To Daddy.*

He let go of the flower and it dropped onto the wet, warped wood. Jillian bent over to pick it up.

"Leave it go," he said.

She remained in a half-crouch. "But don't you want it? To talk to the police or something?"

"It's probably nothing. Some sicko. I'm sure a few fans will start appearing too now that people know where I am." His voice sounded smooth, glib. He couldn't remember when he'd learned how to do that. Somewhere in the mid-seventies, after he'd been acting for a while. The voice control came naturally even when what he really wanted to do was scream and stomp the rose out of existence. "Did you see anyone?"

She stood up and looked across the beach, then back at the driveway as if something would appear now. "No," she said. "And I was looking too. Although I did notice a lot of sand on the porch as if someone had been walking on the beach before they came up here. But who would be walking on the beach in this weather?"

"I don't know," he said. He put his hand on her

shoulder, glad to feel the warmth of her through the flannel.

They went back to the house. He waited until they got inside before he said, "I asked you to stay with me."

She tilted her head up defiantly. "Thomas, I can handle myself. You wouldn't believe the things I've seen. I've made it through—"

"I don't care," he said as he snapped on the overhead light. The room was a mess. The pillows were crumpled against each other, wrinkles and a large wet spot too clearly visible from the other side of the room.

She frowned and drew herself up straighter. He put up his hand to stop whatever she was planning to say.

"I don't care what you've been through," he said. "I came down those stairs one night to find that my daughter had disappeared. I sure as hell don't want to go through that again."

Her entire body relaxed. Her mouth opened and her eyes grew softer. "Thomas, I'm sorry. I didn't think. I—God."

He smoothed the hair from her face. His hands were shaking. "It's okay," he said.

She nodded, her head down, lips tight, eyes focused on the floor. He put his finger beneath her chin and lifted it. Then he leaned down and brushed her lips with his own.

Her mouth opened and he felt the warmth of her breath. He wrapped his mouth to fit hers, finding a kind of comfort in her softness. Finally he pulled away. She remained for a moment with her eyes closed, then she opened them. The irises were clear gray with flecks of brown.

"I am sorry," she said.

"I know," he said. "I was just frightened."

She touched his cheek, stood on her toes, and kissed him lightly. Then she went into the kitchen and pulled open the refrigerator. She took out two cans of diet Coke, set them on the counter, and closed the refrigerator door. He walked to the kitchen door. She opened the Cokes, the pop tabs hissing as the fizz leaked into the air, then set the cans on the table. She pulled back a chair and sat down, wrapping her hands around her can and watching him.

He suppressed a sigh. He hadn't realized until she sat down that he wanted to be by himself. After that outburst, he didn't feel right asking her to leave immediately. He hobbled the last few steps into the kitchen, leaned his crutches against the counter, and sat beside her.

Jillian slid his Coke over to him. The can was cold and damp. "I spent a month in Belfast, early on in my tenure at NPR," she said, pronouncing "Belfast" with a Gaelic lilt. "My first week was really quiet. Belfast is a torn-up city, kind of like Berkeley was in the late sixties, only much much worse. People try to go about their business, but it's hard to ignore the hole in the street where the last car bomb went off or the buildings with the boarded-up walls and the sagging foundations. Some parts of the city hadn't been touched at all, but others . . . I jumped every time a car backfired or someone yelled too loudly. Finally, one of the veteran reporters—his name was Jake—pulled me over and said, 'You blow like a bomb at every little thing, you go home in a body bag. Only this one is white instead of black.'"

She drank from her Coke, so Thomas took a sip from his. It tasted syrupy and more acidic than usual. He waited because he knew she had a point to this story.

"There are two ways to blow, Thomas. The first is to jump every time a car backfires, to shatter every time a bomb does go off. The second is to remain silent, ignore it all, until finally, you become the bomb and you're the one that's ticking."

He clenched the Coke can, his knuckles white. "How loudly am I ticking?"

"Like a grandfather clock," she said.

He nodded. "What am I supposed to do?"

"Talk to me." She took another sip from her Coke. At some point she had put on her glasses, but he couldn't remember when.

"Some sicko put that rose there."

"Probably," she said. "But doesn't it make you angry? Why don't you go to the police?"

He pushed his Coke can away. The liquid sloshing inside the can made little metallic sounds. "My turn to tell you a story." He ran his hand through his hair. It was slightly damp. "About three weeks after I started in *Restless Heart*, people I didn't know started coming to the house, ringing the bell and asking for me. It went on all the time. At first, Marge was irritated, then she got scared. I wasn't home through most of it. We got an unlisted phone number, we took our name off the mailbox, and finally we moved, but somehow people kept finding us. I went to the cops, and the one I talked to just laughed at me. 'Didn't they explain to you the price of fame, Mr. Stanton?' he asked. 'What you got to do is buy one of those houses with the big, locking electric fence and set up a security system and have someone screen your mail. Then the problem will go away.'"

"You're saying you just have to get used to this."

Thomas stared at the table. The Coke can had left a ring on the surface. "Even if it hurts," he said.

Jillian put her hand on top of his. "I'm—"

"I wish they would leave Heather out of this," he said suddenly, surprising even himself. "I can be their Anthony Short or Jason Michaels, but they can't be my Heather. No matter how hard I try, I can't get Heather back."

She was right; the words felt like an explosion. His breathing was heavy and his heart was pounding. Jillian's hand tightened on his. After a moment, she got up, came over, and held his head against her chest. The flannel was warm against his cheek, her fingers soft in his hair. No one had held him like this when Heather disappeared. No one had held him when he knew that she was dead either. Marge had stood on the other side of the hospital bed, lines etched in her face, her eyes wet with unshed tears, but she had stood far enough away that he couldn't touch her, even if he'd wanted to.

"Why don't you come home with me tonight?" Jillian said.

He shook his head against her belly. "No. I want to stay here."

She kissed him lightly. "I love you, Thomas," she said softly.

He tightened his grip on her waist. So many women had said that to him, expecting a response from Jason Michaels. But he thought Jillian saw him.

He wondered if she wanted an answer. If he said "I love you" it would cheapen the moment. He had said those words too many times to too many women for them to ever sound sincere again. He buried his face in her hair.

The ache in his heart had grown deeper.

13

When he woke up the next morning, he was alone on the cot. He reached for his crutches, seeing in his memory Heather's rumpled linen on the edge of the sofa. He fumbled, nearly fell, and then remembered. Jillian had left in the middle of the night. He had walked her to her car, watched as she backed out of the driveway, and waited until her lights had faded on the highway before he went back inside. She had called him eight minutes later to let him know that she had arrived safely.

That didn't stop the worry from eating at the back of his throat. He put the crutches under his armpits and swung, naked, over to the phone. For a moment, he stared at it, knowing that he was being superstitious: just because he felt worried didn't mean that anything had happened.

But something could have. He sat down in the chair, the upholstery sharp and scratchy against his buttocks, picked up the receiver, and punched Jillian's number.

The phone rang four times. His breathing grew

more irregular with every ring. He was about to hang up and dial again when someone picked up the other line.

"Yes?" Jillian, sounding angry.

He let out the air he had been holding. He felt ridiculous. "Hi," he said.

"Hi, Thomas." Her voice relaxed slightly, but still held an edge.

"Bad time, huh?"

"Actually, good time. Alicia just left."

He waited, hearing anger in the silence.

"She was out all night. She comes wandering in this morning, acting as if nothing happened."

"You didn't know?"

"I don't check her room like she's a child!" He heard Jillian take a deep breath. "Sorry, Thomas."

"It's okay," he said.

"It's just that she's so damn passive-aggressive. I was with you, so she decided she could go do whatever she wanted."

He was getting cold. Through the window, he could see the ocean melting into the gray sky. "You ever thought of having her see someone?"

"Yeah, who in Seavy Village?"

"Maybe not in Seavy Village. Maybe in Portland or Eugene."

"I'm afraid to ask. I'm afraid she'll say no."

"If she doesn't go," he said, "why don't you? At least you'll learn how to deal with her."

"You don't think I'm handling her right."

"No," Thomas said. "*You* don't think so."

Jillian sighed. After a moment, she said, "I enjoyed last night."

"So did I."

The silence again, thick and heavy. Thomas didn't want to break the connection, although goose bumps were running along his arm.

"Why did you call, Thomas?"

I was worried about you. I'm afraid I'll lose you like I lost Marge, like I lost Heather. "I thought maybe I could make you lunch."

"I've got a meeting I'm suppose to cover in five minutes. I don't know when it'll end."

"How about I don't put anything in until you arrive."

"Sounds good. Thanks."

He thought she was about to hang up when he heard, "Thomas?"

"Yeah?"

"I'm glad you called."

"So am I." Then he waited until she hung up before he ended the connection.

The living room seemed as gray as the sky. He squinted. The clock on the mantel read 10:30. He had slept longer than he had planned and he was cold. He wished he could take a shower. He always used to take long, hot showers, to think and to get warm. The sponge bath he took every morning left him feeling only semiclean and even colder than when he started. He got out of the chair and was starting across the room when someone knocked at the door.

"Shit," he said. He hurried the rest of the way to the cot and grabbed the robe he kept tucked at the edge. A key rattled in the lock. Carolyn. "Just a minute!" he called.

He grabbed the robe and swung it over his shoulders.

The door opened. "Mr. Stanton, sir? You okay?"

He closed the robe over his lap. "Fine."

Carolyn was standing beside the door frame, her hand over her mouth. A slow blush was building in her cheeks. "I'm sorry, sir. I didn't realize—"

"It's all right," he said. "I'm usually up by now. I had a late night."

"I could leave, sir, and come back later."

"No," he said, then realized the word sounded harsh. "I was awake."

Carolyn's smile returned. She set some envelopes and a package on the end table. "I brought your mail," she said as she went over to the fire. She crouched beside it, opened the screens, and began to assemble the wood.

"I bet it's cold outside." Despite his robe, Thomas felt naked.

"Not so bad as last night. That storm kept me up all hours." She stuffed newspaper in the empty spots between the logs. Then she reached to the top of the mantel and picked up the tin of matches.

Thomas felt the chill seep up under the robe and lie against his naked hips. "I'm going to get cleaned up."

He hurried down the hall to the bathroom. The shower curtain was open, just as Jillian had left it. He smiled, remembering her arm brushing against the plastic, the steam rising in the room, and the smell of soap. He used the toilet, then ran hot water in the sink. Too late, he realized he had forgotten to bring a change of clothes. He belted the robe again, tighter, and opened the door.

Carolyn had set a clean shirt, underwear, and a pair of cast-jeans on the clothes hamper. He smiled at her sensitivity, grabbed the clothes, and closed the door once more.

He dropped his robe and looked at the body reflected in the full-length mirror on the back of the door. His bruises were fading and he was beginning to look like himself again. The pain had receded a little, taking the grayness from his skin. He had gained weight and his tan was gone, but the ugly, discolored patches that made him look like a refugee from a horror film were gone as well. He looked a lot less movie-star perfect and a lot more like an ordinary Joe. Maybe Jillian liked that. Or maybe she was just interested because he was Thomas Stanton.

Thomas grimaced. He hated it when thoughts like that surfaced. Jillian cared because of who he was, not because of his profession. She had never once asked him the typical groupie questions. In fact, she had hardly spoken of his work at all. It had been Alicia who had made constant references to his acting.

He grabbed the half-used bar of Ivory, dipped it in the water, and proceeded to lather his body. The skin felt soft, rather fine, a bit alien. He remembered Jillian's fingers on it, her lips, brushing against his nipples, planting kisses near his groin. She had felt so good, her body warm against his.

After he set the soap down, he grabbed a washcloth and ran it under the faucet.

Then he sponged the soap off of his body. Every time he took a sponge bath, he remembered a commercial he once did—"Most soaps leave a soap film," he whispered to himself, and then smiled. Acting had made him an expert on everything trivial.

And nothing important. He remembered the feeling in his stomach as he had awakened, knowing that Jillian was in trouble, but not knowing how. She had been in riots and done tours in Belfast. He, on the other hand, had only played at danger, let other people fall for him—except accidentally—and had watched curiously from a window as a cloaked figure ran across the beach moments after his daughter had probably died. Jillian knew how to handle trouble. He did not.

Thomas wrung out the washcloth and tossed it over the side of the bathtub. Carolyn would take care of it later. He grabbed the shirt Carolyn had laid out for him and slipped into it. Then he propped himself against the toilet and slid on his underwear. The position embarrassed him, made him feel helpless and ugly. Jillian had helped him the night before and that had been embarrassing enough. But every morning he had to watch himself in the mirror, a slightly overweight, too-white man, attempting to pull boxer shorts over a large white plaster cast. Funny that something like that wouldn't bother him on film, but in the privacy of his own bathroom he felt strange.

He eased on the jeans and stood up. The morning ritual/ordeal was done. It was time to go back to the living room and finish the scripts Connie had sent him and then to see what mail she had decided to forward to him.

He made his way back down the corridor. Carolyn was bustling in the kitchen. Her humming echoed through the entire house. He liked having her here. If he decided to make Seavy Village his home, he might ask her to take the position full-time and permanently. The house wasn't really big enough for a live-in housekeeper, but Carolyn just lived a mile or so away. She could handle his needs and her own family's with ease.

And besides, he liked her.

"I put some food in the freezer," she said when she saw him. "And I put some casseroles in the lower part of the fridge."

"Going away?" he asked, half seriously, trying to think what he would do while she was gone.

She shook her head. "I was just thinking that I don't give you much of a choice. I just make what I make. But now there's shrimp casserole in there and chicken and a whole bunch of other things, not counting what I have in the freezer. I put the instructions on them so that you can fix them any time you like."

"You're a marvel," he said.

She smoothed back her already neat hair. "I like to do a good job, is all. Besides, now there's more for you and Miss Maxwell."

His palms ached from leaning forward too hard on the crutches. "Did I mention anything about Jillian?" He honestly didn't remember.

"Oh, no, sir." Carolyn shrugged, then leaned

back against the counter. "It's just that Seavy Village is so small."

Thomas nodded. He walked toward the mail Carolyn had left on the end table as her words played back in his mind. Small. If the city was small— "Carolyn?"

She had found a glass cleaner and a sponge, and as she turned, her pose reminded him of a commercial he had once done the voice-over for. *Happy women use . . .* "Mmm?"

"I, um," he found himself staring at the half-empty spray bottle. The label was turned away from him and he wondered what the product was. "I—had noticed that I'm not really bothered by fans out here."

"Oh, no, sir," Carolyn said. "Folks around here know that you like your privacy. They're not going to disturb it. Unless you want—?"

"I had expected at least the tourists."

Carolyn set the spray bottle down. It wasn't the one he had advertised. She was frowning. "I thought you wanted to be left alone."

"I do," he said, then realized why no one was bothering him. Carolyn had sent out the word that his beach house was off limits.

"No one has said anything to those tourists." The vehemence in her tone struck him. "The less they know about Seavy Village, the better."

He nodded, wondering why he had been accepted into the fold so easily. The old nagging guilt, returning. Of course they had let him in because he was famous. Whether they would let him stay was another issue altogether.

He sat down on the sofa and pulled the mail off the end table. Another large package from Connie. A script, probably. She would bombard him with them until he decided to return to work. He probably should call his accountant, figure out his own income if he lived on residuals and his accumulated earnings so far. Filming another Short sequence brought back memories of the rain-drenched afternoon and the scream of that damn cat.

Carolyn banged a cupboard in the kitchen. He set the package aside, opened the few envelopes that Connie had forwarded. She had a list of names whose mail got forwarded without being opened, friends mostly, although a few were fans he had never met. He scanned the letters—two from old girlfriends and one from an old college buddy—and then picked up the final envelope.

It had been mailed from a local address. The handwriting was thick and blocky, almost as if it were being deliberately concealed. He turned the envelope over. No return address. The postmark read midnight and it had been mailed from the Seavy Village exchange.

He nearly ripped the envelope as he tore it open. The paper felt blunt against his fingers. He pulled the letter out and looked at it. A simple sheet of notepaper, folded in half. Along the top, written in a flowery, half-familiar script was a simple line.

I miss you, Daddy.

The handwriting looked like Heather's, but it wasn't Heather's. She never called him Daddy, not even in her little, cute moments. He was always

Dad or Father or even, when they were experimenting, Thomas. But never ever Daddy.

He took a deep slow breath, feeling the ache build in his heart. He remembered the warmth of Jillian's arms around him, the pain as she had told him she loved him. How loudly was he ticking? He didn't know.

"You all right, Mr. Stanton?"

Carolyn was crouched beside the couch, concern on her homely face. He was ticking louder than he thought.

"I'm fine," he said. "Would you mind opening the screens on the fireplace?"

The look she threw him was confused, but she stood up anyway. He crumpled the paper, hearing the satisfying crackle as its edges bit into his hand. Then he tossed the letter into the fire. It stopped just inside the grate. A spark fell on the edge and ignited the letter slowly. The fire grew along the top and then, suddenly, the entire paper burst into flames. Carolyn closed the screens.

"Bad news?" she asked.

Thomas looked at her, wondering what she would say if she knew that one of those nice villagers that she kept away from his house had decided to start playing pranks on him. "Just junk mail," he said. "I hate it."

"Me, too. You know those circulars the Safeway sends—"

The ring of the phone saved him from whatever insight she had about Safeway circulars. She picked up the phone and moved it closer to him. He answered. It was Jillian.

"I'm still down here," she said. "It looks like the meeting's going to take most of the afternoon. Can I skip lunch and meet you for dinner instead?"

He took a deep breath against the disappointment—he had been looking forward to seeing her—and then said, "Sure. Where?"

"Newspaper office. I'm driving because I'm buying."

"Jillian—"

"I don't have time for arguments, Thomas. I have to grab a cheese sandwich before the session starts again. White bread and someone tore the damn crusts off."

He laughed. "What time?"

"Five okay?"

"You'll be there?"

"I can't survive on crustless cheese sandwiches much past that. Some blue-haired old lady must think these things are art or something." Jillian made a sound of disgust. "I gotta run. Five all right?"

"Five is fine." He hung up the phone, stretched, sighed, and glanced at the package. Maybe he would read that script. It was either that or think about that note. Whoever was sending them knew a lot about him. That wasn't hard, given the tabloid coverage. But not many people had seen Heather's handwriting. Coincidence? Or purposeful? He didn't know. And he wasn't sure if he wanted to care.

14

 He heard voices as he went down the walk to the newspaper office. The front office had its lights out, but he could see light reflected across the lawn from the main windows near the side. Jillian was there, even if her young receptionist wasn't.

He balanced himself carefully as he opened the front door. Sometimes it felt as if he were going to wear that cast forever. He sighed and pushed his way in. The voices grew louder.

"Stop it, Allie."

"He doesn't care about you."

"How the hell do you know? And what does it matter to you?"

"It matters."

"Sure. Frankly, Alicia, I don't think you give a fuck about anyone."

Thomas felt heat rising in his cheeks. He banged loudly at the desk to call attention to himself so that he wouldn't walk in on Jillian and her sister.

"Did you hear something?" Alicia asked.

Thomas made his way through the hall. "It's just me."

Jillian stood beside her desk. She was wearing a large green sweater with the sleeves pushed up past her elbows. Her short hair was mussed, as if she had been running her fingers through it.

Alicia was wrapped in a ski jacket, her hands deep in the pockets. She faced Thomas, her mouth drawn back in a thin, harsh line. "How long have you been listening?"

The question was impossible to answer. He had overheard, but not purposely—at least not for long. He stopped on the other side of Jillian's desk, caught her gaze, and smiled at her. "Dinner?"

"We have to take Alicia," Jillian said sullenly.

He bit back the irritation rising in his throat and looked at the young girl. "I'm glad you're finally joining us," he said.

"Smooth, smooth. Why don't you go ahead and admit that you don't want me around."

"Why should I?" he said. "I've been looking forward to this. I figure maybe after some time together, we won't be in combat mode anymore."

Alicia's eyes narrowed and she tilted her head back. He had surprised her, and that made him feel good. The girl was intriguing, perhaps because her hostility was so inexplicable to him. Perhaps because she reminded him of Heather.

"I'm still buying," Jillian said. She didn't even try to force any lightness into her tone. "Where do we want to go?"

"Since Alicia's joining us," Thomas said, "let's go somewhere fairly nice. Let me buy."

That was the wrong thing to say. He could see Jillian's anger rise with the flush in her cheeks before she opened her mouth. "I can—"

"I want to pay for dinner," Thomas said. "You spend time with Alicia all the time, but I never get a chance. Let me, and you can catch it later. I *was* supposed to make lunch, you know."

Jillian took a deep breath, grabbed her purse, and slung it over her shoulder. "All right," she said. She closed the top drawer on her desk and locked it. "But if you're going to eat with us, Allie, you're going to eat. Understand?"

Alicia shrugged. Her hands pushed deeper into her pockets. Thomas got the sense that the girl had trapped herself. She had probably insisted on coming to dinner and then discovered that dinner wasn't really what she wanted.

"You still driving?" he asked Jillian.

"Sure," she said. She picked up her keys, then reached over and shut off the lamp beside her desk. As they went through the reception area, she punched on the answering machine. Alicia opened the door and left it wide for Thomas to pass through.

The night was dark and slightly damp. The ocean was louder than usual, although they were nearly a mile away from it. Thomas took a deep breath of the salty fresh air. Dinner was not going to be the quiet romantic evening he wanted. In fact, it could come close to a nightmare, if he didn't play things right.

Jillian locked the door behind them and lightly touched his arm. "I'm sorry," she said softly.

He made sure his smile was gentle. "I under-stand obligations."

Alicia had gone on ahead. He couldn't tell by her straight-legged stance in the center of the sidewalk if she had heard or not. She went to the passenger side of Jillian's car and waited. Thomas hobbled up and stood beside her. Alicia looked down at the door, studying it the way people studied the floor numbers in elevators. He said nothing. He wasn't going to force anything with this girl except, per-haps, a little kindness.

Jillian unlocked the car door, then walked over to her side of the car. Thomas got in slowly, easing his cast into the front seat while holding his crutches outside the door.

Jillian sat beside him. "Allie, take Thomas's crutches."

"No," he said. "It's okay. I—"

Alicia yanked the crutches out of his hand and tossed them in the back. They landed with a clatter against the floor. Jillian's grip on the steering wheel was so tight that her knuckles were white. Thomas pulled his door closed, careful not to let it bang.

"Inn at the Sea, please, driver," he said. The tone wasn't quite light, but appropriate enough for the tense atmosphere in the car.

"Inn at the Sea?" Alicia said. Thomas could see her through the rearview mirror. Her hands were folded on her lap and she sat straight without lean-ing against the back of the seat.

"It's expensive, so you better eat," Jillian said. Thomas put his hand lightly on her knee. The constant harping about Alicia's lack of appetite did no good. If Thomas had heard as much about the way he ate, he'd probably rebel too.

Jillian looked at him without moving her head. She nodded almost imperceptibly, then released the emergency brake and turned the key in the ignition. The little car started with a roar. The muffler was going. Thomas almost spoke up, then decided against it.

Dinner on pins and needles. Each word measured, weighed, and considered before spoken. Not the relaxing evening he had planned. Relaxing, romantic evening he had planned. But he'd had too many of those in his life. He had always searched for the romance and the passion. Romance and passion were exciting. Tense dinners filled with measured words were not.

Jillian pulled out onto the empty street. Her lights illuminated the rows of trees lining the side of the road. The houses they passed looked warm and comfortable, shaded against the coastal weather, their curtained windows holding in a host of secrets. When he was a kid, he used to imagine what life in those houses would be like. He imagined dinners where the entire family talked happily about their daily adventures, a mother who baked pies and a father who read the paper in the living room, his slipper-clad feet crossed in front of him. A combination of *Leave It to Beaver*, *Make Room for Daddy*, and *Father Knows Best*. Maybe that's why he'd had so much trouble with Marge. Life with her achieved that warm hominess only rarely. Most of the time, behind the pies and the newspapers, were bills, a crying child and, toward the end, bitter silences. He always expected perfection and he never got it.

Was that what he expected with Jillian? Was he bringing Alicia along tonight to prove that things between him and Jillian could never be story-book perfect?

"You look lost," Jillian said. They were on the Coastal Highway, passing the darkened storefronts and the video stores with posters of Mel Gibson lining their windows. He didn't remember the car turning onto that street.

"Just thinking," he said.

"What about?"

"Home." He wondered how stupid it would sound to tell her about his fantasies. Maybe he had become an actor because picture-perfect families were possible only on celluloid.

"The beach house?" Jillian asked.

He shook his head. "Where I grew up."

"Where did you grow up?" The question was sharp. Alicia. As if she resented not knowing.

"All over," he said. "No one special place."

The Inn by the Sea rose along the beach like a mansion in a forties gothic. The ocean slapped the rocks below, sending spray against the side of the building. The inn was fairly new, built at odd angles to protect it from the sea winds. Large glass windows faced the beach. Candlelight flickered and dim shapes moved behind the glass.

Jillian pulled in. Only a handful of cars dotted the parking lot. They were still early, but Thomas knew the parking lot would fill as the evening wore on. Inn by the Sea was a tourist favorite.

Alicia got out of the car, slammed the door, and started up the walk. Thomas opened his door and grimaced. The damn girl had left his crutches in the backseat. He swung his legs out the side and said, "Jillian, would you mind grabbing my crutches?"

"Didn't Allie—?"

"I didn't ask her to." He watched Jillian reach into the backseat and he wondered how so much resentment could build up over such a short period of time. If he proved to be demanding and difficult—which he was, no doubt—would she start resenting him too?

She leaned over and kissed him before handing him the crutches. "Love you," she whispered.

The words sent a tremor through him. He touched her cheek, but said nothing.

She stood beside the door and waited as he hauled himself out. Damn the insecurity. It wasn't like him. None of this was like him. Alicia was right; he usually wanted a piece of ass. A piece of ass was easy. Wham, bam, thank you, ma'am—here, have a rose, it's for remembrance and oh, what was your name again? Love. That required guts. Would Jillian hate him if he decided that he couldn't do it?

This close to the beach, he could see the surf rising hard against the sand. Birds stood in pools of water along the edge, flying low if a wave came in too far. The sea always looked different. Tonight it looked romantic, the kind of shots a director in that old forties gothic would edit between the love scenes somewhere toward the start of the film.

Alicia was waiting by the door, first leaning on one foot, then the other, in a sort of instinctive dance against the cold. Jillian glanced at her sister, then back at him. "I *am* sorry," she said again.

"Don't apologize anymore," he said. "I was serious when I said I wanted Alicia to come along."

"I really wanted to talk to you," Jillian said. "I've done a little digging on Hargrave's information."

"Then tell me." Thomas carefully stepped over a concrete parking bump. Life was full of hazards for the feet. "We can't edit ourselves just because your sister is along."

Then he realized the truth in what he said. Conversations measured and weighed were not the way to make it through an evening. That only brought tensions and resentments, the things Alicia rebelled against anyway. The girl had an uncanny knack for spotting his insincerity. He decided to see what she would do with Thomas playing Thomas.

As he approached the entrance, he said, "Alicia, would you mind getting the door?"

She made a face, but she pulled the door open and held it as he made his way through.

"Thanks," he said.

She didn't reply. The dark entry smelled like liquor, day-old cigarettes, and cooked seafood. His stomach rumbled. He hadn't realized how hungry he was. A girl not much older than Alicia hugged menus to her chest. "Three?" she asked, her gaze on Thomas. He recognized the look as one of a shy fan: *Notice me, Mr. Stanton. I'm somebody you should remember. Please?*

He nodded and added, "Nonsmoking," knowing that she would probably cherish those words for the rest of her life. He could imagine her talking with her girlfriends: "And when he spoke, he sounded just like Jason!"

She led them up two stairs, waiting for Thomas to maneuver his way to the top. Then she put them in a table at the corner between the two large windows, overlooking the sea. The chairs were deep brown, plush, with heavy padded arms. The tablecloth was linen and large linen napkins stood like hats in front of each plate. A candle flickered in a glass cone. The perfect romantic setting and there he was, acting like a father to a recalcitrant sixteen-year-old.

Which is what he would have been in exactly a year if Heather hadn't died.

Jillian pulled his chair back for him and took his crutches as he sat down. "Such service," he said to hide his discomfort.

She tucked the crutches beneath his chair, within reach of his hand, but out of the traffic pattern for the servers. Then she sat down across from him. Alicia was already sitting in the only chair facing the dining room, her back to the spectacular view. She still huddled in her coat.

"Cold, Allie?" he asked, Jillian's nickname for her sister harsh against his tongue.

Alicia looked at him, her eyes dark circles in the planes of her face. "I'm comfortable," she said.

"When you get to be as thin as Allie," Jillian said, "you need a coat just to stay cold. Getting warm is damn near impossible."

Alicia seemed to wrap her body against itself even tighter. Thomas brushed his fingers against the back of Jillian's hand. "Let it go tonight," he said.

"What, you want me to ignore the fact that this girl is killing herself?"

He shook his head and sighed. Maybe he wasn't strong enough for this. "No," he said. "I just want to have a nice dinner."

Both women looked at him, identical expressions on their faces. He hadn't realized how deep the resemblance was until that moment of dual confusion. They really didn't know what they were doing to each other. The constant sniping and the small bombs planted beneath each other had become as commonplace as the faint odor of a cat box in the place a person called home.

He opened the menu. The prices here were middling. He would be able to buy them all dinner for under fifty dollars, unlike L.A., where an expensive restaurant meant that he would lose a few hundred dollars without really trying.

"Order whatever you want," he said, and remembered his father using those same words on the few occasions he had been able to take them out. Then the bill would come and his father would stare at it as if it had wounded him. Thomas learned early to look for the cheapest item on the menu.

He still did that. He skimmed the menu and

found it, a simple hamburger, weighing in at seven dollars. Then he scanned until he found the most expensive—a two-course seafood dinner for twenty-five. He chose the shrimp, which came in somewhere in the middle.

He closed his menu to find Alicia and Jillian still studying theirs. A waiter had given them bread and tall crystal glasses filled with water. He took a sip, and gazed out at the ocean as he waited.

The birds were gone and waves were lower than they had been before. The light from the windows reflected off the foam. Under the carefully blended tones of a piped-in hit that he recognized but couldn't name, the roar of the waves sounded more musical, more in tune with the disquiet he was feeling.

The waiter came and took their order—Jillian the oyster strips and Alicia the fillet of sole diet plate—and then left them to their silence. Thomas took a piece of bread from the basket in the center of the table. The bread looked homemade, its crust hard and flaky, its middle warm and doughy. He slabbed butter on it and bit in, savoring the taste. Alicia watched him, her lips pursed. A line came to him from the after school special he had done: *They're like famine victims—starving, yet their every thought is of food.*

Jillian also took a piece of bread, started to shove the basket toward Alicia, then glanced at Thomas and stopped. She grabbed a slice for herself and set it on her bread plate. "I've been checking on the information Hargrave gave us," she said, dipping her knife into the butter.

Thomas watched her spread the butter on the bread. Her fingers were long and slender with short, well-kept nails. "What are you finding?"

She took a bite from the bread. Alicia watched her, waiting, as Thomas was. He felt very adult during this moment, like a parent, like he was sitting in his father's chair, in his father's body, listening to the woman he had married talk about something that excluded the kids. He wished he hadn't asked the question, hadn't told Jillian this topic was all right, but it was too late now.

Jillian dabbed at her mouth with the napkin. "The old stuff is hard to trace," she said. "I think I'm going to have to dig through county records—and even that might not turn up anything. Seavy Village didn't have a newspaper until the late twenties, and it was published irregularly through the thirties. So I mostly used the *Oregonian* and the Newport paper."

He didn't care how she got the information, just the information that she got. Alicia straightened the napkin on her lap. Her gaze kept darting to the bread in the middle of the table.

"They had several short one or two paragraph squibs on the murders. Some of them were called accidents. Some had 'evidence of foul play.' But none of them were linked. It was as if the paper took no notice of the fact that they all happened on the same stretch of beach."

"Maybe some of the linking information wasn't released?"

Jillian shrugged her shoulders. "There was

barely enough information in the articles to verify that they were the ones I was looking for."

The waiter set salads down before them. Thomas's rested on a clear ridged plate. Lettuce, cucumbers, tomatoes, sprouts, and croutons sat beneath a pool of blue cheese dressing. Alicia got cottage cheese and peaches. She shoved the peaches aside and picked at the cottage cheese with her fork.

"What does all this matter anyway?" she asked.

Her flat tone sent a shiver through him. Jillian must have seen Thomas's reaction for she touched the back of his hand. "Allie, a lot of people have died on that stretch of beach, not just Thomas's daughter."

"Heather," Thomas said softly.

Alicia had flattened the cottage cheese on her plate. "She's dead. It's over. Why don't you just move, then you don't have to worry about it."

"I thought of that," Thomas said, concentrating on each word. "That's why I haven't been to Seavy Village in two years. But I can't forget it. When we were doing the Anthony Short filmings—"

He stopped, realized who he was talking to. Jillian had stopped eating and watched him expectantly. Alicia put a forkful of cottage cheese in her mouth and chewed slowly, her eyes dark. What the hell. Alicia couldn't think any less of him than she already did.

"When we were doing the Anthony Short filmings on the coast, I kept getting little reminders. Things creep through the subconscious when you're trying to suppress them. Once I even saw a caped figure run across the beach." He smiled. "Turns out it was my own reflection in a piece of glass. I was wearing the cape. The glass was moving. But it was eerie. I couldn't concentrate. I couldn't work. I had this feeling that something awful was going to happen. And then it did."

He shoved his salad around, much like Alicia playing with her cottage cheese. "Sometimes I think the fall was because of my attitude. And sometimes I think it was because of what happened to Heather. And sometimes I wonder if I even fell at all."

"You mean someone pushed you?" Jillian asked.

Thomas shook his head.

"He means," Alicia said, "he wonders if he jumped."

He stared at the girl. She stared back. There was an understanding between them, even if she didn't like him. Even if he wasn't sure he liked her. What he had felt from the beginning—and the reason she could attack him so effectively—was that she understood him.

"Yeah," he said softly. "I do wonder that sometimes."

Jillian set her salad plate aside. The fork rattled against the glass plate and tumbled onto the tablecloth, but Jillian didn't notice. She was staring at Thomas. "You don't mean that," she said.

He smiled noncommittally and put another forkful of salad into his mouth. The lettuce tasted fresh and green, the tomato soft and succulent. Alicia sat rigidly in her chair, her gaze on Thomas. He did mean it. That was the problem. And the person who understood was a sixteen-year-old girl who hated him.

"What else did you find out?" he asked Jillian.

Her frown remained, but she seemed as eager to change the subject as he was. "Nothing seems to link the people that died there. Some were from California. Others were locals. A handful of tourists that could have been killed by the sea. The only thing they have in common is the place they died."

The waiter swooped by and picked up their salad plates. He shoved Alicia's aside, since she was not done. "You looking for some kind of murderer or what?" Alicia asked.

"I don't know what we're looking for," Jillian said.

The waiter stopped in front of their table. He placed the diet plate in front of Alicia, another plate brimming with food in front of Jillian, and then set the shrimp down before Thomas. The smell, warm and rich, seeped up to him. The shrimp was artfully arranged around a seashell bowl of cocktail sauce, everything sitting on lettuce. His potato steamed beside the lettuce and a mixture of carrots and peas lent color to the remaining corner of the plate.

Alicia took a small bite of fish and chewed it for a long time, as if the fish were tough and stringy. Thomas dipped a piece of shrimp into cocktail sauce. "You don't think all the deaths are coincidence, though, do you, Jillian?"

She shook her head. "The deaths are too similar."

"Some kind of cult, maybe?" Thomas asked. Oregon had had its share of cults, the last being the Bagwan Shree Rajneesh whose followers had poisoned food in small town restaurants along the Columbia Gorge.

"I don't know of anything like that near here," Jillian said. "And besides, it would have to be a cult of long-standing."

"Like Catholicism," Alicia said.

Thomas grinned. He ate some of his potato, pushed aside the peas and carrots, and continued to pick at the shrimp.

"I just wonder if it's the beach," Jillian said.

"God, Jilly." Alicia's fork clattered on the plate. She took a drink of water, then wiped her mouth with the back of her hand.

"You don't believe that stuff Hargrave told us," Thomas said.

Jillian shrugged. "I have learned over the years that people have wide and varying beliefs. And sometimes there are reasons for those beliefs. Sometimes it's real simple. Sometimes there is no explanation at all."

"No explanation that you can find," Thomas said. He ate the last piece of shrimp, then dabbed at his lip with his napkin. The conversation sounded too much like the dialogue in that horror movie he'd starred in here at Seavy Village. *Professor, I think the only explanation we have is the supernatural one. I'm sorry, sir. I know that isn't very professional of me.*

"Maybe the murders are familial," Thomas said. "Or maybe some of those deaths really were accidents and a few were killings. It's easy to die on that beach. Turn your back to the ocean while you're alone and it'll grab you, dash you against the rocks and smash you into little bits before anyone even knows you're gone."

"If you believe that," Jillian said stiffly, "then why are you doing all this looking?"

"Because he doesn't believe that," Alicia said. "He just wants to believe it. It lets him off the hook. He's the one that bought a house where a woman had been murdered. Then his daughter disappears. Damn careless of him, isn't it, not to protect her better when he knew that someone had already died in that house?"

The food was twisting in Thomas's stomach. He'd had enough food, enough talk. He signaled the waiter for the check. The waiter set the check down in front of him on a little tray. Thomas placed a credit card on top of the paper.

Alicia took a last bite of food. "Didn't mean to make you mad."

"You didn't make me mad," he said. Voice smooth, body rigid, hands in perfect control. "I can just only talk about this topic for so long."

"Sure," Alicia said. She dropped her napkin over her plate, hiding the huge piece of fish that remained. "I'll meet you guys outside."

They waited until she walked to the door. "You okay?" Jillian asked. Thomas nodded. He wanted to be by himself. He wondered if he could tell her that without offending her.

"You want to come to my place for a nightcap?" She smiled softly. "Or something else?"

He shook his head. "Not tonight, Jillian."

Her smile faded. "I'm sorry about Alicia."

"I know what kind of person she is. I should get used to it, I guess."

"Come home with me. We can talk—"

He felt stifled, as if her words were suffocating him. *I love you. Love you.* He put his hand out and touched her fingers. They were cold. "I'd just like to be by myself tonight," he said.

"I understand." But her tone told him that she didn't. She didn't understand the fall from the rock, or his desire to be alone; she rarely asked him about his work or how he felt. He took a deep breath and pushed the thoughts away. Those kinds of resentments belonged to Marge. He hadn't known Jillian long enough. He was upset at her because she was touching a tender side of him. The side that frightened him.

"Why don't you take me back to the newspaper office and I'll call you in the morning."

"Fine," Jillian said. She stood up. The waiter brought back the credit card. Thomas picked up the card. Then he grabbed his crutches and stood too.

"I'm sorry, Jillian," he said.

She nodded, but said nothing as she rummaged through her pockets for her keys. He recognized the silence. It would be a long and frosty one. He took a deep breath and steeled himself for the chilly drive back into town.

15

Thomas was still chilled as he drove the remaining stretch of the way home. The traffic on 101 was heavy. Headlights loomed large before him, stabbing his eyes as they passed and leaving little red and green afterimages. He squinted and tried to follow the white line on the side of the road.

Jillian hadn't said more than two sentences to him during the ride back from the Inn on the Sea. Once he had put his hand on her knee and she casually moved away. He reviewed the conversation at the restaurant, trying to remember what he had said, and coming up with a thousand possibilities, none concrete. Perhaps she was reacting to his mood. He had felt irritated with her; perhaps she had merely responded to that.

The answer seemed wrong to him, but he could think of no other. He turned onto the road leading to his house. The darkness was thin. There was a light hovering over the ocean—a long light, like sun reflecting off clouds.

He pulled into his driveway, hearing the tires of

his truck crunch against the gravel, and then stopped near the house. He stayed in the truck for several minutes as the cold seeped into the cab, staring at the waves. The ocean looked flat, almost calm, although the waves rolled against the beach with their usual energy. The constant hush of the surf was softer than usual, and no birds flew overhead. The entire effect was that of an eerie calmness of the kind he hadn't experienced since he was a young boy.

His first set of foster parents had lived in the woods in Northern Wisconsin. Mr. Hally, his foster father, had been a longshoreman. During the off season, from November to April, he sat in his house and drank. Thomas, and his foster sister Barbara, counted the days until they would be free of him. Only when spring arrived they weren't free. They had to do all the errands Hally sent them on. As spring eased into summer, they picked berries. Raspberries, blueberries, and blackberries. But the summer began picking strawberries.

Thomas had been a city boy before his arrival in the North woods. He hadn't known anything about the outdoors. Barbara tried to show him, but he figured she was just a girl and ignored her advice. The first time they picked strawberries, he got separated from her. He picked and ate until his stomach grew queasy. Then he wandered into a clearing and collapsed in a warm patch of sunlight.

He woke up because he was cold. Something crawled across his cheek and he swiped at it, his hand pushing against a hard, tiny bug. He sat up and called for Barbara, but she didn't answer. It was dark, even in the clearing, and the temperature had dropped about twenty degrees. Thomas shivered. He kept calling for Barbara, his voice echoing in the darkness. And then, he stopped.

Long bands of whiteness fell across the meadow. He looked up and saw those same bands outlined against the black sky. The woods were quiet. He couldn't hear birds, animals, or crickets chirping in the darkness. His heart pounded against his chest. He was alone in a strange place. No one knew where he was and no one cared.

Then a crash echoed to the left of him and he screamed. Lights flickered in and out of the trees, and someone called, "Thomas!" They had found him. And they took him back. He said nothing to anyone about his fear in the woods, how the eerie white calmness upset him so. He later learned that the lights he saw were the northern lights and that the woods were probably quiet because of his foster family tramping down the path, but he always believed that he had been on the edge of something, something that watched him and was waiting until he was alone.

Thomas shivered. The front of the cab had grown cold. The dampness on the coast penetrated everything, made fifty degrees feel like twenty. The waves were more active now, the froth leaping into the air, spreading across the beach like laundry soap. Thomas opened the car door and the *cathunk!* of metal releasing metal sounded two times louder in the stillness. He reached around behind the seat for his crutches, grabbed the thick rubber ends, and pulled them out. Then he stepped down from the cab.

Outdoors it was warmer than he had expected. The air had a sultry quality, even though its temperature was only about sixty degrees. He sniffed, smelling salt and rain. A storm was somewhere off the coast. It would arrive in an hour or two, bringing with it heavy rain and large waves. He had been here long enough now to know how the storms worked. And he wasn't sure he liked it.

The unease remained at the bottom of his stomach. He made his way across the gravel to the porch steps. The light was fading, darkness growing as the clouds worked their way in from the sea. He placed his crutches on the first step, then pulled himself up. Stairs frightened him. He always leaned forward almost too far, afraid that if he stood straight he would fall and land on his back, the wind knocked out of him and pain racing up his leg. The idea of falling so paralyzed him that sometimes he wondered if he could do scenes from any kind of height again. He took the next step with equal caution, and the next, finally relaxing as he reached the top of the porch.

Something screamed near the ocean, piercing and high, and he looked over, seeing a lone gull flying against the darkness of the night. His heart was pounding in his throat and his breath was coming too rapidly. It was time to go in, to leave the night behind him. He started forward, but his crutch landed on something squishy, something that cracked as he put his weight on it. The crutch slipped out from underneath him—he was falling! —and he landed on his leg. Pain shot up from the ridge at the bottom, sending tears into his eyes. He tried to right the crutch, but couldn't. It collided with another squishy thing and another, until, finally, he looked down.

A large bunch of tiny birds—the small ones that chased waves—sandpipers?—lay in a heap against his door. They were all dead.

"Holy Christ," he whispered and tried to back away, nearly falling again. Running wouldn't solve this. Running was the last thing he should do. He grabbed his free crutch, leaned on the other one, and, grimacing, shoved the birds aside. The smell was that of the ocean, briny, with an undercurrent of rot. The birds couldn't have been there too long. He brushed them off to the side of the porch, figuring that Carolyn could clean them for him in the morning.

He grabbed the screen door and pulled it open, then fumbled with the lock on the main door. Finally the door snapped and he went inside, flicking on the overhead light.

The house was as he had left it, an overturned script on the sofa, an open diet Coke on the end table. No one had been inside. He shut the door and let out his breath. Goddamn prankster. How the hell did he kill so many birds? If this continued, Thomas would have to do something—go to the police, something. Probably, in the morning, he would find a note out there, saying something about little lost birds. A note and a prank. Why couldn't they leave him alone?

The tips of his crutches were covered with blood and feathers. He grabbed a scarf from the coat-rack, sat down on the stool beside the door, and proceeded to clean the goo off his crutches. Damn them.

The phone rang, its sound shrill and shrieking in the silence. Thomas dropped the crutch he had been working on and stared at the instrument across the room. It rang again. Goddamn asshole calling to find out Thomas's reaction to the prank. Thomas took one last swipe at his crutches, then slid them under his arms and hobbled across the room.

The phone rang again. He flopped onto the couch and picked up the receiver. "What?" he said.

"T-Thomas?" Jillian. He didn't really want to talk to her right now. She seemed part of another life, a different consideration.

He sighed. "Yes, Jillian?"

"I—wanted to say I was sorry."

Sorry. A simple word that was supposed to make things all better. Even when nothing was really wrong. He almost said something about finding the birds on his porch, then decided against it. "Apology accepted," he said, but his voice sounded cold.

"I was wondering if I could see you tomorrow?"

He didn't want to think about tomorrow. Tomorrow there would be another note or something else decaying on his porch. "I'll call you," he said and hung up.

He stared out at the ocean through his large picture window. The sea looked so benign, so picture-perfect. And yet he could feel something out there, something powerful. Something—*he needs it to ease his guilt. He bought a house that a woman died in. Then his daughter disappeared. He has to find something—*

The phone rang again. He stared at it, but didn't answer. He had said he would call Jillian in the morning, and that was what he was going to do. He waited until the phone stopped ringing, then he got up and locked the door. Then he closed all the curtains and eased himself down in front of the fireplace. He had things to do, scripts to read, decisions to make. In a few hours, he would go to sleep. And when Carolyn arrived in the morning, he would have her clean up the birds, maybe see if she could find a note. He would decide then how to handle the entire affair.

16

He still hadn't called Jillian when Carolyn's key turned in the door late the next afternoon. He was sitting on the couch, deeply engrossed in an Anthony Short script. In it, Short and Skeezits rescued an elderly woman who was being harassed by person or persons unknown. His leg itched, and he wanted to reach inside the cast and scratch until the skin was raw.

The knob turned and the door opened. Carolyn was tugging the knot down on her scarf as she walked inside. "It's cold," she said.

He nodded although he hadn't been outside. The wind whipped around the house, seeping into the cracks and making the fire seem as if it weren't even blazing. The storm had come and gone during the night, leaving the chill and the wind in its wake.

He set the script aside and watched her take off her coat. She moved easily, without any sense of discomfort, and he knew that she had not seen the birds.

"You didn't pick up the mail," he said.

She froze as she hung up the coat, her hands resting on the coat's shoulders. "I didn't come that way. You want me to go get it?"

"No." He smiled, in case she took his words wrong. "I need to get out. I'll pick it up in a little while."

She finished hanging up the coat. She brushed its sides, then stepped away from it into the living room.

"Carolyn," he said, "Is your son home?"

"He's in and out today." She picked up a vase from the end table and headed into the kitchen. "You need something?"

"I have a job that I think I'd rather have him handle."

He heard her set the vase down. She came out of the kitchen, her hands on her hips, a smile creasing her face and showing her bad teeth. "Mr. Stanton, I didn't think you were that kind of man. I can handle anything my boy can, as good, maybe better."

"Yes, well. It might be better if he just arrives, picks this up, and takes it away." He didn't want her handling those birds; something superstitious had risen in him. He felt as if she was too pure, too homey, to touch such ugliness.

Her smile faded a little. "Why don't you just let me look at it?" she said.

He had aroused her curiosity. He wouldn't be able to calm it. "I'll show you." He grabbed his crutches and lifted himself off the couch. "I'm surprised you didn't notice when you came in."

He hobbled to the door. Carolyn followed. He yanked the door open and stepped out into the chill.

"Your coat, sir!" she called.

He shivered. The wind bit into the flannel of his shirt, but he pretended not to notice. "It's just for a minute."

A few feathers still dotted the front of the porch, but most of the birds were piled off to the side. Anyone coming up the stairs would have had to look for them in order to see them. He shivered again.

The door banged shut. Carolyn came out, holding her coat tightly across her chest.

"Over here," Thomas said.

She walked over beside him, and said nothing as she knelt down. She stayed in that position for a long time. Then she looked up at him. Her cheeks were dotted with tears. "There must be close to a hundred of them."

"I found them in front of the door last night."

"I can't see how they were killed." She reached out.

"Don't touch them!" Thomas cried.

Carolyn pulled her hand back as if she were stung. "I've touched dead things before," she said.

"Let's just leave them for your son, shall we?" He started back to the house. He had been curt with everyone lately. Maybe the quiet was finally getting to him. Or the pranks. He looked back. Carolyn was still hunched over the birds. "Carolyn."

She wiped her hands on her jeans and stood up.

Her eyes were red-rimmed, her mouth a tight line. "Did you call the police?"

"There's nothing they can do," he said. The damp cold made his leg ache. He opened the door and went back inside. The house was too hot. Carolyn followed and closed the door behind herself.

"Who would have done that?" she asked.

He shook his head. The thought of those creatures stacked carefully against his door made his stomach ache. He grabbed his coat. "I don't want you touching those birds," he said. "Call your son and have him take care of them."

"Yes, sir," Carolyn said.

Her tone made him pause. It sounded as if she still planned to do it herself. "I mean it," he said. With her help, he slipped on his coat. "I'm going to run a few errands. I'll be back later."

He couldn't stay in the house any longer. Seeing the birds again sparked a restlessness in him. He said good-bye to Carolyn, and let himself out. Halfway to the truck, he stopped. A group of sandpipers ran along the beach, dodging the waves and playing in the surf. Someone had gone down there, without scaring them, and killed an entire gaggle of the birds—and didn't leave a mark on them. Thomas frowned. Last night he had assumed that the birds had all died at different times, that someone had merely gathered the corpses and placed them on his porch. But none of them had decayed. They all appeared to have died at the same time.

Thomas frowned. He made his way to the truck,

opened the door, and got in. The steering wheel was cold against his fingers. He blew on his hands before turning the key in the ignition. Hard to believe that it was summer sometimes. The truck roared to life, and he backed it up, carefully avoiding Carolyn's car.

She would get her son to take care of the birds. He knew she would. She had never directly disobeyed him before. He couldn't imagine her doing it now. Although really, he could. He had given her no reason for leaving the corpses alone. He had simply said that he wanted her to do so—and he had come across as a sexist in doing so.

He turned onto Highway 101 and immediately slowed down behind a Winnebago. He felt like honking and passing on the shoulder, even though he had no destination and was in no hurry. Something was bothering him, something besides the birds. He felt distant from himself and he had avoided doing things all day—a clear sign that he was distracted. He hadn't even called Jillian and he had promised he would do so.

Jillian. The twisting feeling had returned to his stomach. The problem stemmed from Jillian. But he didn't want to think about that.

He found himself turning into the driveway of the post office. He hadn't planned to stop here, had, actually, planned to leave the mail for another day. But something had made him turn off the highway and since he was here, he might as well see what Connie had forwarded to him.

He parked the truck one spot away from the

handicapped parking and got out. Only two other cars were in the lot. Through the large glass window, he could see a young woman leaning on the counter, talking with the clerk as he weighed a package. The owner of the other car wasn't visible.

Thomas headed inside. The automatic doors swung open for him, and he was thankful that the building was new. Even so, it had the smell of a post office—the musty, thick scent of a place that hadn't had good circulation in a long time. As he rounded the corner hiding the row of boxes that contained his, he saw the owner of the other car, an elderly man reading mail in front of his small box. Thomas yanked out his key and shoved it into his box. Two more manila envelopes waited— damn Connie and her slave driving—and a letter size envelope.

He pulled out the letter. It was postmarked from Seavy Village, morning of the previous day. There was no return address. His hands shook as he tore the letter open.

Dear Daddy, it read. *Why don't you love me?*

He dropped the letter. They were getting to him. Whoever was planning this was getting to him. He grabbed the manila envelopes out of the box and shoved them under his arm. As he started to walk away, he heard someone call out.

He turned. The elderly man stood behind him. His face was lined and his expression seemed solemn. He held out the letter, neatly folded so that he couldn't read it. "I think you dropped this, sir," he said.

Thomas took the letter and shoved it in his coat pocket. "Thank you," he said and watched as the automatic doors swung open.

17

 He bought a book, thumbed through the scripts, and had dinner in a tiny spaghetti house next to the bookstore, but he didn't call Jillian. The letter burned in his pocket. Dead birds, notes, and Heather. But, like the birds, Heather was dead.

The lights in the spaghetti house were low, the tables small. At his request, the only waiter on duty had given him a secluded seat in the back of the restaurant. Thomas had eaten in silence, staring at the book cover, thinking about the note.

It wasn't written by anyone who had known Heather. And it was mailed in town. But to what purpose? Making him leave? The birds seemed to indicate that. Or was it something else, something by some twisted soul who resented his celebrity status? He didn't know. He had to have help in figuring this out. He would call Jillian.

He paid his bill and left the restaurant, but by the time he had reached the truck, his resolve was already waivering. He didn't want to see Jillian. Seeing Jillian frightened him. He remembered parking the car at the Inn by the Sea. *Love you*, she had said as she helped him with his crutches. And he had almost responded as if he had been saying those words all of his life. And he had, he supposed, but not to Jillian. To different women he had liked and slept with over the years. He had only married one of them. Marge. Because she had been the first. And the strongest.

He climbed in the cab and closed the door, resting his forehead on the steering wheel. With all the other women, he had disappeared shortly after the first "I love you" and never looked back. Sometimes he had received nasty phone calls in the middle of the night, sometimes he got nasty letters and one, the worst, had contacted Marge. But the walking away had never bothered him before. It had been subconscious, inadvertent—until now.

The thing he should do is drive up to the newspaper office and see if Jillian was there. Then he would take her out for coffee and talk with her, explain his problem. She would understand. She always did.

He started the truck and pulled out of the parking lot. Instead of turning onto the highway, he turned away from the ocean, heading into town. He took a side street that led him to the newspaper office.

Jillian's car sat out front and lights shone in the back. He stopped and stared at the curtained windows for a moment. He could see her silhouette against the light, a figure hunched over a typewriter, fingers bouncing. He wondered what she thought, and knew that she was probably angry at him for hanging up on her and then not calling. Any other woman would be.

The metal door handle felt cold under his fingertips. He pulled his hand away and rubbed his palm on his shirt. He would wait until later, when she was calmer. And she would be calmer later.

He pulled the truck forward and headed down the drive. His heart was pounding as if he had just had a fright. And maybe he had. He had gone to talk to Jillian when he wasn't ready. Wasn't ready at all.

About seven cars passed him before he could turn on the highway. The city lights eased some of the brightness of the headlights, but they still bothered him. Maybe he needed glasses. Or maybe the darkness here was thicker, more noticeable.

He was spooking himself. Thomas the neurotic, unable to handle changes, excitement, or deep emotional relationships. *I'm sorry, Jillian, but it was fun. Now that you love me, well, I'm leaving.*

The traffic got thicker as he headed out of Seavy Village. Winnebago after Winnebago passed him, followed by an occasional Airstream, all looking for a place to park their massive, gas-eating frames and relax for the night. The trailer parks or whatever those things were called (camper homes?) were probably booked solid. So many people traveled in those things, leading normal lives, spending their vacation money in the best way they knew how.

He could imagine them, Mom in her nipped waist dress, looking like Jane Wyatt, and Dad in his traveling suit, resembling Robert Young. But

he didn't see their three kids. No, instead, Wally
and Beav sat in the back, playing, and fighting,
Mom occasionally looking back from her spot beside Dad, the driver, telling them to "Hush, boys,
we're nearly there."

Thomas almost missed his turn. No one looked
like that any more. Mom wore tight jeans and no
bra under her blouse and Dad left all of his suits at
home. The kids in back were probably complaining because there was no television and Mom
was probably driving while Dad pretended to
sleep.

He bounced along the gravel driveway in front
of the house and stopped. Carolyn's car was gone,
but she had left the kitchen light on for him. He
got out of the truck and braced himself against his
crutches. The wind had died down. The sea rolled
calmly against the beach, and the air carried with
it the scent of salt and decaying seaweed. He
grabbed the envelopes and the book out of the
truck.

Inside, the phone rang.

Thomas eyed the door, then the steps. There was
no way he would make it. He made himself go
slowly, ignoring the urge to hurry up as quickly as
he could.

The phone rang again.

He mounted the first step, noticing that they
were darker, almost as if it had rained. But it
hadn't rained. He climbed higher.

As the phone continued to ring.

He mounted the second step, and the third, noticing the dark spot glisten in the half-light. The

sea smell was fainter now, but the decay had grown. A red, rusty, carbonized smell, the smell that had invaded his nostrils for weeks after his fall from the rock. Blood. He was smelling blood.

The phone cut off in the middle of a ring.

His hands were shaking as he found the right key. The porch light hadn't worked for sometime, and for the first time he regretted not telling Carolyn so that she could change the bulb. He wanted to see what he was walking in.

He shoved the key in the lock, hearing a grate as the teeth slid into place. The bolt turned with a thunk, sending his heart pounding even harder. He tried not to breathe that awful, bitter scent as he grabbed the doorknob. It slipped under his fingers and his hand came away wet.

The panic had risen to his mouth now. "Carolyn!" he called. Dammit. If something had happened to her, he would—he didn't know what he would do—sue the police department for not acting? He grabbed the knob again, grimacing as the slime oozed between his fingertips. "Carolyn?"

He shoved the door open and flipped on the hall light. His hands were covered with blood. The doorknob was covered with blood. The porch was covered with blood. But the blood ended at the threshold, except for drops slowly appearing on the hardwood floor. He looked up.

A gull had been impaled against the door. A nail stuck from its chest and its head lolled. Blood ran down, dripping, leaving a trail as the door continued to swing open.

Thomas stared at the gull. The feathers on its

head were ruffled, its eyes opened, staring at him, accusing him for placing it on the doorway. Its beak was closed and resting against its breast. Its tiny legs jutted forward, claws bent as if it had been holding something when it died.

He let out a deep shuddering breath. Blood dripped from the bird's tail feathers onto the floor. If the blood was dripping, either it wasn't dead or it had bled an excessive amount. He turned and looked at the blood trailing down the porch. No bird contained that much blood. Something else had happened. Something else had died.

Let the police find it. He wiped his hand on his shirt, then made his way into the living room. The tips of his crutches left little red marks on the hardwood floor. He stopped in front of the sofa and picked up the phone. He wasn't going to sit down for fear of staining the cushions.

He dialed 911, reported trespassing and possible violence, and ask that help come right away. He didn't say a word about the gull on the door for fear they would think him crazy. He hung up the phone and stood in his living room, shivering. Carolyn could be out there. The bird on the porch could be simply a warning, an appetizer, for her.

Thomas swallowed heavily. He could go out and look, but he kept picturing himself, crutches slipping in the blood, falling and rebreaking his leg. Then the memory rose, unbidden, of the cloaked figure running across the beach in the moonlight, trailing its cape behind it like a bat in a horror movie. Thomas had watched from the window as that figure ran, taking Heather's destiny with it. Thomas had watched, while Heather died.

He grabbed the phone, opened the drawer, and found Carolyn's number. Frantically, he pushed the buttons, listening to the near musical beeps as each number registered. Finally he got through. The phone rang. And rang. And rang. And then it clicked as someone answered.

"Yes?" A woman.

"Carolyn?"

"Yes? Who is this?"

He let out an audible sigh of relief. "Thomas. This is Thomas. I was calling to see if you made it home all right."

"About an hour ago." Her voice had softened when she had learned that it was him. "Is everything all right, sir?"

No, he wanted to say. *Some little prankster is scaring me witless.* "I'm having some more trouble with the birds. I just wanted to make sure you left before whoever it is came back."

"I didn't see anyone," she said, sounding confused and a little scared. "What happened, sir?"

"Nothing, really," he said. The trembling was beginning to travel through his entire body. Part of him had really believed that she had died. "This time they killed a gull."

"Oh, sir."

"Carolyn, look." He heard sirens wailing faintly in the background. They were approaching his house. "I want you to be really careful if you're here and I'm not, okay? At least until we figure out who is doing this and why."

"All right."

"Good." The sirens were getting closer. He had to hang up. "I'll see you tomorrow then."

"Yes, sir," Carolyn said. "And, Mr. Stanton?"

"Yes?"

"Be careful."

"Don't worry, Carolyn, I will." He hung up. The sirens were close now, almost deafening. Beneath the screaming sound, he heard the crunch of tires on gravel. Slowly, because he was still afraid that the tips of his crutches were slippery, he made his way to the door.

Car doors slammed. Thomas stopped beside the dripping gull and watched two policemen stop at the base of the stairs. "The blood begins there," Thomas said.

Both men looked up. Thomas was startled to see how young they looked. One appeared to be part Asian, with black hair and dark eyes. The other seemed even younger. The mustache crossing his upper lip barely covered the skin. "Mr. Stanton, sir, is this the trouble?"

"The blood on my porch, the gull on my door. I'm not really in any condition to see if there is something else waiting around the corner. That's why I called you two."

The men looked at each other. The Asian went back to the car and brought out a flashlight while Mustache's hand slipped to his gun. "We'll check it out for you, Mr. Stanton, and then we'll take your statement. Is the house okay?"

"So far as I know. I've only gone between here and the porch."

"Then let's check the house first," Asian said. They started to make their way up the stairs around the blood as another car pulled into the driveway. Jillian's. Thomas watched as she got out.

"Jillian," he said. "What are you—?"

"Any time there's a 911 call in the area, the second person contacted is me." She nodded at the two officers. "Tiger. Ed."

"Miss Maxwell." They finished climbing the steps, moved around the blood, and came inside. Then together, they disappeared up the stairs, their shoes leaving bloody marks on the floor. Carolyn would love that.

Jillian made her way into the house as well. "I'm sorry I didn't call," Thomas said, less because he was sorry, more because he felt he was expected to apologize.

"Something came up, right?" Her tone was bitter, although her expression remained neutral.

"No," he said, the words shooting out of him. "I just needed some time to think, that's all."

She looked at him, her eyes wide behind her glasses. "What happened here, Thomas?"

The crutches were digging into his armpits and his leg was tired. "Is it you asking the question or is it Jillian Maxwell, girl reporter?"

"I am Jillian Maxwell, girl reporter."

He shook his head. "I don't want the publicity, Jillian. I'll tell you, but I don't want this in the paper."

"The police report is public record, Thomas. It'll go in the paper with or without quotes from you."

Bitter. Tough. Yet she looked fragile in her oversize sweater and blue jeans.

"Then take what the police do," he snapped. He could hear the officers clomping around upstairs. He didn't have time for relationships right now. He wanted to be left alone.

She stood quietly beside him for a moment, then said, "Do you mind if I look around?"

"Yes." But not because she was a reporter. Because she was Jillian and the cops still hadn't finished checking out the place.

The two officers came down the stairs. "Nothing," the one Jillian had called Ed said. In the light of the room, he looked older, about Thomas's age, and very serious. Tiger, the mustache, slipped around into the kitchen.

They finished searching the house and moved outside. Jillian went over to the fireplace and built a fire. Thomas watched her, and then they both watched the flames. The door remained open, but the gull had stopped dripping. The ocean air was making Thomas cold.

Finally the policemen came back inside. They closed the door as they entered. "There are two more gulls, sir, on the back of the porch," Ed said. "They've—been ripped apart. I think it's probably their blood all over the porch."

"Do you know who's doing this?" Tiger asked.

Thomas shook his head. "But it's not the first time. Last night, I found a bunch of dead sandpipers in front of the door."

Both Tiger and Jillian were taking notes. "Stabbed?" Ed asked.

Thomas shook his head. "I couldn't tell how they died. Neither could my housekeeper. Her son cleaned them up this afternoon."

They took down Carolyn's name, and a few more details about the birds. Then they asked if anything else had happened.

With his clean hand, Thomas pulled the note from his pocket. Wordlessly, he handed it to Ed. Jillian peered over his shoulder and gasped.

"I got that today," Thomas said. "I've been getting one every day for the past three or four."

"And the other notes?"

"I destroyed them."

"You don't know who could be sending them?"

Thomas shook his head. "They were all postmarked Seavy Village."

"And your children live elsewhere?" Tiger asked.

Ed, Thomas, and Jillian stared at the young cop. He shrugged and looked perplexed. "My only child died here a few years back," Thomas said as gently as he could. Tiger reddened and mumbled an apology. Thomas merely nodded.

They questioned him, about the birds, about the notes, and about the gulls. Then they checked the house one more time. As they started to leave, Ed said, "I want you to contact us the minute anything else happens. This is a strange area, Mr. Stanton. We want to make sure that nothing happens to you."

Thomas nodded. They left, closing the door behind them. Jillian looked at him. " 'This is a strange area, Mr. Stanton'? What the hell did they mean by that?''

"You're the reporter," he said. "Why don't you go ask them?"

"Thomas," Jillian said, "What's going on? Why all the chill directed at me?"

He shook his head. He didn't want to talk about anything. "I'm tired." He eased his crutches out from underneath him and sank onto the couch, not caring if he got blood on the cushions. "I think I need some sleep."

"Well, you can't stay here," she said. "Why don't you come home with me?"

He stared at her, surprised and tempted by the offer. Then he shook his head. "I'll be all right here," he said. "Whoever did that isn't coming back tonight."

"Then at least let me help you clean up."

"No." The superstition ran through him again, deep and fine. He didn't want her touching those birds. "I'll get it in the morning, with help. Okay?"

"Thomas, you can't stay here like this with all that everywhere." Jillian wrinkled her small nose in disgust.

"I'm really exhausted, Jillian," he said. "I promise I'll take care of it. Promise."

She sighed and put a cool hand to his cheek. "No matter what, Thomas," she said. "I'm always there for you, okay?"

He nodded, feeling stupid. Feeling grateful.

"I'll see myself out," she said. She bent over, kissed his forehead, then opened the door. From Thomas's angle, it looked as if the gull's feet brushed against her coat. But they couldn't have, or she would have jumped away in horror.

"Good night, Jillian," he said, managing to keep his voice calm. "And thanks."

She smiled. Then she hooked one foot around the door, pulled and the door swung shut behind her. Thomas stared at it for a moment. The fire crackled in the grate. Bloody footprints graced his floor. He was alone.

He got up, locked the door, and watched Jillian get into the car through his window. She waited a minute, almost as if she knew he was staring at her, then she backed up, turned around, and drove away.

Exhaustion overwhelmed him. He didn't know if he could make it to the cot before he fell asleep. But somehow he did and eased himself onto the softness without even taking his clothes off. As he lay there, he realized that the lights were still on, but he didn't care. And that was the last thing he remembered until morning.

18

Light seeped into the living room through the curtains of the picture window. Cool light, morning light, resting on his face, digging into his eyes. Thomas rolled over and groaned.

Someone on the porch giggled.

He sat up. The light was the gray haze of a rainy day. The clock on the mantel read noon. He had overslept and Carolyn hadn't arrived yet. Good. He didn't want her to clean the gulls off the porch.

A shutter banged.

Thomas's grip tightened on the crutches. There was no wind. The shutter banged and there was no wind.

He got off the cot and shrugged on his robe, first one arm, then the other. He belted it tightly across the middle, not wanting to approach whatever it was, whomever it was, naked.

Someone giggled again.

His mouth was dry. He hobbled across the room to the front door, nearly knocking his cast against an end table. *Careful, Thomas, careful,* he thought.

He reached the door, pulled it open and it felt too heavy, it swung too fast. He had to back out of the way.

The door slammed against the wall, sending a movie poster crashing against the floor. But Thomas wasn't looking at the mess. He was staring at Alicia.

She had been impaled against the door like the gull the night before. Her head lolled to one side and a single nail pierced her breast. Blood had run down her white clothing, mixing with the dried bird's blood already on the floor. Her hands were clenched as if she had been beating at something and her mouth—

Her mouth was full of feathers.

Thomas sat up. His throat was raw. He had been screaming. That was the sound that woke him up. Damn dreams. He wiped the sweat off his forehead and took several deep breaths to calm his heart. He hadn't dreamed much at all before he came here. It would be ironic if, through all this, it was the dreams that drove him away.

The light caressing the edges of the windows was softer, brighter than that of his dreams. Early morning sunlight. He glanced at the clock. Seven A.M. He almost lay down to go back to sleep when he remembered the feeling in the dream.

He should clean up the porch before Carolyn arrived.

He got up, put water on the stove, and dressed. He would clean up later, after he had disposed of the gulls.

The water boiled and he poured his tea, wrapping his hands around the warm mug. Using a single crutch, he limped his way over to the window and pulled back the curtains. The sea looked calm. It slithered onto the beach with an almost unnatural smoothness. A handful of sandpipers ran along the water's edge, and footprints dotted the sand. Footprints, parallel with the water's edge, almost as if someone had been jogging.

But who would jog on this stretch of beach?

The phone rang and Thomas nearly dropped his mug. He set it down carefully and, with a shaking hand, picked up the receiver.

"What?"

"My, aren't we bright and cheerful this morning?" Connie. He let out a sigh of relief. In the back of his mind, he had been afraid that this had been another emergency. Jillian calling him to tell him that Alicia was dead.

"It's seven-thirty in the morning."

"Business hours in New York. And you know New York. It expects the entire world to play along."

"What are you doing in New York?"

"Trying to save your flagging career. Did you get the scripts?"

"Yes," he said, sitting in the large green armchair. "Great kindling."

"Thomas!"

He took a sip from his tea. It felt warm against his raw throat. "I read a few."

"What did you think?"

"I think I'm not ready to go back to work yet."

Connie sighed. He felt her exasperation almost

as if she were sitting beside him, glaring at him. "Look, Thomas, they want to start filming the next Short episode early next week. And Michael is making noises about hiring someone new."

"Let him."

"I think he's serious," she said. "That's why I'm out here. And why I am harassing you at an ungodly hour of the morning."

"Tell him I'm recovering. Tell him it's his own damn fault I'm out here in the first place."

"I have been, Thomas. Why do you think the new Short scripts have an injured Short in them? He's not stupid. He knows that you don't want to come back. I think he's forcing your hand."

"Then let him hire someone new." Thomas held the mug against one cheek and then the other. The warmth felt good against his skin. The house was cold. He hadn't had a chance to build a fire yet.

"Sometimes I feel as if I'm the only one who cares about your damn career."

Thomas took another sip. He had made the tea too strong. He remembered her statement from the last phone call that his career influenced hers. But the thought brought no guilt. Together, they had already made a fortune. "Connie," he said as kindly as he could, "I'm here to decide if the career is going to continue."

"Bullshit. I thought you were working on some project about Heather."

Project about Heather. The Heather Project, subtitled Thomas Stanton's Search for Self. "I'm doing that too."

"Thomas, look. Come back to work. This stuff

can wait. The job can't. You can't play prima donna forever. This has already affected your reputation and who knows—"

"If it's already affected my reputation, then you're not doing your job. The entire world should sympathize with a man who almost dies in a fall and wakes up to discover that his missing daughter is indeed dead. People have taken off more time for less. Celeste Anders left *Restless Heart* for an entire year after her divorce. She was a pivotal character they had to write out in one week, and yet they let her come back."

"Those were the daytime soaps, Thomas. You're in the big leagues now. PBS isn't going to lose a program as popular as Anthony Short because the actor has gone wonky."

" 'Wonky'?" Thomas slammed his tea down. The liquid sloshed over the edge of the cup. "If they think the ratings are going to stay the same with someone else playing Anthony Short, they're wonky. Tell them I don't care what kind of maneuvers they're going to make. I'm coming back—*if* I'm coming back—I'll come when I'm damn good and ready."

He banged the receiver onto the phone. More tea sloshed onto the table and the roses Carolyn kept in a small vase on the end table wobbled. He was shaking. Wonky. Maybe he had gone wonky with dead birds, anonymous notes, and mysterious forces on the beach. But whatever it was, he would ride it until the end.

He got out of the chair and hobbled over to the fireplace. He opened the screens, piled a few logs on the grate, stuffed newspaper between them, and lit the newspaper. The flame licked at the logs, sending a sweet warmth into the house. Damn place was cold. Damn coast was cold. He was cold.

No matter what, Thomas, I'll always care about you.

The fire had taken with the logs. He sighed and pulled himself to his feet. The cast felt heavier than usual this morning. He shot a quick glance at the phone. Connie didn't call back. Not that he expected her to. He had hung up on her several times in the past and she always waited a while, waiting for him to cool down. But he had always suspected that she waited until her anger cooled before contacting him again.

He made his way to the kitchen and dug a garbage bag out of the cupboard. Wonky. It was definitely wonky to clean birds off the porch before his cleaning lady arrived. But he was going to do it. He grabbed the garbage bag with one hand, then stopped at the fireplace and picked up the shovel. He left one crutch leaning against a chair and limped to the door.

He pulled the door open. A blast of chill air hit him and he shivered. The gull remained in its position, looking less malevolent in the daylight. The blood had dried onto its feathers and its curled feet looked pathetic instead of horrific. He set the shovel down, wrapped the garbage sack around his free hand, and pulled the bird off the nail.

It came loose with surprising ease. The tiny body felt soft through the plastic. Thomas grimaced as he turned the bag inside out. A large runny bloodstain remained on the door.

He would worry about that later. He had to get the other two gulls first. He picked up the shovel and headed around the porch. They were stuck in a corner near the spot where the sandpipers had been, under the kitchen window, facing the ocean. He scooped them up with the shovel and dumped them in the sack, their little bodies thumping as they landed against the wood. Then he rounded the porch toward the front door.

Carolyn was standing there, her hands on her hips, studying the bloody path leading down the stairs. "It's quite a mess they made this time," she said.

Thomas nodded, set the bag to the left of the door, and went back inside. The house was warm after standing in the brisk sea air.

"I hear you called the police." Carolyn closed the door behind her.

"Yeah," Thomas said. "This was a little excessive."

Carolyn didn't take off her coat. She stalked into the kitchen, banged a few cupboard doors, and, as Thomas walked in, turned on the faucet to fill a bucket sitting in the sink.

"What're you doing?" he asked.

"Getting ready to scrub that mess off the porch."

"I'll do it," Thomas said. That mess was directed toward him. He was responsible for it. He had to clean it up. Better him than anyone else. Dead birds could never hurt him.

"What's a little blood compared to a pile of birds? And besides, you're in no condition for it." Carolyn took the sudsy bucket out of the sink, then went around to the back closet and removed a mop.

Thomas's heart lurched. "You cleaned up those birds."

"Didn't see no sense in calling Ken about them. I could do as good as any."

"But I asked you not to."

She came out of the back room, shrugged, and smiled sheepishly. "Mr. Stanton, sir, it's my job to keep your house neat, not my son's. If I can't do the work, I'll tell you."

She pushed past him and headed out to the porch. The chill had returned. He staggered over to a chair and sat down. His arm was tired from supporting all of his weight with one crutch.

She had cleaned up the birds all by herself.

He rubbed a hand over his face. It wasn't his fault. He had told her not to. So why did he feel this low-grade horror rising in the pit of his stomach?

Because of the film. Thomas brought his head up. The memory rose clear and cold as if it had happened yesterday instead of eight years before. The townie had followed him around everywhere. She wasn't particularly pretty, but she didn't have to be since she was simply a stand-in for one of the minor characters in the film. He was never interested in her, in fact, he never noticed her one way or the other unless Heather or Suzette said something. Suzette especially: *Why does that woman have to follow you around?* He would always shrug and move on.

Then, after that night on the beach, Suzette left him alone. The townie kept her distance as he searched among the starlets for another conquest. He spent too many late nights drinking in his trailer with all sorts of women while Heather slept in the next room. And one night, he passed out on the couch to awaken to screams outside the door.

He got up and pulled the door open to find Suzette standing there in blue jeans and a knit shirt hitched up, her hands covering her mouth as she screamed. He called her name, twice, then slapped her to quiet her. She took a trembling breath and pointed to the concrete. A little bird lay in front of the threshold, its wings, legs, and head neatly sliced off and placed a half inch from its torso.

People had come out of their trailers to see what the commotion was and the townie pushed past, looking as if she'd spent the night waiting for him to appear. *I got it, Mr. Stanton,* she said, and she picked up the bird with her bare hands and carried it away to the dumpster.

Three days later she was dead.

He got up, grabbed the other crutch, and got his jacket. He knew what he had to do. He had to talk to Hargrave. He had to see what that old man remembered about the shoot that he had forgotten.

Thomas slipped on his jacket and opened the front door. Carolyn was on her hands and knees, scrubbing fiercely. "Damn stuff doesn't want to come up," she said.

Thomas looked at her and swallowed. Part of him was glad that she was cleaning up. He couldn't stomach the blood, the rich metallic scent of it rising from the wood. "Just do your best," he said. He started out the door and Carolyn got up. He made sure that he placed his crutches very carefully on the wet porch.

"I'll be back soon," he said.

She nodded, and for a minute, he felt as if he were eighteen again, looking at his mother for the last time. He had come to visit, finding no one but his mother at home. She had looked frail, her skin almost translucent, as she stood out on the porch to say good-bye to him. *I'll be back soon*, he said. But he had never come back, not even during all those months she lay in the hospital dying of cancer.

He let himself into the truck and turned the ignition. The engine roared into life. He looked back over to the porch. Carolyn was scrubbing again, looking hail, hearty, and as healthy as a woman of her age and occupation could. She saw him watching her and waved at him with the scrub brush.

He forced himself to smile and wave back.

Then he pulled the truck into reverse and backed out of the driveway. He drove fast along the little road, feeling as if he had no time. He had to settle something with Hargrave, and he didn't know what that something was.

Highway 101 was full of campers and cars with out-of-state license plates. Thomas watched them pass for a long time, becoming so hypnotized that he almost missed an opening when one appeared. He pulled in behind a ratty Chevrolet Impala with a Texas license plate. The couple driving didn't look as if they were traveling. They looked as if they were fighting.

He slowed down, giving them a great deal of driving room. He had to take his time and think because he didn't quite remember where the old man lived. It had been dark the night he drove there, and he had been preoccupied with Jillian.

Jillian. He sighed. She would be angry with him for seeing Hargrave without her. Thomas wasn't sure how the old man would receive him either. He wasn't going to stop for beer and flowers—that was Jillian's ritual. This was going to be two men, talking, comparing notes about the problems on the beach.

Maybe he was wonky. The old man clearly hated him. But out of that hatred, Thomas might find a bit of truth.

When Thomas reached Hargrave's part of town, he watched the side of the road more than the road itself. The street Hargrave lived on was un-marked, but Thomas remembered the windswept trees lining its sides. He squinted as he drove, as if he could create darkness by half-closing his eyes. Once he almost rear-ended the Impala and as he hit his brakes, he heard the squeal of two other sets of brakes behind him.

He glanced into the rearview mirror and saw a Porsche on his tail. The driver glared at Thomas with the move-it-asshole look of a California com-muter. He almost decided to speed up, to give in to the pressure from the car behind him, when he saw the road.

The trees looked less spooky in the daylight, almost like overgrown bonsai trees whose maker had a strange sense of humor. Their branches were frozen in a nonexistent wind and as he turned the truck, Thomas half expected to be buffeted to the side of the road. The drive had a strange, almost familiar feeling. He hadn't noticed the small, dilapidated house off to the right, or the ancient truck parked on blocks on the sandy patch near the trees. But he did recognize Hargrave's driveway with its gravel and clutter. The dogs were back, barking as if the truck were a small animal that they could easily kill. This time, Thomas kept driving, and the dogs kept backing away as the truck moved forward.

He stopped in front of the garage and shut off the ignition. The garage door was half-open, revealing a dirt floor littered with cartons, boxes, old orange crates, and tools. In the deep recesses, he thought he saw wheels, but he wasn't certain.

The dogs stopped barking as soon as he opened his door. As he reached for the crutches, one of the dogs bumped against his arm, and he had to pet the matted fur. He spoke to them softly, and they whined as if they knew they should be scolding him, but couldn't bring themselves to do it.

"Thought you'd come back." The old man was leaning against the side of the garage. He held a single rosebud in his hand.

"I hope I'm not disturbing you." Thomas hobbled on one foot until he was able to shove the crutches under his arms.

"The only thing you're disturbing is a slow, dull death." Hargrave scanned the truck. "You didn't bring Jillian."

Thomas shook his head.

Hargrave nodded. "Didn't want her to hear about you, did you?"

Thomas's jaw tightened. He had been stupid to come back here. Hargrave Lester was in his nineties. He had liver spots and his hands shook. How could Thomas expect any valid information from someone like that?

"Come on in," Hargrave said. "I got some coffee all fixed."

Thomas didn't move. One of the dogs brushed against his leg, then wiped its wet, slimy tongue on his hand.

Hargrave started down the walk, then turned. "Well?"

Thomas took a deep breath and followed. He was here. He might as well go through with it. The old man held the door open, and Thomas hobbled inside.

Daylight cast eerie shadows on the mess in the living room. Dust motes rose in sunbeams and some of the books looked as if they had been folded open for decades instead of days. The plants were greener and lusher than Thomas remembered. The room smelled of eggs, coffee, and wet dogs.

"You want coffee?" Hargrave asked.

"Yeah," Thomas said, although he usually didn't drink the stuff. "I can get it."

The old man put his hands on his hips. The rose jutted out like a sword. "Right now, young man, I can get around better than you. Rule Number One in this house is that I hate to be coddled."

"Yes, sir." Thomas felt as if he were ten years old. He moved two dictionaries, a desktop encyclopedia, and Umberto Eco's *The Name of the Rose* in hardcover before he could sit on the overstuffed chair. More dust motes and dog hair rose from the chair as he sank into it. He set his crutches against an end table so that no one could trip over them.

Hargrave came out of the kitchen clutching two mugs. Thomas took one and wrapped his hands around it so that they would get warm. The old man sat down in a green chair near the only uncovered window. He fit into the contours of the chair so well that Thomas assumed Hargrave always sat there.

"You didn't tell me everything," Thomas said.

"Of course not." Hargrave slurped out of his mug, then set it on top of a copy of *The Tommyknockers*. "Ain't no rule that says I have to be absolutely one hundred and fifty percent honest with everyone I meet. The only reason I talked at all was Jillian. The girl loves you."

"I know," Thomas said quietly.

"No, I don't think you do." Hargrave leaned back and propped one foot on a nearby footstool. "Jillian is probably the loneliest woman I have ever seen. She's never brought a man before, never talks about them, never spends time with anyone away from her work. She was excited when that sister of hers was going to come, but now that the girl has moved in, Jillie has gotten quiet. Then one day, her mood picks up and next thing I know she's out here with you."

Thomas nodded. He hadn't passed much beyond ten in the way he was feeling. Fifteen maybe, and coming home late from a date. "So now you're going to tell me to treat her right?"

"I can't tell you to do nothing. And I don't think you'd know right if it slapped you in the face." Hargrave picked up his mug and took another slurp.

Thomas set his coffee on the end table. "What did I do to deserve all this hostility?"

Hargrave peered at him from over the mug. "You got involved with Jilly."

"She's a little young for you, don't you think?"

"I think a man my age can love a woman like her without wanting to stick his dick inside her. There's more to life than that, you know." Hargrave set the mug down. "I don't like you. I didn't like you the day I met you and I don't like you now. But I'll help you as best I can because you make Jilly light up like a Christmas tree. And as long as you do that, you got me to talk to. The day you hurt her is the day I turn on you."

A shiver went down Thomas's back. The old man was frail and couldn't harm Thomas physically, but the threat felt very real. Thomas took a sip of the coffee. The liquid was bitter and too hot. "I want to know what you remember about the shoot."

"Tall order," the old man said. "It was a long time ago."

"I don't think you'll have any trouble remembering."

Hargrave shrugged. "I told you the last time you were here."

"Some of it. I think most of the time you were talking to Jillian."

"She needs to know what she's getting involved with."

Thomas made himself take a deep breath. Coming here had been a mistake. He knew that now. The old man wasn't going to help him.

Then Hargrave sighed. "I didn't meet you first," he said, looking at his hands. "I met your daughter. She ran out of your trailer, sobbing so hard I thought she'd never stop. Seems that brassy woman you were sleeping with had told her to go home, that you didn't want her. A couple of us comforted her, and told her not to pay any attention to the things that woman said."

"Suzette?"

Hargrave shrugged. "I don't think it much matters what her name was. You didn't care about her, that was clear. But your little girl didn't know that. And we couldn't find you anywhere, so Doreen took care of her that afternoon."

The sides of the mug were burning Thomas's hand. "Who's Doreen?"

Hargrave tilted his head to the side. "You don't remember Doreen? I would have thought she'd be hard to forget. She was the one who was murdered."

She came into sharp focus then: long black hair, wide brown eyes, always wearing a floppy hat a few years out of style. She had been the townie that Suzette hated, and it finally became clear why. "She took care of Heather?"

"Most of the time. At first I thought it was because she had a thing for you. Later I think she came to feel something for your little girl. After all, you were ignoring both of them."

"I didn't owe this Doreen anything."

"No, you didn't," Hargrave said. "But you can't say that about Heather."

Thomas was squeezing the mug so hard he thought he might break it. "I remember something about birds," he said.

Hargrave started, then didn't move at all.

"I remember," Thomas said, "that someone killed a bird outside my trailer, and it scared Heather, and Doreen took it away."

"That's all you remember?"

Thomas nodded.

"What the hell kind of drugs were you taking?"

"What do you mean?" Thomas asked.

"I came in that morning for an early shoot. I watched you slice up that bird. The blood got all over your costume, and I kept wondering how it would be clean enough for later in the day."

"I killed the bird—?" Thomas half stood, but his leg buckled under him, and he fell into the chair. "I would never do anything like that. I was inside the trailer. With Heather."

And then he paused. He didn't know that for

sure. "Are you the one putting the birds on my porch?" he asked.

"Birds?"

"Sandpipers the other night. All dead. Last night, someone impaled a gull."

Hargrave's hand was shaking as he smoothed his hair over his bald spot. "So it's starting again."

"It?"

"I saw you kill the one bird, but not the others. You don't remember the gulls, then, either? Or the blood and feather trail leading to the commissary? You don't remember finding Doreen's body sliced in pieces, with feathers coming out of her mouth?"

The image of Alicia in the dream returned to him. Thomas felt all the color drain from his face. "You think I did this? You think I'm doing this? You think I killed my own daughter?"

"You're saying that, not me," Hargrave said.

"I loved Heather. Goddammit, I would never do anything like what you're saying. I've never killed anything in my life."

"Really?" Hargrave's tone was dry. "Not many of us can say that."

Thomas grabbed his crutches and pulled himself to his feet. "Who the hell are you, old man, to sit in judgment of me?"

"I wasn't judging," Hargrave said. "You asked me to tell you what I remember. I am. I'm not responsible for whether or not you like it."

Thomas turned his back on the old man and headed out the door. He knew he had been wrong to come here. The old man was senile, and he hated Thomas. Probably for that incident in the filming. He probably thought Thomas had taken his one chance at stardom away.

He shoved the door open with his shoulder and started down the walk. The dogs bounded up to him, but he ignored them.

"Hey!" The old man was calling to him, but Thomas refused to turn around. "You can't run away from the truth!"

"You don't know the truth," Thomas said under his breath.

"I'm not done talking to you yet," the old man said. "There's a few things you need to know."

"I'm done," Thomas said. He yanked open the truck door and got inside. After turning the key in the ignition, he revved the engine to scare the dogs, then backed out of the driveway.

The old man's words ran in his head as he drove. He remembered finding the bird, holding Heather as she shook with terror. He didn't remember placing it there. He didn't remember needing his costume cleaned.

The whole thing had happened a few days after he had taken Suzette to the beach. He had pulled open the door at her screams, more surprised to see her there than anything. He never thought he would see her again.

Her left hand was over her mouth, and her right was pointed downward. Heather had crept up between his legs, and that was when she started to scream. The townie had come forward—from inside the trailer? Had he slept with her too?—and thrown the bird away.

And died.

No wonder he didn't want Carolyn to touch the birds. He associated that event with the townie's death. Doreen. With Doreen's death.

He pulled over beside the ocean, to calm himself. If he went back to work now, he could get lost in Anthony Short. He and Skeezits could pretend they were solving crimes. He would come home at night and memorize the next day's lines. He wouldn't have to think about this anymore. He wouldn't have to listen to other people tell him what a horrible father he was, what a horrible man he was. His father had been a horrible man, not him. He had always prided himself on being different. On being stronger.

On not being there at all.

He put his forehead on the steering wheel and wished the entire nightmare would go away.

19

She was sitting on the porch, huddled in her jacket. The wind had come up and the ocean sprayed wildly against the beach. Thomas glanced at the girl again as he pulled into the driveway. For a moment, he had thought it was Heather. Sometimes, when he closed his eyes, he still saw her like that, waiting on his porch for him to come home. In one way or another, she had always waited for him like that.

The girl on the porch stuck out her legs. She was wearing pink tennis shoes and matching socks that folded outside her blue jeans. A cloud of smoke rose beside the railing. When she heard the truck, she threw her cigarette onto the gravel.

Thomas grimaced. She was too heavy for Alicia and too young to be Carolyn's child. His stomach turned slightly. Something had changed.

He stopped the truck. The girl glanced at him, looked toward the beach, and called out. He couldn't hear what she said, but he recognized her demeanor. Worshipful. The great god Thomas

Stanton arriving home after a long day. In his truck. How utilitarian. How human.

He opened the door and got down as another girl rounded the house. She was younger than her friend, but the expression was the same. The girl sitting on the stairs stood up. "Mr. Stanton?" she asked.

Her clothes were new, extremely stylish, and she wore a trace of makeup although she couldn't have been more than twelve. Clearly, she wasn't from Seavy Village. She was a tourist's kid.

"Yes," he said, keeping his tone a mixture of friendly aloofness. His stomach muscles had grown tighter.

"My sister and me, we were wondering—" The pause was excruciating. Garbo at her worst. He nodded so that the girl would continue. She swallowed and then said, "—wewerewonder-ingifwecouldhaveyourautograph."

And so it started again. He felt his shoulders slump, the tension move from his stomach to his back. Inside, the phone started ringing.

The girl looked back at the door. "It's been doing that all day," she said and then blushed. She had been waiting for some time.

He sighed, then held out his hand. "Of course I'll give you an autograph."

The girl smiled and her sister took a few steps closer. The phone stopped mid-ring. The older girl handed him a purple book with AUTOGRAPHS stenciled on in white. The younger girl merely handed him a notepad decorated with Smurfs. He took the notepad and the offered felt tip pen and asked, "Who do I write this to?"

The younger girl blushed and turned her head, but the older one said, "She's Meg."

"Okay, Meg." He scrawled the date and then *To Meg: You're lovely. Thomas Stanton.* He handed the notepad back to her and took the autograph book. "And you're . . . ?"

"Anna."

He opened the autograph book, paged past large youthful signatures and the hastily scribbled names that marked the adult contributions until he found a blank page. *To Anna,* he wrote. *I'm amazed you could find me on the beach. You're quite a detective! All the best, Thomas Stanton.*

He handed the book back. The girl immediately opened to the page and read it. Her blush grew deeper. "Actually, I'm not a detective," she said. "I read about you in the paper."

The paper. All of his muscles tightened at once. Damn Jillian. She knew better than to do that. He made himself smile at the girls. "I'm flattered that you came all the way out here looking for me," he said, "but now I have things to do."

They hung near the porch, and he knew they would hover there all night if he let them. The phone started ringing again. He glanced at the door and searched through his keys until he found the house key.

"I think it's time for you to go home now, girls."

Meg jumped off the porch. Anna climbed down slowly, as if he had rejected her. The phone's shrillness was making him nervous. He had to make himself cross over to the stairs slowly, afraid that he would trip if he tried to move any faster. When he reached the second step, the ringing stopped.

"And girls," he said as he stopped to catch his breath. "I really like my privacy. I would appreciate it if you didn't tell anyone else that I was here."

They nodded before running down the gravel driveway. He watched them go. His request would do about as much good as asking Jillian to retract her article. But he had to try. The solitude had meant more to him than he had realized.

He climbed the rest of the way up the stairs, his eyes scanning the entire porch. He half expected more birds, gutted against the wood, their blood dripping into the cracks and weatherworn beams. But he saw nothing, only the dusty prints of a ten-year-old's tennis shoes.

As he unlocked the door, the phone started to ring again. Someone was really trying to get a hold of him. Probably Connie with a deal that he couldn't refuse. He pulled open the door and stepped inside.

The living room smelled like lemon furniture polish and flowers. Carolyn had placed wildflower bouquets in all of the vases around the room, as if she were trying to ward off his memories of the dead birds. The house was extra clean and had a festive air.

He closed the door, then hurried across the floor to the phone. He picked it up in the middle of a ring.

"Yeah," he said, already planning his speech. He

couldn't do the project. Connie knew that. She was foolish for even trying.

"Thomas?"

He sank down into the couch. Jillian. He could still see her as she had been the night before, notebook in her hand, eyes wide. *I'll always be there for you*, she had said. "What?"

She sighed. "You've seen the article."

"No," he said. "I saw the first wave of groupies."

"I'm sorry," she said. "I had no choice—"

"You had plenty of choice!" All the tension that had been building in him exploded through his mouth. "You censor things for that damn publisher of yours. You don't write about murders, if they happen to be serial killings, and you don't write about food poisoning at local restaurants because all of that is bad for the tourist trade. But, gee, find a poor actor who is enjoying his seclusion, have a few birds die on his porch, and it's front page news. Of course, an actor is good for the tourist business. It doesn't matter how many tourists flock to his front door as long as they all spend money in Seavy Village."

His words echoed in the phone. Gradually the echoes faded out and he would have thought that Jillian had hung up except for the low hum in his earphone. "I suppose I deserve that," she said.

He took a deep breath and felt his muscles relax. She had been calling because she realized that she was wrong.

"But," she said. "It is news."

"News?" He sat forward, the relaxation he had

felt a moment earlier completely gone. "You haven't reported news in years, Jillian."

He slammed the phone down before he realized what he was doing. Damn her. She didn't understand what publicity did to his privacy. And he certainly wasn't going to let her justify her actions just because she wanted his forgiveness.

The phone rang again. He picked it up, knowing that Jillian was on the other end. "What?"

"Thomas, look. I was calling to apologize."

"I know that," he snapped. "Why don't you just wait until I'm calmer?" He almost hung up again, but then he raised the receiver to his mouth. "No, on second thought. Let's not discuss this again. Okay? I hate being this upset."

He hung up and then unplugged the phone. That would teach her. *Jillian loves you,* the old man had said. "Bullshit!" Thomas whispered to the voice echoing in his head. If she loved him, she would have respected his wishes about the article last night. If she loved him, she would have understood.

He leaned his head back on the seat in his lemon-scented living room and sighed. He felt very, very lonely.

20

He found Hargrave's words surfacing at the oddest moments. Thomas took a casserole out of the refrigerator and preheated the oven. He remembered finding the bird, its little body neatly sliced into parts. A frisson of shock had run through him as Heather screamed. If he closed his eyes, he could see that moment as if it had happened the day before. But no matter how hard he tried, he couldn't remember getting to the door or closing it later. Only the moment was clear. Nothing else.

Thomas took a Coke can off the counter and sipped from it. The Coke was warm and stale. He poured the liquid out and tossed the can into a bag with all the others. Carolyn would turn them in for nickels when she got groceries.

He opened the refrigerator and took out another can. The old man was messing with his mind. Thomas hadn't even been in Oregon when the woman who owned the house had died. And a banging shutter woke him up when Heather died.

He had seen a cloaked figure running across the beach.

He had been so frightened. So deep down terrified. He couldn't have been responsible.

Could he?

The oven light clicked off and Thomas put the casserole in. A wave of heat hit him as he leaned over the oven door. He did miss the warmth of California, despite Oregon's beauty. He closed the oven and sat down, his back to the warmth.

The police had thought so, even though they had said nothing. And so did the detectives. Even De-Freeze and Garity looked at that possibility. But he would remember if he had killed his own daughter. Everything else in his life was clear.

Except coming to Seavy Village for the shoot. He hadn't remembered that until Jillian had reminded him years later.

And sometimes he would pass out, losing entire days after a long streak of work and coke. Marge had hated that. She had complained that his drug use was one of the major problems in their marriage.

But he was clean now, and had been clean for a long time, since before Heather died. LSD produced flashbacks, but he had never taken LSD. He had done coke, mostly, with a little joint thrown in for relaxation. Neither drug messed with the memory, so far as he knew.

Thomas sighed. He picked up his Coke and took another sip, wincing at the bittersweet taste. He had run out of diet earlier and Carolyn had brought the wrong kind home. She had probably done it intentionally; she kept telling him that he was losing too much weight. He looked in the bathroom mirror every day, relieved that Thomas Stanton was coming back. His face was clearing and he had cheekbones again. As soon as the leg healed, he would be himself.

And being himself meant confronting how he felt about all the deaths. No, Heather's death. He looked at the clock. The casserole still had half an hour to cook. He stood up. It was time he confronted the beach.

He grabbed his crutches and put them under his arms. It was dangerous going on sand with crutches, but he would make it. He always did. Besides, Carolyn was due later and if he wasn't around (and the casserole was burned), she would look for him. Then he stopped at the door. He was being stupid. This is the part in the script he would tell Connie to change before he even accepted the assignment. *No one would be that dumb*, he would say and she, the director and screenwriter, would agree.

But this wasn't a script. This was his life, his stretch of beach. He would walk out to the end of the grass and stop, surveying it from there. He had handled the crutches on grass; that would be safe enough.

He pulled his coat over his shoulders, pulled open the door, and stepped onto the porch. Somewhere out here, a cloaked figure had lured his daughter to her death. That person was torturing Thomas now, sending him notes, slaughtering birds on his porch. None of the detectives had investigated Heather's death as someone's way of getting to Thomas. Perhaps that was an angle to pursue.

Thomas shivered again. The breeze off the ocean was chilly and damp. The sun was beginning to set —it was later than he had thought. A girl in town had told him that sometimes people saw a green flash of light coming in off the ocean at sundown. There was a legend attached to that light, a legend he couldn't remember.

He made his way slowly down the porch steps and onto the gravel. The ocean looked almost calm. The sun sent golden, not green, rays across the water. Thomas stepped onto the gravel, his crutches slipping slightly on the tiny rocks, and walked to the grass.

The air was fresher here, colder, smelling of salt. Here he was, defending his house against nasty stories of murders and invisible monsters, and he had forgotten why he chose to live near the ocean in the first place. The ocean was beautiful, but more than beautiful. It was primal. It called to something in him. The *shush-shush* of the water calmed him and made him feel as if he were a part of something larger. On the other side of this water, Japan rose. These waves could have been sent from Asia, especially for him. Deep within the cold depths, whales played and dolphins laughed at each other in their strange alien language.

He stepped closer. The ground beneath his good foot felt spongy, the result of constant dampness. The chill was sharp, piercing through his coat. He almost felt like an old sailor, gazing out at the mysteries he had spent his entire life taming. But Thomas had never been on the sea. He hadn't even swum in it, somehow avoiding that during his entire life in California. The only boats he'd ever taken had been small craft on small lakes where the water was predictable and friendly.

The ocean wasn't friendly, not in the traditional sense. She was always there, though, as solid as a constant companion and as difficult as a demanding human being. He never knew what to expect when he opened his curtains in the morning: foaming waves several feet high or near calm, as near as the ocean could get.

Like she was now. He stared at her, feeling no desire to go in her or to ride on top of her, but to stare, simply stare until he could stare no more. He had felt that way about Marge once. Just before and after their marriage, he would stare at her while she slept, marveling that someone as intelligent and passionate as she was would fall in love with him.

And he had stared at Heather like that too. When he first saw her, tiny fist crammed against her mouth, her entire body red and chapped as if she had been through a fire instead of a birth, he had stared so long that visiting hours ended and the nurses had to ask him to leave. He had been reluctant then. Later, it got easier.

He took a few more steps. The ground felt even marshier, although the sand a few feet away was not wet. He was supposed to be looking at the beach, not the ocean. The beach was the problem, with the large protective rocks, the sea caverns, the hundreds of places for someone to hide.

Thomas glanced around. Someone could be watching him now, and he wouldn't even know. The idea made a chill run through him. If someone was after him, why not get him now? He was as helpless as he would ever get, unable to run. Anyone could sneak up to him in his sleep and he wouldn't be able to get away. Why go after Heather?

She wasn't even the thing he had loved the most.

The thought startled him. He wanted to retract it, but it had already crossed his mind and sent a pang to his heart. He had never loved her, not the way she'd wanted to be loved. Not the way he had wanted to be loved when he was her age.

When he was her age, he had already been through a succession of foster homes. His father had molested his sister, and both kids were removed when Thomas was twelve. His parents would visit—supervised visits—through most of his teen years. His foster parents had called him difficult, and had bounced him from home to home, separating him from his sister early on. Finally, his mother divorced his father when Thomas was eighteen. Thomas moved home. His sister refused.

Even then, he had received no affection. No attention. No matter what he did. His mother watched her soap operas, cleaned her house, and left at five for her job as a cocktail waitress at a local bar. Thomas had been company, another person who had helped pay the rent. Nothing more.

And he had ignored Heather in the same way. She was a line item on his résumé, an excuse to go into a toy store. He thought Marge was taking care of the affection side.

The setting sun cast shadows across the rocks, putting half of the beach in darkness. The beach continued on its north end for miles, finally ending at a massive rock face that separated this beach from the beginning of the beach lining Seavy Village. The south side also ended in rock, a large, porous rock jutting out against the sea and the night sky as if by its very defiance it could subdue the erosion caused by the waves and the wind. The rock was mighty, but the sea was mightier. The little stones that formed the sand before him had once been mighty rocks that were defeated by the sea.

Heather had come here, looking for affection, just as he had gone to his mother when he was eighteen. And what did he do? He scolded her a little, didn't know her well enough to see the extreme thinness, and he hadn't even hugged her. He hadn't seen his daughter for years, and he hadn't touched her in greeting.

Thomas stopped at the edge of the grass and gazed at the beach. It was boxed in, a beach unto itself. The rocks were so big that the sand from this beach stretch didn't touch the other beaches unless the ocean took it and deposited it elsewhere. And the strange, curving line of the water's edge left a lot of sand that the sea didn't touch except on those frightening stormy nights when all seaside residents had to leave their homes for safer ground. Such a storm hadn't happened here, but California had experienced one in January, knocking down marinas and even sending a restaurant into the ocean. Storms like that could touch the packed sand before him, but nothing else.

The beach was not giving him the comfort he wanted. In fact, the open air was letting him see things too clearly.

He was about to turn and return to the house when his crutch slipped. He toppled forward, landing with his good leg against the sand, his cast still propped on the grass. His ankle twisted and he would have fallen on it, breaking it too, if it weren't for his crutch dug deeply in the sand he had been studying earlier.

His broken leg ached so badly he was afraid he had injured it again. His heart was pounding. He took a deep breath, leaned on his crutch, and put his good leg back on the grass. Then he stood cautiously, resting on his leg and his other crutch, and pulled the sand-locked crutch free.

"Almost, Stanton," he whispered to himself. He had almost been as stupid as all those characters he had demanded rewritten. Maybe he wouldn't be so harsh in the future. Maybe he would simply demand that their motivation be strengthened instead of their actions changed.

A fire was burning deep within his cast and his breath hurt in his chest. If he went inside, he would be all right. He climbed up the grass and onto the gravel, tears gathering in his eyes. Tomorrow, he promised himself, he would see a doctor. He had been putting that off for too long.

He took the stairs easily so that there was little pressure on his injured leg. As he opened the door to the house, the scent of chicken casserole rose warm and rich, making his mouth water. He was hungry, tired, and in pain. He couldn't imagine leaning over to take the casserole out of the oven, but he had to in order to eat. He sighed deeply and went into the bathroom, opening the medicine cabinet and removing the pain pills he so rarely allowed himself to take. He shook two into his shaking hand and dry swallowed them, then cupped water from the tap and splashed it against his face.

The pills would calm him, and take the pain away. He wished they were strong enough to take all the pain away.

The pills scraped against Thomas's throat as they went down. He stood up and walked through the hallway and the living room to the kitchen. He grabbed a plate from the cupboard, took a sip from his still-cool Coke, and pulled open the oven door. Waves of heat greeted him. The elements were burning red. The casserole bubbled. The smell was stronger, making his stomach rumble. He took the casserole out, closed the oven door halfway, and shut off the stove. Then he dished out some food and watched it steam as he set it on the table.

All of his life he had been solitary, even as that beach was solitary. Even with Marge, he couldn't seem to get any closer than the grass was to the sand, touching but not touching at the same time. He sat down and stared at his food. The chicken bits were large and flaky, trapped in a mushroom sauce. Green peas littered the creation, tiny bits of green against gray. He took a bite, savoring the taste—Carolyn had added a little wine—and swallowed. Eating helped. His ankle itched and he brushed against it. His hand touched something hard and grainy. He brought his fingers up.

They were covered with sand.

21

He was dozing on the couch when the front door slammed. Thomas sat up. He felt irritated, and out of sorts. He pushed his hair out of his eyes and squinted. Carolyn stood in the darkened room, an apologetic smile on her face.

"There was another one," she said. In her left hand, she held a bird. A gull. Dripping blood.

Anger exploded inside him. His entire body shook with the force of it. How could she bring that bird in here? How could she touch it, knowing that it jeopardized her? How—?

He pushed himself off the couch, lunging for her. She stepped back, but he managed to grab the bird from her hands. It was soft, the blood still warm. He could feel the tiny parasites crawling under the feathers.

Stupid. Stupid of her to grab that bird. He swung his arm to hit her, to show her that it was wrong, but his arm caught in his cape. With a quick snap, the material swung free, and his hand collided with her neck. Only he wasn't holding the bird anymore. He was holding a knife. Blood spurted across the room, like the anger inside him, thick and red and ugly—

Thomas sat up. He wasn't screaming, at least, he didn't feel as if he had been screaming. His breath was coming rapidly and his heart was pounding. He could still feel the dream, lurking in the back of his body like a half-felt memory.

The living room was dark, the darkness grainy and almost tangible. He stretched. The air was cold against his bare skin. It was the middle of the night or perhaps later—the darkness before dawn. He swung his body over the side of the cot and winced as his bare foot touched the cool floor. His back ached and he was exhausted, even though adrenaline still pumped through his body.

He grabbed the crutches and adjusted them under his arms. Three deep breaths and the dream would go away.

One.

The air felt good in his lungs—expanded them, slowed his heart.

Two.

The sounds of his exhalation echoed, making him sound like some big swamp monster—no! Darth Vader—instead of a human being. He smiled at the image.

Three.

The feeling again. Deep. Old. So old, he wouldn't have noticed it if he hadn't been looking. What was the dream saying to him? That he couldn't get angry? Or that his anger would cause more trouble than he realized? Or something more sinister? Twice he had mistaken himself for the man in the cape. The first time on the beach in Depoe Bay. The second time in this dream. His shrink back in L.A. would have been able to say what all of this meant, but he wasn't going to call the man for an expensive long-distance consult. No. Something else was happening. Something more important.

He had never had so many nightmares in his life.

He hobbled over to the kitchen and opened the refrigerator. The tiny light bulb cast a feeble glow across the counters. The chill air from the refrigerator made him shiver. He should have put on his robe.

He grabbed some bread—Carolyn insisted on keeping it in the refrigerator—butter and jam and set them on the table. Then he splashed his face and chest and filled the tea kettle with water. Remembering Heather doing that, during one of the last hours of her life, he wiped away the water.

Thomas set the tea kettle on the stove, turned on the burner, and went back into the living room for his robe. He struggled for a moment, trying to ease it on without sitting down to do so, then managed to slip the velvet sleeves over his arms. The material warmed him instantly. He went back into the kitchen, made himself a jelly sandwich, put a tea bag into a mug, and sat at the table, waiting for the water to boil.

Somehow he had to stop the dreams. Connie would say that they were being caused by the other events, the gulls, the sandpipers, and when

Thomas left, everything would cease, including the dreams. But Thomas didn't believe that. The dreams were being caused by the events, but they were tapping into something deeper, something richer, something, in the flurry of being Thomas Stanton Professional Actor, he had never examined before.

The tea kettle whistled and he jumped. He shut off the burner, grabbed the kettle, and poured water into his mug. Then he warmed his hands on the steam rising, sending the faint odor of tannic acid into the room.

Jillian. Jillian provoked the dream. He had asked her not to print the story. He had demanded, in fact. But she had anyway. Then she had tried to apologize.

He should have been angry at her, but he wasn't. The strongest emotion he had felt was irritation. He took a bite out of the sandwich, then set it down. The strawberry jam was too cloying, too sweet. He didn't want it anymore.

Her job had come first. It had been more important than he was. And, oh, that felt familiar.

His mother's voice rang in his ears, yelling at his father, those days just before the split-up, saying that if he hadn't started editing for the magazines (had she said porno magazines?), they wouldn't be in this trouble. The family would still be together. One of his foster mothers had always stated, in a reasonable, matter-of-fact, biting tone, that the reason his foster father didn't know much about the family was because he worked too much. And Marge, always bitching at him, complaining about living apart. Toward the end, he had said that she was using his job to hurt him. And she had been. Just as he had been. No compromise, no giving in. L.A. or New York, no in between. No talk about flying his family out to location shoots like so many other married actors did—like he would later do with Heather. No compromise. Nothing but bitter words and hurt feelings.

He pulled the tea bag out and tossed it onto his sandwich. With both hands, he picked up the mug. The ceramic sides were hot and felt good to his chill fingers. He took a sip, wincing at the strong tannic flavor, but continued to drink.

He felt like he had to call Jillian, to smooth this out. She was wrong printing his problem because she knew how he felt about groupies. But she was right too. He was news. And news that she could print. He would probably have done the same thing.

No. He wanted to start the dialogue again, tell her what he and Hargrave had talked about, tell her about that thread of fear that had grown in the pit of his stomach since he had found the gull on the door.

He set down the almost empty mug and got up. As he hurried into the living room, he realized what time it was. He couldn't call her now. She would wake up, grab for the phone, in a panic and already half-dressed, wondering what emergency they were calling her to now. She would be almost angry—no. She would *be* angry that he had called her in the middle of the night. He would wait until morning, and then he would go see her, at the *Ga-*

zette, maybe buy her lunch, talk with her about what he was feeling and try, try very hard to repair the damage he had already done.

He made his way back to the cot, slipped off his robe, and climbed in. The sheets were cool, like the rest of the house, but a warm spot remained where his feet had nestled an hour earlier. He tugged the blanket up to his neck, closed his eyes, and forced himself to relax. But sleep did not come.

22

Three cups of tea, a large breakfast, and four TV talk shows later, Thomas was sprawled across the couch. He had dozed a few times, but had never really slept again. He needed to talk to Jillian, but he knew that he had to wait until he could show up at the office.

Then she wouldn't kick him out.

He heard the click of a key in the lock and watched as Carolyn pushed the door open. She glanced over her shoulder at someone as she came in, then closed the door tightly and locked it.

"There's a mob out there, Mr. Stanton," she said as she took off her raincoat. He closed his eyes. He had forgotten how much he hated groupies.

"They're not doing anything, really." Carolyn went to the window overlooking the driveway and peered out. "Just waiting."

"They can keep on waiting," he said.

She let the curtain fall and looked over at him. "You've had a rough night."

"I didn't sleep well," he said.

She nodded and leaned against the windowsill. Then she sighed. "I've been meaning to say this for a while, sir, but I never found the right time. Now, with them"—she inclined her head toward the window—"I guess I wonder if you wouldn't be better off somewhere else. There are a lot of houses for sale in Seavy Village. This one just doesn't seem right for you. It—"

"Thanks, Carolyn." He made sure that his tone was flat, but not rude. He didn't want to hurt her feelings, but he didn't want to listen to the lecture either. "What time is it?"

She glanced at her watch. "Almost eleven."

He sat up, stretched, and yawned. His eyes felt gritty and his shoulders and arms cracked as he moved them. If he left now, he would get into town by 11:15. Time to catch Jillian before she headed to lunch.

"I've got an appointment," he said as he stood up. He made his way over to the door and peered through the side panes of glass. Ten, perhaps fifteen, people waited outside. Many of them were teenagers, but a few adults stood with the group. He sighed and grabbed his coat.

"Mr. Stanton."

He turned. Carolyn hadn't moved from her place beside the table.

"If you don't want me to say things like that, all you have to do is say so."

He shook his head. "Your opinions are your opinions," he said. "I'm not going to censor them."

She smiled. He pulled open the door and let

himself out. The crowd perked up as he stepped onto the porch. A few teenage girls leaned over and whispered to each other. Everyone else watched expectantly.

He waved at them, and then started on the stairs. He felt awkward as he walked down, not the slender, graceful actor who was able to push his way through true mob scenes outside, say, the Emmys.

At the bottom of the stairs, he stopped, signed the papers that people placed in front of him, going through the motions, asking names and carefully writing. He wondered what the value of the signature was. Proof that they had actually seen him? Or proof that he had actually seen them?

Finally, he was able to get into the truck. He closed the door, feeling as if he wanted to sit there for a moment, to get his bearings, but he knew that he dared not. He turned the key in the ignition, listening to the engine roar to life, then he shoved the truck into reverse, turned around, and headed for the highway.

Once he reached 101, he slipped in behind a blue sedan. The fans had unnerved him, brought him back to the world he had once thought real, the world that he was beginning to believe was imaginary. A handful of people, standing at his doorway, wanting to see the Thomas Stanton who played Jason or Anthony Short, someone who, in their imaginations, was taller or handsomer or nicer than any other man they knew. Some of those girls probably had his poster on their walls. He remembered watching Donna, one of his foster sisters, stand on her bed every night so that she could reach the paper lips of the rock star who dominated that wall. Every night, she would whisper good night to him, perhaps hoping that he would whisper back.

He hadn't thought of that before. In all the years he had been signing autographs and dodging fans, he had never thought of them, what they were feeling, wondering what their dreams were. He had always seen them as parasites, as people without lives who impinged on his. But Donna had had a life, boyfriends, and she seemed quite content with it all. Except when she faced her poster just before she turned out the light.

Overlapping personalities. If he gave in to the fans, they would be around all the time. He shouldn't even have signed autographs, because that would merely bring more. He knew that and yet he acted anyway. His solitude and the privacy that he had so loved about Seavy Village was now gone.

And he was going to talk to Jillian, calmly, even though she had been the one to take that privacy away.

But how much privacy could he reasonably expect? He wasn't like Jillian. She reported the news, existed as a byline on a piece of disposable paper. No one recognized her when she walked down the street. When she left her post at NPR, she didn't have to worry about people continually asking her why. To them, she was merely another human being, someone they could greet without fear or adoration. Someone normal.

He had been playing at being normal and had forgotten what it was like to be noticed.

The sedan shot through a stoplight on the first intersection in town, but Thomas stopped. The sun had broken through the clouds and caressed the buildings, giving everything an air of freshness and clarity. To his left, the ocean sparkled. It was going to be a warm one, if seventy degrees was warm. He rolled down his window and took a lungful of the tangy sea air.

He would have to find a way to keep people off the property. He would probably have to enlist the help of the police department. Maybe they would think that keeping an eye on a celebrity's premises was fun. But they would probably see it as yet another duty in a world filled with too many of them.

The light changed. He drove for another block, watching the tourists crowd the sidewalk, looking garish in their Hawaiian prints and too short shorts. He had probably looked like that a lot on location, dressed inappropriately for the climate or mood, but he had been a celebrity and then it hadn't mattered.

He turned right on Rhododendron Drive and felt himself relax. In a few short weeks, he had become a villager, hating the tourists and blaming them. At least two of the faces in the group at his house this morning had been familiar; the townies had probably been waiting for an opportunity to scope him out. After he left Jillian, he would see about police assistance, at least until he was able to arrange for a security firm to install a fence.

The houses along the drive were open to the

sunlight and the flowers lining the porches looked brighter than usual. Thomas felt some of the tiredness ease. He pulled in front of the newspaper office and got out of the truck.

All of the windows were open. He could hear the *clack-clack* of typewriter keys and the squeal of a dot matrix printer. A phone rang and someone answered, the voice too soft for him to catch the words. He stood beside the truck's cab for a minute, feeling the sunlight warm his skin. He didn't know how to approach Jillian without apologizing. And apologizing was the wrong thing to do. Thomas Stanton, unable to do anything without the aid of a script.

He took a deep breath and started down the walk. Someone had mowed the lawn recently and the entire area smelled of fresh grass. He shivered a little, even though it was warm, and opened the door.

Jimmy Olsen sat at the front desk, cradling a telephone receiver between his ear and his shoulder. When he saw Thomas, he punched the "hold" button and sat up. "You're h-h-here to see Jillian?"

Thomas nodded, a half smile on his face.

Jimmy Olsen stood up. "I'll get her."

"I'll go back," Thomas said.

The boy ran his fingers through his thick red hair. "She said you weren't supposed to do that. She said no one was supposed to do that." A blush was creeping up his neck. "She said she doesn't want any surprises."

"Okay," Thomas said. He leaned against the empty desk. He really had no choice but to wait.

The poor kid would get in trouble if Thomas showed up in the back. And the boy was already nervous enough. "I'll wait."

Jimmy Olsen smiled and scampered off down the hall. Thomas watched him go. He had no real desire to learn the boy's true name—Jimmy Olsen was a nice conceit—but he felt a compassion for the boy. This was probably the boy's first job and he probably felt as if he were doing something big, something important. He had been working with the town's only celebrity until Thomas showed up. Then the boy had two celebrities to deal with—one a local celebrity and, even worse, the other a national celeb.

The printer stopped. Then a metal desk drawer slammed shut. Jimmy Olsen returned from the back, his face redder than ever. "She'll be right out," he said.

"Thanks."

The boy sat back down at his desk, punched the line button, and murmured into the phone. He grabbed a message pad and began scribbling. Thomas could hear footsteps in the hall. Then Jillian appeared.

Her hair was standing up in spikes along the top of her head, as if she had been running her fingers through it constantly. The deep circles under her eyes were almost hidden by her oversize glasses, but her bloodshot eyes were clearly visible. She wore a bright red sweatshirt with the sleeves pushed up, and her blue jeans were streaked with what appeared to be fresh dirt.

She handed him a slip of paper. There was dirt

under her nails too and she smelled like motor oil. "This is the publisher's name, address, and phone number," she said. Her voice was forceful, clipped, and rich. This had to be her radio voice and the speech he was going to hear had been rehearsed. "If you have any complaints, you can bring them to him."

She turned around to go back into her office, but Thomas grabbed her arm. The force of his action nearly threw him off balance and he gripped her tighter than he had planned. She glanced down at his hand. "That hurts," she said.

He let go and clutched at his crutches for support. "I want to talk to you."

"I think I know what your position is, Thomas, and I am not changing mine, no matter what you say. There's the publisher's name. You can talk with him about policy."

"I don't want to talk to him. I want to talk to you."

She pushed nervously at her sleeves. "I don't see what the point is, Thomas. I did the best I could under the circumstances to protect your privacy. I didn't give your exact address, which goes against company policy. In fact, I just said beachfront. It's not my fault the damn village is so small that people can figure out what beachfront house would suffer from dead birds and gulls. There aren't that many isolated beachfront houses to check out and it doesn't take a great intelligence to figure that a well-known actor would live in an isolated area instead of a popular one. I even debated about putting your name in the paper, but then I decided

that it would be hard not to—people would wonder why—and Thomas Stanton isn't that unusual a
name. I didn't mention your profession, I didn't
say one word about the fact that you were famous.
People deduced it. And it isn't hard. You've been
all over town. I'm sure the tourists just looked at
you and whispered to each other, 'Gee, he looks
like that actor' and then when they saw your name
in the paper, they realized that you were that actor. I'm sorry, but I would do it again."

Thomas leaned back against the desk. "Are you
done?"

She set her lips in a rather grim line. "Yes."

"Then can I take you to lunch?"

Her eyes grew wide and he thought that, for a
moment, they filled with tears. "I don't want to
fight."

"Neither do I. I want to talk."

She swallowed hard, nodded, and swiped at her
hair. "Let me just lock my stuff up, okay?"

Thomas looked over at Jimmy Olsen. The boy
had hung up the phone. He was doodling on his
memo pad. Jillian disappeared down the hall.
Jimmy Olsen looked up. His face and his neck
were still bright red. "She's been like that for the
past couple of days," he said.

"I haven't exactly been cheery myself," Thomas
replied.

The boy glanced down the hall. Then he lowered
his voice. "She really didn't have much choice.
Ever since Mr. Diller—that's the publisher—found
out that you were in town, he wanted some kind of
interview with you or something to boost the cir-

culation of the paper. She's been fighting him off for a while now. But if he found out about the police report and then found out that she hadn't printed it, it would have been her job.''

"And I really can't afford to disappear from one job and get fired from another," Jillian said. She stood near the room dividers. Thomas wondered how much she had heard. "But it was my choice. I decided that it wouldn't hurt much to print what little I did.''

Jimmy Olsen was twisting a pen between his fingers. Thomas stood up. "Where do you want to go?''

"Mo's," she said.

He nodded and started out the door. He pulled the door open and paused. Jillian was saying something to the boy. His flush grew deeper. Then she joined Thomas.

"I hope you didn't yell at him," Thomas said after he had closed the door.

Jillian shook her head. "I told him to relax because"—she grinned—"newspapers deal in gossip.''

"He seems awful young to be working in your office.''

"Summer internship. Although we don't have much for them to intern on." She walked to Thomas's truck. "You drive," she said. "I have car problems.''

"That's why the oil beneath the fingernails, then.''

She pulled open the door, got inside, and grimaced. "It's gross. I can't get it off. I can't imagine working in that junk all the time."

Thomas smiled. He walked around to the other side of the truck. He couldn't imagine it either— for either one of them. He set his crutches in back, got inside and started up the truck. Then he looked over his shoulder and pulled out on the road.

Although their few moments of conversation had seemed comfortable, a knot still sat in the pit of his stomach. The growing silence made him nervous.

Apparently Jillian felt the same way. "You don't mind Mo's, do you?" she asked.

He shook his head. He had never been there, although he had heard about it. Mo's was a coastal chain of seafood restaurants, a well-known tourist attraction advertised all the way down to California. He suspected that she had picked it for its lack of privacy. "I just hope it's good."

"We should barely beat the lunch crowd," she said.

The silence grew as he drove. Once again, he had to cross 101, then take a winding side road down to the ocean. Mo's sat on a pier overlooking the water, a large blue-gray building covered with kites and signs and posters. The parking lot was half full. Thomas frowned. "I thought you said—"

"When they're busy, you can't park here."

He pulled in as close to the building as possible. Jillian leaned over to look in the rearview mirror and tried to tame her hair with the palm of her hand. "You look fine," Thomas said. Actually, she looked better than fine. She looked wonderful. He wanted to reach out, stroke her hair, like she had been doing, then kiss her slowly to chase the uncomfortable feeling away.

"I feel like a mess." She took one last look in the mirror, then let herself out of the truck. Thomas climbed out too.

The wind off the ocean was strong, but warm, and the sky was a clear, cloudless blue. The sunshine made him feel good, but strange, as if he had never been to Oregon before. The Oregon coast, as he knew it, was always cool, sometimes rainy, but never mild. Never like this.

He rounded the truck. Jillian was waiting for him on the other side. She smiled at him and together they walked to the building. She pulled open the big glass door and he stepped inside.

The restaurant smelled of fish, chowder, and coffee. The entryway was filled with touristy things: postcards, earrings, wind socks, coastal artwork, and mugs, all of it overpriced and most of it gaudy. A heavyset woman sat behind the counter, next to a large, humming cash register. Her hair was too black to be natural and her skin too pale. As Thomas stepped up closer, he could see powder gathered on her cheek.

"Two?" she said without looking up. Then she did look up and smiled as she recognized him. The powder disappeared in lines that formed on her face. "Mr. Stanton, where would you like to sit?"

He glanced at Jillian. She was turning an earring tree, pretending to be interested in the large plastic selection. "Somewhere toward the back," he said. "As private as you have."

The woman nodded. She slipped out from the behind the counter, grabbed two menus, and led them into the main dining hall.

Rows of benches half-filled with people lined the room. To the right, a large counter stood where the waitresses scrunched to scribble their orders and hand them directly to the cooks. The rest of the room was lined with windows. The ocean dominated the restaurant.

Jillian had clearly picked the place for its lack of privacy and for its family setting. No intimations of romance here. The place was designed for parties and large groups of tourists, not for a single, quiet dinner. But the hostess did manage to find them a table, tucked off in the corner, near the back wall. They sat down on the straight-backed wooden chairs with the hearts carved into the center of the backs, and immediately stared at the menus.

Thomas didn't feel much like eating. The lunch idea had been more of a ploy to get Jillian to join him than an end in and of itself. He ordered chowder and bread and waited while Jillian ordered breaded oysters. Then the waitress left them.

Jillian took a sip of her water. "What did you want to talk about?"

There. Simple question, but it made the answer freeze up inside of him. Thomas took a deep breath and let it out, slowly. "I—promised myself that I wouldn't apologize, but I guess what I'm doing is apologizing. Sort of, anyway."

She was watching him intently. She neither nodded nor made the small encouraging noises that people normally make, yet he knew he had never been listened to more closely.

"I miss you," he said. "And I'm sorry that things have been so strained between us."

Her shoulders visibly relaxed. "I didn't intentionally try to hurt you, Thomas."

"I know." Thomas glanced up as the waitress brought their beverages. He took his teacup, poured hot water into it, and wrapped his hands around the cup's sides. His fingers were cold, his entire body cold, and he recognized that as a sign of tension. "I realized that last night. I also realized that I miss talking with you."

"I've missed talking with you too." She reached out and put her hand on top of his. Her fingers were just as cold as his were. He picked up her hand and kissed it just as the waitress set down their meals.

Thomas ignored the food. "Truce?" he said.

"I didn't know there was a war," Jillian replied. She squeezed his fingers, then slid her hand away and began to eat. Thomas did too. The chowder was thick and rich, and the bread tasted fresh.

"You haven't found out anything about the gull, have you?" Jillian asked.

Thomas nodded. "I did, sort of. I talked with Hargrave again."

Jillian set her fork down. "You're kidding. Hargrave won't see anyone. It took forever for me to get him to talk at all."

Thomas shrugged. "He doesn't like me. I think he'll do anything to get me out of here."

"And away from me?"

Thomas nodded.

"He means well," she said.

"He may have a point." Thomas ripped the bread apart. He hadn't meant to talk about this. "My history isn't that great."

"I know." Jillian's voice was quiet. "I read the reports."

He glanced up. Her expression was solemn. "Then why be with me?"

She shrugged. "I like you."

"A lot of people like me. They wouldn't stay if they knew my past."

She pushed the food around on her plate. "I think we're a lot alike, Thomas," she said. "Why do we work so hard? What are we running away from?"

He frowned and set the bread down, giving her his full attention.

"I don't think you ever looked at me, not clearly anyway. Alicia is a clue. Anorexics don't appear in happy families."

"What happened?" he asked.

"What didn't?" Then she smiled. "I—don't always know. I can't talk about much because there's not much that I remember, except the need to leave."

"Have you gotten help?"

"Seen a shrink?" She shook her head. "Of course not. I ran away to Seavy Village. People who run away don't deal with things."

He reached out and took her hand. She stared down at her plate. "Great lunchtime topic."

"I'm glad you said something."

"Well, I'm not. Just talking about it makes me want to run away. Let's talk about something else."

"Okay," he said.

Jillian leaned forward. "Why don't you leave, Thomas? You can afford it. Why don't you get away from the groupies and the dead birds. Sell the house or something, and then just buy another place closer to Seavy Village."

"No," Thomas said. "I'm not moving until all of the pieces fit. There's a man in a cloak who is unaccounted for. Something is going on there. I'm not leaving until I know what it is."

"But you're forcing other people to be there too."

Thomas pushed his empty chowder bowl away. "Who am I forcing?"

"Carolyn, for one."

"She works for me. She's been going there for years."

"Me, for another."

"It's your choice, Jillian. You don't have to come out to the house."

"What about all the fans you say you've been having trouble with? They're on that beach now too."

Thomas sighed. "I know. That's also their choice, but it's a choice I hope to take away from them soon. The group this morning was five times bigger than anything I'd seen in Seavy Village before."

Jillian set aside her oysters. She wiped her

hands on the napkin, paying special attention to her fingernails. "What do you plan to do?"

Thomas shrugged. "I was wondering if the police had any ideas. If I stay here much longer, I'll have to install some kind of security system. I really don't want to do that. What I liked most about Seavy Village was the privacy."

Jillian looked out at the ocean. A child was playing on the beach, throwing pieces of driftwood to a small dog. A woman watched from a nearby log. "I really screwed that up for you, didn't I?"

Her mouth turned downward. From the sideways angle he viewed her face, he could see the deep circles under her eyes. He took her hand. "It was bound to happen sooner or later. The first time, I wasn't here long enough. This time, I was bruised and battered, hard to recognize. The fans are part of what I do. It's stupid of me to expect that I can live like a normal human being."

"It's not unreasonable—"

"Yes, it is, Jillian," Thomas said softly, "if I expect to continue doing what I'm doing."

Her entire body tightened and she pulled back from him. "When are you going back?"

"I don't know if I am or not," he said. "That's one of the things I'm thinking about. I don't know if I want to go back."

She was studying him, saying nothing. He smiled. He felt closer to her now, less frightened, and he couldn't quite put his finger on why. Perhaps it was the talking. Or perhaps it was something as simple as being together.

He picked up the check. "I suppose I should take you back."

"Actually, what I would really like to do is go home and try to get some of this oil off. I felt silly asking someone if I could borrow their car just to go home and change." She picked up her purse and slung it over her shoulder, then stood up as Thomas threaded his way back to the cash register.

The benches were full now, and many people looked up as he passed. He ignored them. He didn't want to deal with autograph seekers or obsequious fans right now. He wanted to pay for lunch and hang on to the mood that he and Jillian were beginning to recreate.

He had almost made it to the front when a little boy stopped him. Then another joined, and another, until he was surrounded by a handful of children. As he signed autographs, the parents approached him. He signed and said hello, and tried to keep moving forward. Once he glanced back and saw Jillian standing patiently at the edge of the crowd. Finally he handed the last pad and pen back.

"I have to go, folks," he said. The people parted and let him by. He moved forward, a bit stunned. Oregon seemed to bring out the polite side of people. He had never before had fans move just because he had asked them to.

Jillian caught up with him at the cash register. "God," she said. "Is it always like that?"

"No." Thomas glanced back into the main dining room. People were still watching him, but most had returned to their seats. "Usually it's a lot worse." He got his change back from the black-haired woman and followed Jillian out the door.

The parking lot was full and so were both side streets. Thomas and Jillian got into the truck. He had to ease it out of the parking space, since the cars on the other side were parked too close.

As he drove, she slid closer to him and put her hand on his knee. A wave of warmth ran through him. He looked down at her and smiled. She smiled back. He stopped at a stop sign at the intersection of 101, leaned over, and kissed her.

Her lips enfolded his, caressed his, and her tongue brushed against his teeth. A honk behind him made him jump. He glanced in the rearview mirror to see two cars waiting behind him. Jillian squeezed his knee and slid back over to her side of the car. He waited for a break in traffic and then pulled out onto the highway.

The drive to Jillian's was short; it was only a few blocks away from Mo's on the other side of the highway. Thomas pulled into Jillian's driveway.

"Come on in," Jillian said.

He had been hoping she would ask. He shut off the ignition and got out of the truck. Jillian was already at the front door, struggling with her keys.

"Alicia's not home?" he asked.

"She never is this time of day." Jillian found the right key and pushed the door open. The house was just as messy as ever. A stack of newspapers and empty cans sat near the door. The table in the entry was littered with open mail, jewelry, and books. Thomas closed the door behind himself. A thin light still filtered in from the picture window. Dust motes rose in the rays of the sun.

Jillian disappeared down the hall. A light went on. He assumed she was in the bathroom. "God-damn oil," she called. "You know how to get it off?"

He followed the voice. She had left the bathroom door open. The room itself was neat. The towels hanging beside the shower matched the rug. Most of the bathroom counter, however, was covered with books and magazines. He squinted at some of the titles. Four romance novels, two horror novels, a science fiction novel, a biography of Reagan, an analysis of the Carter Administration, the transcripts from Oliver North's testimony before Congress, piles of the *New York Times Book Review*, *The Washington Monthly*, and *The Nation*.

"Where do you find time to read all of that?" he asked.

She glanced at the stack, then reached for the towel. Water dripped off of her hands onto the books. "It should be obvious." She dried her hands. "I take it you don't know anything about motor oil."

"You're right."

"What kind of man are you?" she asked and grinned. She came forward and unbuttoned the top button of his shirt. "Do you have any meetings this afternoon?"

He looked down. The oil was still on her fingertips, only the smudge was fainter. "No, but I'll bet you do."

"Not a one. Or if I did, it wouldn't matter." She

unbuttoned the next button. Her thumb brushed against the hair on his chest. "You sure? No appointments?"

"No."

Another button opened.

"Phone calls?"

"No."

The next button and the next.

"Dates?"

"No."

She stood on her tiptoes and kissed him, pressing her palm against his chest. His heart was beating hard. She tasted like cinnamon. "That's where you're wrong," she said against his mouth. "You have a very important appointment."

He was standing awkwardly. If he let go of one of his crutches, it would fall. "Where?"

"Down the hall and to the left." She stepped back and unbuttoned the remaining few buttons on his shirt, then gave him a slight push. "What are you waiting for? Get going."

He backed out of the room, then followed her instructions. Down the hall and to the left was a bedroom filled with more books and unhung paintings leaning against the walls. A queen-size water bed covered with quilts dominated the room. He glanced back over his shoulder. He could see Jillian in the entryway. She locked the door. He stepped into the room, leaned his crutches against the wall, and eased himself onto the bed.

A large wave rippled underneath him, hit the side of the bed, and then rolled back. He hadn't been on a real water bed—one that allowed waves —in years. He wondered if his cast would harm it, then decided that it wouldn't.

Jillian came into the room just as he was about to put his legs on the bed. "Wait," she said. She bent over, unzipped his pants and pulled them down over his cast. Then she took off his shirt. She ran her hand along his skin and he watched as well as felt himself grow hard.

"I like it when the man is naked first," she said, her eyes twinkling. Then she helped him put his legs on the bed. He put his head against the pillow and watched her.

She pulled the sweatshirt over her head, breasts bobbing as they swung loose. He reached out to touch her nipple, but she stepped back. "Not yet," she said. Then she unzipped her own jeans, tugged them over her hips and let them fall to the floor. Her underwear was lacy and see-through. Little strands of hair curled along the top. She slipped both hands along the sides and wriggled out of that too, then joined him on the bed.

The warmth and softness of her skin made him groan. He ran his hands along her side, her back, her buttocks, feeling all of her. She kissed his neck, her own hands roaming. She rolled away from him, turned around, and took him in her mouth. He wriggled with pleasure, slipping a hand along her thigh, caressing her, then sliding a finger inside of her. Jillian squirmed against him. He grabbed her hips and gently turned her around. His mouth met hers at the same moment that he slipped inside of her. She felt warm, wet, and good. They moved with each other, rocking, the bed splashing. Her mouth caressed against his in time to their bodies. The pleasure ran up from his groin and back down again, making him shiver. Her hands grabbed him tighter, pulled her against him, and she came, once, twice, and yet another time. He moved deeper inside her, deeper, faster, deeper, faster, until she came again and at the height of her climax, he came too.

It felt as if he were turning inside out. He clung to her, to prevent losing too much of himself. Jillian wrapped herself around him, holding him in.

"I like that kind of appointment," he said when his breath came back. "Is there another scheduled?"

She cupped his buttock with one cool hand. "This kind of appointment is never scheduled," she said. "Either you're there or you're not."

"Mmm," he said, kissing her. "I'll make sure I'm there, every time."

He rolled off of her, still holding her against him. She ran her hand through his hair and kissed him. He waited for her to tell him that she loved him, but she said nothing.

"I would love to fall asleep," he said. "But I suppose I should take you back to work."

"Work." She spoke the word as if it were anathema. "I suppose you're right."

She stretched and yawned. He watched her torso move, watched her breasts flatten and then regain their shape. He ran a finger along the underside of her left breast. She caught his hand in her own. "That's nice," she said and climbed off the bed.

There was no ceremony in the way she dressed. One moment she was naked, the next she wasn't. She reached over and helped him off the bed, then handed him his clothes. While he dressed, she went down to the bathroom. He heard the toilet flush, then heard the sound of water running. He felt good, but tired. This "talk" had gone better than he ever could have expected. Coming back to her had been the right thing to do.

He grabbed his crutches and met her in the hall. She put her arms around him, kissed his ear, and whispered, "I liked that, Thomas."

"I did too."

She patted his bottom and let him go. She went into the other room, grabbed her coat and purse, and opened the front door. Already she had slipped back into her reportorial mode. The woman who had seduced him in the bathroom was gone. He found that he liked the switch; it meant that Jillian would never cling to him.

He followed her to the truck. She was inside before he even had his door open. As he started the vehicle, she grabbed his hand, but he could tell her mind was back on her job. He drove her to the newspaper office, kissed her, and watched her walk up the sidewalk.

He almost didn't want her to go. He felt as if he had found her again and even being separate meant that they would lose precious time together. The birds, the talk of murder, everything was mak ing him superstitious, and he found that he didn't like it.

The drive was clear all the way to 101. He turned away from the highway, determined to find the police station by the back roads. As he passed the lake, he saw a familiar figure walking along its edge, hands shoved in her coat pocket, shoulders hunched forward. He pulled the truck onto the side of the road and rolled down his window.

"Alicia!"

She saw him. A hand came out of her pocket, smoothed the hair away from her face in a gesture reminiscent of Jillian. Then she trudged across the grass to the truck.

"What?" she asked.

Thomas leaned over and opened the passenger door. "Need a ride?"

"Not from you," she said.

"I'm going downtown."

"Not to the newspaper office?"

"I just came from there."

Alicia's frown grew. "I thought you and Jilly hated each other."

Thomas smiled and shrugged. "We made up."

"You know," Alicia said, "She doesn't need her heart broken. I wish you would leave her alone."

"What makes you think I'm going to break her heart?"

"You've already started." Alicia slammed the truck door and started back toward the lake.

"Alicia!" Thomas called.

"I'm done talking," she said as she walked. "Go away."

"Go away," he murmured. The words made an anger rise in him. Damn girl didn't seem to care about any of his overtures. He had thought, after the dinner, that they at least had grown to respect each other. He had obviously been wrong.

He rolled up his window, started the truck, and pulled onto the road. Amazing how one encounter with Jillian's sister could alter his entire mood. He tried to concentrate on Jillian, but Alicia kept returning to his mind. Too-thin Alicia, who reminded him too much of Heather.

The police station was just off the highway near the burned-out bakery. Thomas pulled into their lot, got out, and walked into the building. The officer on desk duty eyed him coldly. "What can I do for you, Mr. Stanton?"

It seemed as if everyone knew who he was. "I'd like to talk with someone about some troubles I'm having near my house."

"Tiger's handling that. You can talk to him. He's over there."

Thomas leaned around the corner and saw the mustachioed policeman who had been to his house the night the gull was killed. Then he realized that the on-duty officer thought Thomas was coming to talk about the bird incidents. Oh, well. He didn't need to tell her.

He walked over to Tiger's desk.

"Mr. Stanton." Tiger kicked a chair back away from the desk for Thomas to sit on. Thomas leaned his crutches on the desk, then used the chair's arms to assist him in sitting. "We don't have any more on the birds yet. Sorry about that."

"The birds aren't concerning me," Thomas said. "Although they're the cause of my problem. The publicity about the whole thing brought curiosity seekers, autograph hounds, a few fans, to my door, and I'm afraid that the problem is going to get worse."

Tiger nodded. He folded his hands on top of a stack of folders on his desk. "It probably is."

"I came to see if you could help me."

Tiger got up, went over to the coffee machine, picked up a styrofoam cup, and filled it. "You want some?"

Thomas shook his head.

"I think you know what we can do, Mr. Stanton, because I suspect this isn't the first time you've had this problem. Put up a few no trespassing signs and we'll make sure that someone drives by a couple times a day. That won't solve your problem, but it'll cut it down. The best thing to do is put up a fence and make the place inaccessible."

"I know." Thomas sighed. "I was kind of hoping that you would have a different solution."

"I'm afraid not." Tiger sat back down. He slurped the top off the cup of coffee. "The security system is a good idea. It'll probably solve the bird problem you're having too."

"Think so?"

Tiger shrugged. "Nobody can get in. How can they massacre gulls on your porch?"

Thomas leaned forward. "How long have you worked here?"

"Except for going to the Academy, I've lived in Seavy Village my whole life."

"And what do you know about my place?"

Tiger set his cup down and ran his hands along his pants. "Mr. Stanton, you don't really want to know—"

"I do," Thomas said.

"There's been weird things going on at that stretch of beach since the late seventies. People were always finding dead animals, dead birds, and not the way the sea kills either. A lot of them were mutilated."

"And then there are all the murders."

Tiger tilted his chair back on two legs. "Only one murder, Mr. Stanton. The rest all seem to be accidental deaths, including your daughter's."

"What about the girl who died in '79 when we were shooting that film?"

"Same thing. Can't prove it was murder, even though we investigated it like it was. We investigate most of those deaths like they were murders, but we don't find anything."

"Not even anything linking them together?"

Tiger shook his head. "The cause of death always seems to be something different. There are no prints, no fibers, nothing."

"Why haven't you been investigating this like a serial killing?"

Tiger brought his chair back down. "Because it's been going on too long. Serial killers have a standard M.O. They use a knife or a gun or they rape their victims. They don't change weapons and they don't operate over a decade. They appear, commit a rash of killings, and get caught or move on. They don't concentrate their work on one stretch of beach.''

"So what do you think it is?"

"I tell you, Mr. Stanton. If we knew, the entire department would be happy.''

"I don't care what the department thinks," Thomas said. He was gripping the chair so tightly that his knuckles were turning white. "I want to know what you think.''

Tiger smiled and finished off his coffee. "What I think sounds a little crazy, Mr. Stanton, but then I've lived in Seavy Village my whole life." He crumpled the cup and tossed it in the wastebasket. "I think we're dealing with an unlucky stretch of ground. Perhaps it's more dangerous than some people think, and more people die there. Or maybe we just hear about what goes on there more than other places. Maybe it's Seavy Village's equivalent of a haunted house.''

"But you don't believe that.''

Tiger shrugged. "I could believe a lot of things. People die around you, Mr. Stanton. We have no record of deaths before you arrived in Seavy Village.''

"I was gone for some of them.''

"I know." Tiger leaned back. "That's what blows that theory. Of course, we haven't really checked on your location during the other killings. We only have your word, and the fact that no one saw you in town before or after the deaths.''

"What do you believe?''

Tiger's gaze was level. "Before your daughter

died, I believed that you had nothing to do with any of the deaths. Now I don't know."

"You think I killed Heather?" Thomas's heart was pounding inside his chest. His throat had gone dry.

"Stranger things have happened," Tiger said. "And frankly, any man with a background like yours is bound to be a bit off."

Thomas frowned. He wasn't that unusual. Abuse in the home, yes, and foster homes that followed. But a lot of people had gone through that. "You're saying that because I was abused as a kid, I'm more likely to kill people."

"You know that's not what I'm saying," Tiger said. "It must have been pretty awful, seeing your sister ripped up like that."

"My sister?" Thomas could barely get the words out. He had lost track of his sister when he was thirteen, when they had been sent to separate foster homes. She hadn't come home when he did, and his mother never spoke of her. She didn't even come to his mother's funeral, and Thomas figured that she had found a new family, one that cared about her, and gave her a new life. "What happened to my sister?"

Tiger studied him for a minute. "You don't remember?"

"I remember how my father hurt her, and how they took us away from him."

"And you don't remember him finding you and coming to get both of you?"

Thomas shook his head. He felt as if he were

under water. "I never saw him again. Not even after I went home when I was eighteen."

"He was in prison, Mr. Stanton. I'm surprised that the tabloids never picked up on this, but then Stanton isn't that uncommon a name."

"Prison?" Thomas's throat hurt. The words could barely emerge. "For raping my sister?"

"For killing her," Tiger said. "In front of you."

23

Thomas didn't remember leaving police headquarters. He found himself standing on the public beach between the Shilo and the Sand & Surf hotels. The air was brisk, filled with a salty mist, coating his cheeks. His entire body felt like it was going to explode.

Shards of memory rose like embedded glass. His father's hand, raised, blood-covered. His sister, screaming. Thomas running up the stairs of his foster family's house, seeing his father inside, seeing the blood coating the walls. Hearing her voice grow fainter and fainter.

Tiger said Thomas had gone to a neighbor's and called the cops. Then he had come back to the porch and watched, doing nothing, as his father beat his sister to death.

And his father had never spoken a word about it. Not to the police, not during his trial. He had been angry, and his anger had gotten out of control. There was no way a man could apologize for that.

Tiger said his father had killed her for telling, for splitting up the family.

Thomas squeezed his hands into fists. The surf pounded against the shore, along with the rhythm of the headache pounding in his skull. She had gone to another foster family. They had been separated. She was still alive somewhere, living a good life, with a happy family. He knew that with the firmness of two decades.

He also knew it was a lie.

A family walked by, the father holding his daughter's hand, the little girl kicking at the waves. Thomas turned away. No wonder they all thought he had done it. Like father, like son.

The crutches were digging into his armpits. It hurt to breathe. His shrink used to tell him that it was okay to remember the past. Thomas would say that he did remember. He did.

He just remembered it wrong.

And his daughter disappeared. And then died. When she was reaching puberty, just like his sister.

Only he never molested Heather. That he did know. The idea so repelled him that he couldn't imagine even trying it. And he didn't kill her. He had been asleep. He had seen the figure on the beach, running away.

And he had mourned for her.

Murderers didn't mourn, did they?

24

Thomas had gathered the detective reports and read the parts about him, the parts he had previously skipped. They confirmed Tiger's story in graphic detail. After reading DeFreeze and Garity, he put his head on his arm and let sleep take him.

He slept for the rest of the afternoon. His dreams were jumbled, a mixture of faces he hadn't seen in over twenty years. He awoke with his headache gone, but a feeling of disquiet in the center of his chest.

He had just sat down to yet another casserole dinner when the phone rang. He grabbed his crutches and struggled out of his chair, counting the rings as he moved. One. Two. Across the kitchen. Three. Four. Into the living room. Five. Six.

Don't hang up yet, Jillian, he thought. *I need you.* Seven. Eight—

"Hello?" He grabbed the phone, talking into it before it reached his ear.

"Is this late enough for you?"

Connie. He sank into the couch and set his crutches aside. "This is fine," he said. The disappointment was deep. He didn't know why he had expected Jillian, but he obviously had. "What now? Touchstone wants me to bring Anthony Short to the theaters?"

"I wish. I want to know what's happening with you. The tabloids are screaming about a voodoo curse against you and the legitimate papers are talking about dead birds taped to your door."

Thomas sighed. "I'm having some troubles up here."

"Good. Maybe it will bring you back to work where you belong."

"Lay off, Connie. I think it's related to Heather's death."

"You want me to put that in the retraction?"

Thomas picked at the upholstery. "I don't want you to retract anything. Some birds were massacred on my porch and it made the local paper. So far it's no big deal."

"What are you going to do if it becomes a big deal, Thomas?" Connie had lowered her voice. She almost sounded concerned.

He thought for a minute. That was the important question. If the killing started again, would he jeopardize himself and his whole career for some answers? "I suppose I'll see it through," he said.

"I think that fall hurt your head. I really do." She sighed. "Do you want me to leave you alone, Thomas, let you work this thing out on your own?"

Life without the voice from the past forcing him to remember who he was and why he had gotten into trouble in the first place. Acting and arrogance. Connie and more projects. "Yeah," he said. "If you haven't heard from me in a month or so, then call again. Deal?"

"And I'm supposed to ignore voodoo curses, dead birds, and any other sort of tabloid headline."

"You got it."

"All right, Thomas." Connie's voice was firm. "One month. But I expect you to have some decisions for me on the scripts I sent, and on the types of projects you plan to do in the future. I think I can hold off production on Short for another month, but after that, kiss that role good-bye. And losing Short will hurt your entire career."

"I know," Thomas said.

"Okay. As long as you understand." Connie paused. Thomas listened to the silence echo through the phone lines. He wondered if he was hearing the fiberoptics that phone company had paid him to ballyhoo, and then decided he was being silly. He shifted slightly, wondering what Connie's silence meant. Was she waiting for a specific type of response from him?

"Thomas," she said slowly. "Whatever the voodoo curses are and the dead birds and everything, be careful okay? And I'm saying that as a friend lest you think it's the money grubbing side of me talking. Even if you decide to never take another project—I can't believe I'm saying that!—but even if you do, I'll miss you a lot. So be careful, okay?"

Thomas smiled into the phone. "I will, Connie. I promise."

He hung up and stared at the phone for a minute. He wasn't sure if he was glad or not that she was going to leave him alone. He almost liked the nagging, the constant pressure to go back to work. It gave him something to think about that had nothing to do with Seavy Village. Or his past.

He got up and started back toward the kitchen. When he reached the entryway, he stopped and stared out the window. The groupies had disappeared with the darkness. They were relatively tame, as groupies went. The bulk of them merely waited until they saw him once, and then they got his autograph and moved on. About six lingered, hoping for more glimpses, perhaps hoping for something else. In the morning, he would have Carolyn put up NO TRESPASSING signs and he would politely ask whatever fans were waiting outside to leave. He didn't want to anger them, but he didn't want to be harassed either. Maybe he would explain that to them, tell them how hard it was to conduct a normal life when people constantly waited for him outside his door.

A normal life. Something he'd never had.

He went back into the kitchen and sat down. His dinner was cold now, but it didn't matter. He ate it anyway, sitting in the silent, semidarkness, hoping that Jillian would call.

25

Voices echoed around him, young voices, but he was so tired, he didn't want to open his eyes. He drew the blanket up to his shoulder and shivered.

"Maybe I came to see the great PooBah. What the fuck business is it of yours? You don't own the porch." Alicia. He would recognize her voice anywhere with its underlying current of bitterness. If he opened his eyes, he would see her, tacked to his door, blood covering her shirt, feathers in her mouth. God, he hated dreams. He wished they would go away.

"It's just kind of strange that you're wandering all over in the dark." Another girl's voice. Different. One he didn't recognize.

"No stranger than you sitting here, waiting for the great man himself. He's really just a fuckhead, you know. He's screwing my sister and then he's going to dump her. Men like him, they don't have anything inside."

Marge had said the same thing. No feeling. No soul. Nothing but surface. Thomas frowned. He wanted out of the dream. It was making him sick to his stomach.

"I thought you were staying to see him." The other girl again. Her voice had a nasal, whining quality to it.

"I lied."

Thomas sat up. The darkness was beginning to thin. Dawn was breaking.

"He's not going to be happy to find you there." Alicia again. He hadn't been dreaming. He actually was awake and Alicia was on his porch.

"Why don't you just go away."

"I think I will."

Thomas grabbed for the crutches under the cot. He slipped his robe on, got up, and walked to the window. It was still dark outside, but he could see the first rays of the sun peeking over the coastal range, sending little tendrils of light across the lawn. Four girls sat on the front porch, each on their own step, two on one side and two on the other. They had blankets and looked as if they had been trying to sleep. None of them looked like Alicia.

He scouted the lawn and the beach for her. The waves were breaking slowly across the sand. The ocean sounded tame this morning, its roar more like a murmur. The lawn was covered with dew that sparkled in the growing light. The only place she could be was behind his truck, in the driveway, or trudging up the road. He squinted, but could see nothing.

Then he looked back at the girls. One of them held out a candy bar to the others. They shook their heads. A six-pack of 7-Up sat on the top step. He should really go out there, chase them away, but they weren't hurting anything. The signs would be up soon enough. Besides, it was cold and he wore nothing under his robe. Opening the door, looking sleepy and grumpy, might make such a wait even more worthwhile the following morning. And he wanted to do his best to discourage them, not encourage them.

Thomas sighed and let the curtain fall. He went into the kitchen, grabbed a glass, and without turning on a light, poured himself some water. Then he downed it. The exhaustion was overwhelming him, making him feel as if he had run six miles, not simply bummed around town the day before. He started back to bed when he stopped.

Alicia had been here. At five in the morning. She didn't seem like the kind of person who would trudge all the way out to his place just to hassle four girls she probably didn't know very well. She'd had another reason. He started to reach for the phone, to call Jillian, to ask her if Alicia was there, but then he thought the better of it. Alicia had obviously come out here to do something in secret. He didn't want her to know that he had heard her. He would figure out what she was doing and then he would contact Jillian. But first, he would go back to bed.

He wandered back to the cot and collapsed on it, sinking back into sleep as easily as if he had never really awakened from it.

26

Thomas awoke to the sound of a key turning in the lock. He leaned over, grabbed his robe, and threw it over his chest as the door opened. Sunlight poured in and he knew that he had overslept.

Carolyn shut the door behind her. She was holding a sack of groceries in one arm and some envelopes, along with the keys, in her other hand. She saw Thomas and stopped.

"I didn't mean to wake you up," she said.

"It's all right." He rubbed the sleep out of his eyes and stretched. "How bad is it out there?"

"There's a bunch of them. But they're pretty quiet."

"Wonderful."

Carolyn took the groceries into the kitchen. He heard the bag rattle as she set it on the counter. Then she mumbled something.

He slid his robe on, one sleeve at a time, the blanket still pooled around his waist. "What was that?" he called.

"There's something on the kitchen window. You should come here."

"Just a minute. Let me get on my robe." Thomas belted his robe at the waist, then slid his legs over the side and stood up, checking to make sure the robe covered everything. He grabbed his crutches and hobbled into the kitchen.

Carolyn had set the groceries next to the refrigerator. She was standing in front of the sink, staring at the window. A white envelope had been taped to it on the outside. Thomas felt his stomach flutter.

"Did you bring the mail?"

She turned to him, frowning. His question clearly didn't make sense to her. "It's right here." She grabbed three envelopes off the counter next to the bag. He looked at them. Two more letters forwarded from Connie and another bill from De-Freeze and Garity. He tossed the envelopes on the table.

"Well," he said. "I suppose we should see what that is."

"I'll go," Carolyn said, scurrying around the table. "There are quite a few people out there, and you're not dressed."

He heard her scramble through the living room, slam the front door, and then he heard her footsteps echo softly on the porch. He wondered if that was what had awakened him at dawn, the sound of footsteps outside his house.

Her slender hand came up and yanked the envelope off the window. Then he listened to her footsteps trace her path to the front door. This time she closed the door more gently. He walked out into the living room. She handed him the white envelope. *Daddy* was scrawled on the front.

Carolyn bit her lower lip. Thomas turned the envelope over and slid his finger along the seal. A small piece of notepaper was folded inside. He pulled it out.

I miss you, Daddy, the note read. *Why don't you ever come to visit me?*

"Damn her," Thomas said. He shoved the paper back in its envelope and started for the door.

Carolyn touched his arm. "What are you doing, Mr. Stanton?"

"I'm going to go see if anyone knows who put up this note."

"Then maybe you should get dressed first. They'll all still be there."

Thomas looked down at his robe. It gaped open, showing slightly more thigh than he wanted it to. He nodded, tossed some clothes from the top of the hamper over his shoulder, and made his way to the bathroom.

So Alicia was the one leaving the notes. He should have realized that. The girl was sick, clearly sick, and she hated him. He had the scenario figured out. Alicia heard Jillian talk about him, knew how obsessed he was with Heather's death, and decided to haunt him a little. When that didn't work, she killed a few birds, and finally tacked the gull to his door.

He grimaced. How could a sixteen-year-old girl bring herself to kill a live gull, gut it, and pound it into the door, then do the same thing again until the entire porch was covered with blood? He would have to call Jillian now. Then she would have to do something with Alicia before the girl hurt something larger than a gull.

He sat on the toilet cover to pull on his jeans. He would have to talk with Jillian in person. This wasn't the sort of thing to do on the phone. She would be hurt, disbelieving at first, and then she would need help deciding what to do with Alicia. He would wait before he went to the police. He would give Jillian a chance to get used to the idea.

He finished buttoning his shirt, got up, and left the bathroom. Carolyn was still in the same place in which he had left her. She was staring at the note. "Who did this, Mr. Stanton?"

"I think I have a pretty good idea," he said. He pulled the front door open. Several teenage girls sat out front, a few boys, and about ten women, ranging in age from thirty to fifty. As he stepped out, a camera clicked and whirred. He put up his hand. "Who was here around dawn this morning?"

"I was."

"Me."

"Me too."

Three girls stepped forward. Thomas frowned. "I thought there were four of you."

One of the girls, the blonde, shrugged. "Kari was with us, but I guess she went home."

Thomas nodded. He would talk with Kari later. "Did anything unusual happen?"

The three girls looked at each other. They all wore sweatshirts and had their socks rolled up over the cuffs of their jeans. One girl, whose dark brown hair was pulled back into a ponytail, shrugged. "It was pretty quiet," she said.

"I thought I heard voices around five A.M."

"We were trying really hard to be quiet," the blonde said.

"But that one girl wasn't." The shortest girl looked at him. She had a pug nose, and her hair curled around her cheekbones, making her face seem fat. "She was pretty loud when she saw us."

"What one girl?"

The girl glanced at her companions. They shrugged a little. "I don't know. She was really thin." The girl's tone was envious. "And kinda pretty. I guess she lives around here. She says her sister knows you."

Alicia. Thomas nodded encouragement.

"She came around from the back of the porch and seemed kinda surprised to see us. She was really rude."

Thomas inhaled slightly.

"Did something happen?" the blonde asked.

"Not really," Thomas said. "But I do want your names and where I can reach you if I need to."

The brown-haired girl blushed. The others nodded. They each pulled out paper, wrote their names and addresses down, and handed them to Thomas. He skimmed over the sheets, then stuck them in his back pocket.

"You said there was another girl?"

The blonde nodded. "Kari. But I think she left."

"How do I reach her?"

"She's staying at the same hotel I am," the blonde said. "I'll tell her."

"Thanks." Thomas smiled at her, using what Marge called his wide, wonderful, award-winning smile. Then he took a deep breath and looked at the remaining people. "Listen, folks, I have a lot to do today. I would appreciate it if we broke this up. It was really nice of you all to come out here."

The crowd started dispersing. A few people wandered up to the porch and asked him for autographs. He signed distractedly, watched them go, and then went back inside.

Carolyn had watched everything from the entryway. "You think little Alicia Maxwell is doing all of this?"

"She's not so little," Thomas said as he closed the door. His entire body was tense and the tiredness had returned. He really didn't want to talk with Jillian.

"Mr. Stanton," Carolyn said. "She could have left those notes. In fact, I wouldn't put it past her. She's a pretty bitter little girl and probably very jealous of the time you spend with her sister. But she couldn't have killed those birds."

Thomas frowned. After the things he had learned from Tiger the day before, he didn't believe anyone could know how another person would act. He made his way to the couch and sat down. Taking the weight off his legs eased them a little. His bad leg was throbbing in its cast. "Why not?"

"Because I got a good look at them when I was cleaning them up. Those sandpipers all died abou the same time. And there were no marks on them. Their necks were broken, but not twisted, if you can fathom that. No teenage girl could do that. At least not by herself."

"So you're saying she had help."

Carolyn shook her head. "I'm saying that the birds are something different. The notes, yes. I believe it. But the birds—Mr. Stanton, she's so thin, she doesn't even have the strength in her fingers to kill that many birds."

Thomas sighed. "We'll see, Carolyn." He ran his hand through his hair. "I just don't know how I'm going to tell all of this to Jillian, that's all." He reached over and picked up the phone, cradled it between his shoulder and his ear, and started dialing. The tones of Jillian's number sounded familiar, like a jingle played too long on the radio. He stopped dialing before he reached the last number, waited for a moment, and then hung up.

Carolyn was still watching him from the doorway.

"I think I'll see her in person instead," he said.

Carolyn nodded. "You'll be back for lunch?" she asked.

"I'm not sure." He got up, grabbed his coat, and started out the door. The ache in his leg ran down to his foot. He would have to call that doctor in Newport soon. "I'll see you later," he said, and let himself out.

All of the groupies were gone. Only a few empty pop cans and some candy wrappers even let him know that people had been there. The grass was trampled and flattened. He could see footprints in the dampness. Some of them ran to the beach. He shook his head and wished that people would leave him alone.

Thomas got into the truck, backed it up, and headed for the highway. 101 was full of traffic, Winnebagos, small cars with California plates, all bumper to bumper. Thomas sat for nearly five minutes before there was a break in the line, then he scooted forward and immediately slowed to a crawl behind the rest of the cars.

He was content to wait. Talking to Jillian didn't seem like the best idea, but it was the only one he could think of. He didn't want to talk with the police. That would get Alicia in more trouble than she already was. Talking to Jillian, however, made him feel like a schoolboy tattling on friends. Strange thought, considering he really didn't like Alicia at all.

As he neared Seavy Village, he could see the sunlight sparkling off the ocean. People wandered along the city's main beach, admiring the multicolored wind socks twirling in the breeze. He reached the first set of touristy shops—the ones selling shell necklaces and Seavy Village T-shirts—and pulled into a parking lot.

The person to talk to was not Jillian. It was Alicia. He had to find out what motivated her, what she was trying to accomplish. Letting her know that he knew about the notes, and that he hadn't told Jillian, would give him a bargaining chip. Alicia would quit as soon as she knew that he had caught on. If she started causing trouble again, al he had to do was tell Jillian. Then big sister could deal with little sister properly.

The problem was how to find Alicia.

He backed up and took the parking lot's other exit to a side road. He drove down the windy, hilly streets, past the one-bedroom houses with an ocean view by virtue of their height in the city, and finally reached Jillian's street.

Her car was gone. He stopped the truck and got out. His crutches slipped slightly on the sloped pavement, but he was able to right himself. He went to the front door and knocked.

The knock sounded loud and out of place. He glanced at the other houses on the street. All of them were built at an angle against the hill and all of them had picture windows facing the ocean. Two houses were empty; FOR SALE signs stood in their front lawns. The house next door was half-constructed. Waist-high weeds covered the lower half of the project. The construction money and the housing market in Seavy Village had died years ago.

The house in front of him was silent too. He knocked again, this time concentrating on any noises within the house. He heard nothing. The curtains were drawn and the place was dark. He tried to peer in through a side window, but was unable to see anything. Finally he sighed and went back to the truck.

He took more back roads to the newspaper office. Jillian's car wasn't there either, but that didn't mean anything. She had never really explained the kind of trouble she'd been having with it. The car could still be in the shop. He scanned the building's exterior. No Alicia waiting to harass her sister. The windows to the office were open, soaking in one of the coast's few warm days. He could hear the clack of typewriters, but couldn't see either sister through the window.

Maybe Alicia was just out walking. The last time he had seen her, she had been near the lake. He drove there, scanning the sidewalks as he passed. The tourists had infiltrated Seavy Village's back roads. Fat women in too-tight pantsuits puffed up one of the hills. Another couple was staring at a house with a FOR SALE sign in the window. He watched them with a disdain that was not natural. He wasn't a permanent resident of Seavy Village. In his own way, he was as much of an intruder as those tourists. But the city had become his, and he didn't really want to share it with these people, who didn't understand that life went on here, even in the winter, when business was down sixty percent and the village became a true village again.

The park beside the lake was filled with people. Toddlers wandered in and out of the bushes. Young couples lay on blankets, necking or staring at the water. Near the water's edge, an old man sat, his arms wrapped around his knees. Thomas pulled the truck over and looked. No Alicia. Anywhere.

He leaned his head back against the plastic seat. Clearly this was not the way to find her. He would have to wait for Alicia to come to him. Now that he knew who was sending the notes, he would be fine. He moved the truck forward, away from the lake, and drove to the bottom of the hill. As he waited at the stoplight, a VW Bug rounded the corner and honked at him. He glanced over. Jillian was behind the wheel. She pulled over and rolled down her window.

"Like it?" she called.

Thomas rolled down his window too. "Little small, isn't it?"

"It's a rental." She pushed her glasses up the bridge of her nose. "Can I see you tonight?"

"Sure." His heart leaped. He wanted to talk to her. About everything. "Call me when you're done."

"Will do." She waved and drove up the hill. He watched her disappear in his rearview mirror. It would take some discipline not to talk about Alicia, but he thought he could do it. The light changed and he turned onto the highway.

Some dark gray clouds were blowing in over the ocean and the beaches seemed to be clearing. The surf was up, rolling over the sand like soapsuds from an out-of-control washing machine. The beach was beginning to tire him, or perhaps it was the events, mixed with the presence of the groupies. Maybe he should start looking at those scripts Connie sent him more seriously and consider going back to L.A.

As he turned onto the road leading to his house, he saw a squad car sitting in his driveway. His stomach lurched. Something had happened to Carolyn. He pulled up beside the squad car and got out. The front door was ajar.

"Carolyn!" he called. He forced the truck door

open, grabbed his crutches, and hurried along the gravel. His heart was pounding against his throat. "Carolyn!"

She came to the door and looked out. "A couple of policemen are here," she said.

He nodded, too relieved to say anything else. He slowed down and took the stairs carefully. Carolyn went back inside. When he went in the front door, he closed it behind him.

Tiger and another police officer sat on the couch. Carolyn had pulled a chair into the living room and was sitting on it. She had left the easy chair across the room for him.

"What's going on?" Thomas asked. He remained standing.

"Got a phone call this morning from the parents of one Kari Andrews," Tiger said. "Seems she hasn't been back to the hotel since early yesterday. I guess she's a big Thomas Stanton fan and has been hanging out a lot here."

"A lot of people have been around here lately."

"I was trying to tell them that, Mr. Stanton," Carolyn said. "But they seem to think I should have noticed her."

"She's about fifteen or so. Been hanging out with other girls staying down at the Shilo hotel with their parents. I guess they were here before dawn this morning."

Thomas frowned. His stomach still hadn't settled down. "What did you say her name was?"

"Kari Andrews."

Kari. Kari. The three girls that had seen Alicia had mentioned a girl named Kari. "I did see her,"

Thomas said, "although I can't tell you which one she was. Some noise woke me up around five A.M. and I looked out the window over here. Four girls were sitting on the porch, talking and drinking pop. Then later, when I talked with three of them, they said Kari had already left."

"We've already talked with those girls," Tiger said. "They didn't actually see her leave. They had fallen asleep and when they woke up, she was gone. They did say that you were asking about a note?"

Thomas sighed. He pulled the note out of his pocket and handed it to Tiger. "Carolyn found that on my kitchen window this morning. Apparently the girls saw the person who did that."

"Alicia Maxwell," Tiger said.

Thomas looked at Carolyn. She shrugged. "He already knew most of it," she said.

Thomas nodded. "It must be some kind of prank thing. I haven't talked to Alicia or Jillian, and I would like to."

Tiger handed the note back. "You want us to stay out of it?"

"Yeah."

"What about the birds?"

"Carolyn thinks Alicia had nothing to do with the birds. I agree." Thomas's leg was aching so bad that he could barely stand. He crossed the room to the easy chair and sank into it. "Even if she did kill those birds, I think I want you to stay out of that part of it for now."

Tiger's smile was sly. "If you say so," he said. He glanced at his partner. "What I'm really out here for is permission to comb your property. We'll probably concentrate on the beach."

"You think the girl is out there?"

Tiger shrugged. "I don't know. But it wouldn't hurt to check. There aren't many places to go in this town. She has to be somewhere. She's probably hiding out from Mom and Dad, doing something she isn't supposed to do, but we still have to check."

"Go ahead," Thomas said. He leaned his head back. Pain killers. That was what he needed. A good strong dose of pain killers.

"Thanks," Tiger said. "And thank you, ma'am." He stood. His partner stood too.

Carolyn saw them out. When she closed the door, she turned to Thomas. "What do you think of that?"

Thomas shrugged. "I think Tiger is probably right. I think the girl is doing something for attention."

Carolyn nodded and looked away. Thomas watched for a moment. "You don't think so, do you?"

She brought her head back up. Her eyes were a deep blue, round and almost scared. "I don't know what to think," she said. "Too many strange things have happened around here for me to believe the simple answers anymore."

Then she went into the kitchen. Thomas sighed. He didn't believe the simple answers either. The problem was, he had nothing to replace them with.

27

Thomas was rereading one of the scripts Connie had sent him when two more squad cars and an ambulance without lights or sirens pulled into his driveway. He got up and went to the door. Four officers got out and started for the beach. Thomas pulled the door open.

"Wait!" he said. Two of the officers stopped. Thomas hobbled to the porch rail. "What's going on?"

One of the officers looked up. He was a tall, slender man with thick red hair. His clear blue eyes and freckles made him look as if he could be Jimmy Olsen's father. "We've found her, Mr. Stanton."

The man's tone was ominous. Thomas shivered. Carolyn came up behind him and he could feel her body heat warming his shoulder. "Is she all right?" he asked, although he knew the answer already. Empty ambulances didn't make silent arrivals if someone was in trouble.

"She's dead, sir." The officer watched Thomas for his reaction.

"Dead?" Thomas felt as if he had been punched in the stomach. He remembered standing on this very porch two years before, watching officers comb the beach for his daughter, and the cop coming up to him, saying, *I'm sorry, sir, we can't find anything. Maybe she went back to your wife?*, even though they all knew that Heather had done no such thing. "What happened?"

"I'm not at liberty to say, sir, and I'm not even sure I really know. You can talk with Tiger when he gets back. He's the one in charge."

Thomas nodded. He made himself swallow. The lump in his throat was large and uncomfortable.

"It was probably the sea," Carolyn said. She put her hand on his arm. "We lose a good dozen tourists to the sea every year."

Thomas turned slightly and made himself smile at her. Then he pulled away and walked to the side of the porch facing the beach. The surf had gone down. The waves were low and almost gentle. Large spots of wet sand ran almost up to the grass line. As he watched, a cloud passed overhead, blocking the sun for a moment. When the sun returned, it kissed the beach, adding sparkle to the grains of sand. He had seen sparkling beaches before, knew that it was a trick of the light reflecting off tiny clear stones in the sand, but he had never seen a sparkling beach this far north. Funny that he had never noticed it before. The twinkling sand almost seemed to be winking at him, as if they shared a joke.

He closed his eyes and tried to remember the girl. All that he saw were the four girls, sitting on his porch steps, two girls on one side, two on the other. Their legs were stretched out and they were dressed almost identically. Only their skin was rounded, soft, healthy, their cheeks pink with the fresh air and good nutrition. Heather's skin had been sallow, her arms and legs like matchsticks. She lacked the strength to run and hide from whatever pursued her that night—the man in the cloak—but this girl hadn't. She had—they had all had—the look of young athletes, strong, confident, and invincible.

In the back of his head, his sister's voice echoed, screaming for help.

A car pulled up, crunching gravel. He heard the squeal of brakes, the engine die, and then the slam of a car door. Thomas didn't turn. More cops probably. Whatever happened on the beach had to be ugly.

Footsteps resounded on the porch steps.

"Hello, Carolyn." The voice was Jillian's.

"Miss Maxwell."

"Where's Thomas?"

Thomas didn't hear the answer, but he heard more footsteps moving toward him. He took a deep breath and opened his eyes. "I thought you didn't cover this kind of story," he said.

Jillian put her arms around his waist and pressed her face against his back. "Don't start, Thomas. This is ugly enough."

"I suppose you're right." He continued staring at the beach. The body was probably too far away for him to see. The beach looked empty. "You going down there?"

"No," she said. "I brought a photographer along. He's going to the site. I'll talk to everyone when they return."

Thomas turned. Jillian had to let go of his waist. He leaned against the porch rail, holding the crutches to one side. "You could have waited then. You didn't have to be here."

She sighed. She had a tape recorder slung over one shoulder and an equipment bag over the other. Her hair was tousled and her cheeks too red. "I came to talk to you first."

"I don't want this covered, Jillian."

"It's going to be covered," she said. "And the stories are going to focus on you. Even if I do a puff piece for the paper, the national press is watching us now. They'll pick it up and those reporters will be down here in a second, covering everything. This happened near your house, where other murders have happened, where your daughter disappeared. You're at the center of this, Thomas, whether you like it or not."

"God." He closed his eyes again. He had forgotten about the publicity. Jillian was right. It was going to be ugly. The girl was dead. The presence of all the squad cars meant that the cops were treating it as a murder. *We treat them all like murder*, Tiger had said. That meant questions and court appearances and a coroner's inquest. Connie would be upset, more than upset. She would insist that he hire a lawyer. She had been livid the last time, when he answered questions about Heather's death without a lawyer present.

Jillian touched his arm. He opened his eyes. Her expression was solemn. She looked like a little girl who had broken her mother's favorite vase. "I wanted to talk to you about this," she said.

"I think I could have figured out the publicity problems on my own."

"I know that." She took her hand away. "But I didn't think you would have such a strong handle on the solution."

"There is no solution." He could hear Connie now. The only solution would have been never to have been there in the first place.

"I think there is," Jillian said. She glanced out at the beach, then at the cars. Seemingly satisfied that no one was around, she said, "I want to handle the publicity on this. I'll write the stories that go to the *Oregonian* and I'll cover the piece for NPR. I still have contacts there. They'll let me cover something as simple as this. That means I'll control the information that goes out of here and make sure the coverage of you is accurate, not sensational."

From around one of the rocks, two men in white appeared carrying something between them. Thomas squinted. It was a stretcher. "Where are the parents?" he asked. He didn't want them to know that he was thinking of his own reputation when their daughter was being carried off a beach in a body bag.

"Back at the station house. Why?"

He didn't answer the question, just watched.

They had taken Heather off the same beach in the same manner. Only he hadn't been there to see it. And Heather hadn't been a few hours dead. She had been dead for two years.

"Do what you want, Jillian," he said. "I guess in the scheme of things, it doesn't really matter."

He pushed past her and walked over to Carolyn at the edge of the steps. Carolyn's left hand was clutched around her collar. Her fingernails were blue. Thomas moved one crutch, leaned on his good leg, and put his arm around her. "You're cold," he said.

She nodded.

"Go inside and get a coat. You can't do anything out here."

She looked up at him. Her eyes were lined with tears. "I can pray," she said.

Her words surprised him. Then he remembered what she had said when he first arrived back at Seavy Village. *I got to say I was awful worried when I read about your accident,* she had said. *They weren't real sure there for a time what was going to happen to you, and, well, I did my talking to the Lord.* He squeezed her shoulder tighter and then let go.

"I'm sure that the Lord can hear just as well inside," he said.

She wiped at the back of her hand and nodded. As she went inside, Thomas looked across the porch at Jillian. She was fiddling with the dials on her tape recorder, a microphone clutched in her right hand. She looked up and saw him watching. Her expression was tight, guarded. She finished working with the machine, then walked toward the steps.

"Jillian," he said.

She stopped. Her expression hadn't changed.

"Thanks. I appreciate you thinking of me."

She nodded and stepped down onto the driveway. The men were loading the stretcher into the ambulance. She went over to them, stuck out the mike, and pushed a button with her left hand.

He didn't know why he had pushed her away, and yet he had. He couldn't talk to her now, about Alicia, about his past, about anything. The girl's death had changed it all.

He grabbed his other crutch and made his way down the stairs. Through the corner of his eye, he saw Tiger and another officer round the same rock that the ambulance attendants had.

". . . you really have to talk to him," the attendant was saying.

"No theories, even?" Jillian asked.

The attendant shot her an exasperated look. "Listen, Jillian. Tiger is heading the investigation. He asked that no one talk to you or anyone else. Just him. No theories, no statements off the record, no nothing."

"Must be pretty gruesome," Thomas said.

The attendant looked up. "You don't know the half of it," he replied and closed the ambulance door. Then he made his way around to the front.

"You're good," Jillian said.

Thomas shook his head. "Just famous."

"In my business," she said, "that can get in the way."

"Mine too," Thomas said.

The ambulance attendant climbed into the driver's side of his vehicle. He started the engine. Thomas and Jillian moved away.

Tiger stepped onto the driveway and stopped to watch the ambulance drive away. His hair was windblown and his face pale. His mustache stood out in sharp relief to the rest of his skin. Jillian walked over to him. "What happened?" she asked.

"In a minute, Jilly," he said. "I have to talk to your friend over here."

"Thomas?"

"Thomas." Tiger stepped around one of the squads and over to Thomas.

Thomas leaned over slightly. His hands ached from clutching the bars on his crutches too tightly. "What happened?"

Tiger stopped right in front of him and leaned against the bumper of the nearest squad. "I can tell you one thing," he said. "The sea didn't get her. Her body was ripped and torn so badly it made your gulls look pretty."

Thomas looked away. He could feel the wind off the ocean riffling his hair. Jillian stood beside them, her microphone forward. "So why are you talking to me?" he asked.

"I want you to get into my car. I'm taking you down to the station."

Jillian's gaze met his. Thomas shrugged slightly. "Am I under arrest?"

"Not yet," Tiger said.

"Then I would like to use the phone before I go with you," Thomas said.

Tiger nodded and waved his hand in dismissal. "Be my guest. I'm sure that Jillian has a few questions for me."

"Yeah. I do." Jillian stepped forward. She pushed her glasses up and looked at Thomas. Tiger had his back turned slightly. She mouthed "I love you." The words sent a feeling of warmth through him. Thomas smiled at her.

Then he turned his back and climbed up the porch steps. Carolyn was standing at the top. She wore a coat now, but otherwise her position hadn't changed. "They can't suspect you," she said. "You couldn't have done anything."

"I suppose I'm the logical one right now." He clomped across the porch and into the front door. The inside of the house was warm. The script was still overturned on the couch. Nothing here had changed, although everything outside had. He made his way to the couch, moved the script, and sat down. Connie was going to love this. He dialed her number and waited. When the secretary answered, he asked for Connie.

"Who may I say is calling?" the secretary asked, as if she didn't already know.

Thomas had no time or patience for games. "Thomas Stanton," he said. "Tell her this is an emergency."

The line clicked into silence for a minute, then another click signaled Connie's entrance. "No emergency," she said. "I'll just tell everyone they can start producing Short next week."

"I doubt that, Connie." Thomas rubbed his hand

over his face. He had a lot of thinking to do. "I need your help."

"Sounds serious, Thomas. More dead birds?"

"Another dead teenager," he said and winced. The first dead teenager had been his own daughter. No. The first dead teenager had been his sister. "I need the best criminal lawyer you can get your hands on."

"Criminal—? Thomas, they're not blaming you?"

"Not officially," he said. "It's kind of like Heather, you know? It happened near me and no one seems to have a motive. Two mysterious deaths around the same person don't exactly add to my appearance of innocence."

"I suppose you want someone from Oregon," she said.

"I don't give a shit who you get. I just want someone good and someone soon. I'm going to the police station for questioning now. They're not going to book me yet. That much I know. But it'll be soon if they're going to do it."

"Jesus, Thomas." Connie sounded angry. "All right. I'll get you someone. And then you're going to leave that godforsaken place and come back to work. You hear me?"

"I hear you." He picked up the script and tossed it to the other side of the couch. "And I agree."

She hung up without even saying good-bye. He stared at the phone for a minute. If these charges got out of hand, no one would take him back. Stacy Keach had come back after time in prison, but that had been on a drug charge in a foreign country. A forgivable offense. Murder wasn't. Suddenly he was very glad that Jillian was trying to control the publicity.

Thomas stood up and went back outside. Jillian and Tiger appeared to be in a heated discussion. Thomas stopped beside Carolyn. "What's going on?"

"Nothing important, really," Carolyn said. "That poor little girl."

Thomas sighed. That poor little girl would still have been alive if he had handled the groupies right. But there was no changing that now. He started down the stairs.

"Mr. Stanton?"

He turned. Carolyn was watching him. Her face was mottled, almost as if she'd been crying.

"If there's anything I can do—"

"I'll let you know," he said. He crossed the driveway to Jillian and Tiger. They stopped talking when they saw him.

"Ready, Mr. Stanton?" Tiger said.

Thomas nodded. Tiger opened the back door on the nearest squad car and Thomas slid in. Jillian leaned over to him. "I'll be talking to you soon, Thomas."

"Thanks, Jillian." He leaned his head back and closed his eyes. He had been in real police cars before, always for movies. He had never realized how claustrophobic they made him. Plexiglas separated the front seat from the back, and the doors had no handles. He strapped on the seat belt, making his confinement complete.

28

The drive to the police station was uneventful. The car stopped around back, in the officers' only slots. Names had been spray painted onto the building wall, marking each parking spot. No room for promotion or job transfers in this outfit. People either had their names on the wall or they didn't.

Tiger let Thomas out of the backseat. He grabbed his crutches and stood on the pavement. Somehow it seemed colder in town. Perhaps that was because the sun was slowly sinking over the ocean. Thomas stared toward the west, wondering what it was that made one stretch of beach more dangerous than another.

"Let's go inside, Mr. Stanton." Tiger's line sounded like something out of a bad TV movie. Thomas turned, half expecting to see Tiger holding out handcuffs. But the police officer was merely standing beside the squad car, waiting.

Thomas hobbled down the slanting pavement. A small door with a metal knob stood at the bottom of the parking lot. Tiger leaned over and unlocked the door, then held it open for Thomas.

This part of the station was quiet. It smelled of concrete and old cigarette smoke. Thomas's shoes whispered against the hard concrete floor. Behind him, the door swung shut with a metallic bang.

"To your left," Tiger said.

Thomas followed the instructions. The left corridor led past a series of painted metal doors with metal knobs. At the very end of the corridor stood another door, this one with webbed glass. Tiger opened that and they walked into the back area, where the officers sat at their desks.

"Wait here a minute, Mr. Stanton," Tiger said and walked to the front of the room. Several people sat in the chairs. Two overweight women talked in hushed voices. An elderly man, wearing grubby jeans and a flannel shirt, leaned forward, his elbows on his knees. He was staring at the cigarette cupped in his right hand. Off in the far corner, a couple sat hand in hand. The woman was slender. Her blond hair curled around her shoulders and her makeup was light and tasteful. She wore a white blouse and pale pink pants with sandals on her feet. A pale pink sweater hung loosely from her shoulders. Her husband was dressed very similarly except he wore deck shoes and neatly pressed blue jeans. His dark curls were short and made him look younger than he probably was.

Kari Andrews's parents. Thomas recognized their bleak expressions. He remembered sitting in the same chairs with Marge, holding her hand, for comfort more than anything. The comfort never came and neither did the answers, not for many months. At least these folks would know what had happened to their daughter.

Tiger pulled up a chair and sat in front of them. His demeanor changed. It was still professional—very much so—but he was warmer, more giving. Thomas didn't have to hear the words. He could see them on the parents' faces. The husband blanched and then turned dark red. The wife gasped slightly, let go of her husband's hand, stood up and wrapped her arms around her chest as if to hold her heart inside. The husband asked a few more questions. Tiger responded, but shook his head. Then he handed the other man a card, stood up, and spoke for a moment longer. Words that the parents would never forget, Thomas was certain. He still remembered every detail about his first visit to this police station.

Finally, the husband put his arm around his wife and led her out of the building. Tiger watched them go. Then he patted his pocket, pulled out a pack of cigarettes, tapped it against his hand, and stuck a cigarette in his mouth. He fumbled for another moment until he found some matches, lit one, and puffed on the cigarette. He waved the tiny flame out, tossed the match into the garbage can, and took a long drag off the cigarette. Then he stubbed that against the wastebasket and came back to Thomas.

"They took it better than I would have expected," Thomas said.

The look Tiger gave him was cold. "They're in

shock. They'll be back once what I said really sinks in. Then they'll want me to have some answers."

Thomas nodded. The not knowing was the worst part. Day in, day out, seeking answers to questions that no one should have to ask about their own children.

Tiger touched his arm. "Why don't you come with me, Mr. Stanton?"

Tiger's remark wasn't a question, but a command. Thomas followed Tiger to a small office. Tiger shut the door and closed the blinds. "We can talk here," he said.

"I have an attorney flying in from California," Thomas said.

Tiger nodded. He took his cigarette pack out again and set it on the desk. He sat down in the swivel chair behind the desk, then he pointed to a chair across from him.

It was the only other chair in the room. A wooden slatted chair with rounded arms. Hardly functional, but Thomas didn't complain. He sat down, leaned his crutches on the file cabinet, and looked at Tiger.

Tiger leaned back, his head touching the large city map on the wall behind him. "You're not under arrest."

"I know," Thomas said. "You told me that already. You also told me that I was a suspect."

"In an odd sort of way, yes, you are. So maybe it's good that your attorney is flying in. And maybe it's good that we're talking here without him." Tiger opened all of the drawers, then held out his hands. "I'm not going to tape this. I'm not even going to write anything down—at least, not until we're nearly done and then I'll show it to you. If we get into the messy stuff, the real police procedural stuff, we'll do it later. Right now, I just want some answers."

Thomas swallowed heavily. He almost wished that Tiger would follow procedure. "And you think you can get those answers from me."

"I don't know what to think," Tiger said. "I'm going to be real up-front with you, Mr. Stanton. This is a mess. A big mess. Another teenage girl is dead. A tourist no less, so the news is big. The news is even bigger because she was last seen on the property of a well-known actor at five in the morning."

"She was sitting on my porch!"

"Nonetheless. The national press is going to pick it up. Out-of-staters are involved. I want this investigation to run like clockwork. Better yet, I want an answer to all the mysterious happenings on that beach."

"So do I." Thomas sighed. Suddenly he felt very tired. "What do you want from me?"

"When did you last see the Andrews girl?"

"Like I told you earlier," Thomas said. "The first and last time I saw her was through my window at 5 A.M. this morning. I know she was there because her little friends told me that Kari was the one with them. I saw four girls, heard five, since Alicia was there. And that's it. That's all I know."

"Let me tell you what I know." Tiger reached across the desk and tapped his pack of cigarettes against the metal surface. The taps punctuated his sentences. "I know that Kari Andrews had a crush on you. When she found out you were in town, she got her friends together and went over to your place. She was there yesterday, although her friends said that they didn't speak to you. And she was there this morning, waiting to be the first to see you when you got out of bed. In fact, it was Kari's idea to wait on your steps. The girls were out all night, talking, giggling, making plans on how they could actually spend some time with you."

"That's normal groupie stuff," Thomas said.

Tiger took out a cigarette and stuck it in the corner of his mouth. "They brought food and blankets and arrived about four-thirty A.M. It was still dark and kind of creepy. No sound came from your house, at first anyway. Then they thought they heard footsteps. It turns out they were hearing Alicia."

"I think she woke me up too."

"They exchanged words with her and then she left. The four remaining girls decided that you wouldn't be up for another hour or so, so they drifted off to sleep. One girl wasn't able to sleep. She was uncomfortable. Too cold there, so close to the sea, a little hungry, and not used to snoozing while sitting up. She saw Kari leave."

"She didn't say anything to me when I asked about Alicia," Thomas said.

Tiger took the cigarette out of his mouth and tapped the filter against the table. He tossed the pack into a drawer and concentrated completely on the cigarette. "There was no reason to talk to

you," he said. "She figured you already knew
where Kari was."

Thomas felt as if his heart had stopped. He
frowned. "What?"

"You heard me. She thought you already knew.
You see, Kari was sitting on the bottom step, the
closest to the driveway. After the other girls drifted
off to sleep, Kari drank 7-Up and stared at the
ocean. Our observer watched Kari through her
eyelashes. I don't know why she pretended she
was asleep. She wouldn't tell me. Anyway, a man
came up off of the beach. He was tall, slender,
dressed in black and wearing a cape—like you do
when you're playing Anthony Short. In fact, that's
what the girl said it looked like. Anthony Short.
When he saw Kari, he smiled, bent over, and
kissed her hand. He asked her what her name was
and she told him. Then he told her that the name
was beautiful. She laughed, and he led her back to
the beach with him."

"And you're saying that was me."

Tiger tapped the cigarette so hard that it bent in
half. Tobacco spilled across the papers littering the
top of the desk. "You tell me."

"Was he walking?"

"She didn't say anything about a cast."

Thomas looked down. "I can't just take this
thing off and on at will."

"I know," Tiger said. "And the terrain we found
the body on would have been difficult for you to
reach on crutches. But I can't rule anything out.
You work in illusion, Mr. Stanton."

This time, Thomas did roll his eyes. "I'm an actor, for crissake. I pretend I'm someone else all the time. That's not illusion. That's a simple child's game that I happen to be good at and I get paid for."

"Exactly. Playing two roles isn't hard for you. And I know there are all sorts of makeup tricks and ways of making casts and seeming to be hurt. There's also a back way out of the house. You could conceivably have walked across that beach, taken that little girl, and ripped her to shreds."

Thomas winced at the language. The picture in his mind was vivid—the young girl sprawled across the rocks, her clothing in tatters, a bloody trail leading to what remained of her skin.

"But I don't think you did that."

"Thank you," Thomas said sarcastically. "Why not?"

"Why?" Tiger brushed the remaining tobacco off the desk and threw the cigarette into the garbage can. "Why go to all that trouble to kill a girl you don't even know? It makes no sense, follows no pattern I know of. By all accounts, you had never seen that girl before. Your daughter's death could have been a crime of passion. She said something, did something to irritate you, and you killed her."

Thomas was clutching his hands together. His knuckles had turned white.

"But you had no reason, passionate or otherwise, to kill Kari Andrews."

"It would be a great way to keep the groupies off my lawn," Thomas said. He couldn't keep the sarcasm out of his tone. He felt as if he had been cast in the starring role of Kafka's *The Trial*, rewritten, of course, for television."

Tiger smiled. "Believe me, I thought of that. I also know that there are hundreds of better ways to get rid of them, many of which you had already started to try. No, Mr. Stanton, I don't believe that you killed that girl. But I think someone wants me to think you did."

"How do you know that one girl just isn't lying?"

"Her story is too consistent. And beside, I had to pry it out of her, bit by tiny bit. She's a Thomas Stanton fan too. She thought she was betraying you. She cared less about her friend's death than she did about the possibility of hurting you."

"Jesus." Thomas looked down. He had cut off the circulation to his fingers. He separated his hands and flattened them on his cast. "Why are you telling me all of this?"

"Because I want your help." Tiger leaned forward, assuming almost the same stance he had had when talking with Kari's parents. "I'm not stupid, Mr. Stanton. The fact that all of this happened on your lawn means a lot to my investigation. I told you before that the deaths on that beach have always intrigued me. Now I get a chance to figure them out. And the biggest stumbling block to the entire investigation could be you."

"Me?" Thomas finally had enough. He sat up straight. "I'm the one who was in here in the first place, asking why the fuck you people weren't investigating these things harder. You gave me some

mumbo jumbo—more than you gave Jillian, I
might add—and then let me go off to see if I could
figure out what happened to Heather all by myself.
Now you tell me, after someone has been murdered a few yards from my house and the investigation has become yours, that I am going to get in
the way.''

"Yes," Tiger said. "That's exactly what I'm saying. Think about it, Mr. Stanton. The press is going
to be all over this place. Fascinating story, death
and murder near a famous actor's house—and one
of the dead happens to be his daughter. You can
use those media people any time you want to hamper my investigation if it impinges on you too
much. And then there's this hotshot criminal lawyer coming in from California. I can't remember
the last time I dealt with a lawyer in this building,
let alone one who spends his days ambulance
chasing in Los Angeles. He could tie up the investigation quicker than I can say Jiminey Cricket and
probably put a few demerits on my service record
at the same time. I want to solve this. You want to
solve this. And the only way we can do it is to work
together. That's why I'm telling you all of this. The
first step toward working together.''

"And what happens if I did murder that girl?''

"You didn't," Tiger said.

"It seems to me that a good detective has to
keep his mind open to all possibilities," Thomas
said. "And someone who looks like me led that
little girl away from my house.''

"All right.'' Tiger leaned his chair back again,
resting his hands behind his head. Circular swea

stains marred the shirt of his uniform. "We will be continuing that side of the investigation. I can't tell you anything about that, either. But if we find something linking you, you and that hotshot attorney will be the first to know."

"I just wanted to be up-front about everything," Thomas said. "Even the things we can't be up-front about."

"You won't get in the way of my investigation, then?" Tiger asked.

"I'll do my best to help you," Thomas said. "On one condition."

"Shoot."

"You keep looking at Heather's death as well."

"It won't be my first priority," Tiger warned.

"I don't care," Thomas said. "As long as you do it."

The policeman nodded. "I hope to have some answers for both of us in a few days," he said.

29

Carolyn came to pick him up at the police station. She pulled up in her 1975 Oldsmobile with the wide rear end and long body. It belched blue smoke, but she didn't seem to notice. Thomas climbed down the steps and into the front seat. Carolyn smiled at him, but the smile was small and frightened.

"They aren't going to book me, if that's what you're worried about," he said.

"I don't know how they could think you could have done anything. You can barely walk."

He reached over and patted her hand. She blushed and concentrated on pulling the car onto the street. "Your agent has called twice. She's really worried."

"I am too," he said. He had a lot of thinking to do. Clearly he couldn't stay in the house much longer. The killing, the dead birds, and the fact that someone had linked him to all of that meant that he wasn't safe either. Much as he liked the place, it was time to close it up.

But he didn't want to move to a hotel in town.

And he did want to see the investigation to its logical end. The correct move for him would be to find another house, again on a secluded area of beach, move to it, and close up this house. Maybe even tear it down and keep the land, depending on what Tiger found.

"Do they know what happened?" Carolyn asked.

Thomas shook his head. "Just that she was killed. In a particularly gruesome manner. I saw her parents. I wish there was something that I could do."

"I'm making up a food basket," Carolyn said. "I could add your name to it."

Thomas smiled. "Thank you, but no. I think it's better if I don't contact them at all right now."

Carolyn took the car along side roads that Thomas had never seen before. The Oldsmobile bumped and clattered along the uneven pavement. When she reached the side of town, she pulled onto a dirt road almost hidden by trees. The road wound along the beach, rounded a few large rocks, and ended up dumping onto the side road that led to Thomas's house.

Thomas looked at her, amazed that she had found such a circuitous route. She pulled the car into the driveway and got out. Apparently she always drove in from Seavy Village that way. No wonder the car was belching blue smoke.

Thomas got out too. Ahead of him, along the grass line, the police had erected small barriers and yellow tape marked POLICE LINE. DO NOT CROSS. Perhaps they hoped that would keep people off the beach. Or perhaps they hadn't finished their investigation yet. But that seemed unlikely since the investigation had to proceed rapidly, before the tide swallowed up all of the evidence.

He turned toward the house. No one waited for him there. The groupies had all gone home. He found that he almost missed them. The human presence made the beach less forboding. He crossed the driveway and mounted the stairs, remembering the blood running across it, the gull pounded into the door. Blood had run across those stairs more than once; a woman had died here in a manner as horrible—or more horrible—than the girl on the beach.

He shivered and took another step up. Heather had waited for him on this porch on her last full day of life. So had the teenaged girl that had died this morning. She was led off by someone who looked like him, someone in a cape. Had Heather been led away by someone also? Someone she thought she knew? Someone she trusted? She hadn't screamed. He would have heard it. He had heard the shutter banging, the screen door slamming against the frame. But he'd never heard Heather.

He took the final step up and let himself into the house. Carolyn was already inside, washing dishes and putting them away. The house had a stark feel. The walls were too white. Their paint hid the blood that had decorated the plaster and lath so many years ago. His movie posters seemed to come alive, daring him with times that weren't necessarily happier, just saner. The cot in the corner looked too small and uncomfortable. The fireplace, with its gray ash and fake brick sides, was a sad addition to an already gloomy living room.

When he had moved here, he hadn't been searching. Searching had been his excuse. He had been hiding. Hiding from the fact that his beautiful daughter had run away from her mother to be with him. Hiding from the fact that his daughter didn't know him, that even to her, he had become a fantasy—a picture on celluloid, so unreal as to be whatever she wanted. When she got here, she had learned that he was a human being, less than she'd imagined, and then she had died, without them being able to work through that realization.

Even now, with all the revelations, her death bothered him less than her life. He had let her live without getting to know her. Heather had always been in the way. First she'd been someone for Marge to hide behind. Then she'd been Thomas's excuse to come home, to a place that was no longer home. And finally, she'd ceased to matter, except when Marge wanted her out of the house. Then Heather had become a burden, someone to take care of, another role assigned to him at odd moments—that of father, requiring no script and allowing no retakes.

This house was the symbol of his emptiness. A place where something brutal had once happened. But it had happened to someone else, not him. He'd merely resided there, absorbing the death, the feeling of the place through that slot in his imagination that had allowed him to act.

Maybe, in the memory of such violence, he had felt at home.

It was time to leave. He would pack his things and move back to the hotel. Then he would decide what he wanted to do, whether he wanted another house or whether he wanted to go back to work.

He wandered over to the phone and dialed Connie's number. The secretary put him through immediately.

"How bad is it?" Connie asked without preamble.

"Oh, it's pretty bad." Thomas sat on the couch. The upholstery bit through his clothing. He hadn't realized how rough it was. "I'm not being held or anything, but I have a hunch that attorney might come in handy."

"I couldn't get anyone to you today. I got a woman from San Bernardino. She comes highly recommended. But she won't be there until tomorrow. She's taking a red-eye to Portland and driving down."

"Does this famous lawyer have a name?"

"Elizabeth Gordon. Ring a bell?"

"Is it supposed to?"

Connie sighed. "She handled that slaughter in the Hollywood Hills a few years back and—"

"Christ, Connie. They were convicted."

"Thomas, those men brutally murdered fifteen women. She got them reduced sentences and a chance for parole."

Thomas rubbed his hand over his face. His fingers were cold and clammy. "Hiring someone like that is almost like admitting I'm guilty."

"No, Thomas," Connie said. "Hiring someone who is tough and competent is the only smart thing to do. Maybe she can stop this thing before it gets underway."

"I suppose you're right," Thomas said.

"Good. Then I expect you to cooperate with her. She should pull in sometime around ten-thirty, eleven o'clock. Then she'll call you."

"Here?"

"Where else would she call?"

"I'm not staying here tonight," Thomas said. "I'm going to one of the hotels. I think I'm going to sell this place."

"Fine. Wonderful move. You should have done it years ago. But be there by ten-fifteen tomorrow, okay? You're paying a small fortune for this woman. You may as well take her to lunch and explain the situation."

"Okay." Thomas leaned his head back. A headache was building at the base of his skull. He wondered if, after his talk with Tiger, he even needed this hotshot attorney. "I'll call you when I know where I'm staying tonight."

"Leave a message," Connie said. "I'm heading out the door now to catch the end of happy hour. I feel like getting pleasantly sloshed."

Thomas dropped the receiver into its cradle. Pleasantly sloshed. As if she were the one suffering through all of this. He was the one who should get drunk, and he hadn't even suffered a true tragedy. The people who needed to forget was that good-looking couple he had seen in the police station. A simple getaway to Oregon had turned into a night-mare for them.

Carolyn came out of the kitchen, rubbing her hands on a towel. "You're leaving?" she asked.

Thomas nodded. "I think I'll go to one of the hotels on the beach and then decide what I'm going to do. But I think I'll close up the house."

"Are you leaving Seavy Village?" Her question was soft, worried.

"I don't know, Carolyn," he said. "Not for a while, anyway. I'm sure they want me to be here because of the murder."

She nodded. "I'll take good care of the house for you."

"No." Thomas's answer was almost too quick. "I don't want you in this house without me."

"Mr. Stanton, I've been here alone before."

"I don't care," he said. "Promise me."

"Mr. Stanton—"

"Promise me."

She took a deep breath, shook her head slightly, and then said, "All right. I promise. But I think it's silly. That girl died with a whole bunch of her friends around. If something is going to get me, it's going to get me."

Thomas stood up. A little shiver was running up and down his spine. He wished he could reach around, clamp his hand on it, warm it, and make it go away.

"If you're going to get a hotel room," Carolyn said, "You had better do it quickly. The rooms fill up fast in the summer."

Thomas nodded. He picked up the phone book,

dialed the Shilo, and reserved a room. He suspected, from the clerk's harried tone, that it was
one of the last. Then he called the agency and
asked for Connie. As he had expected, she was already gone. He left a message as she had re-
quested.

When he got off the phone, he looked over at
Carolyn. She was digging in the bureau, pulling
out clothes and filling one of his suitcases. "You
don't have to do that," he said.

"It goes faster." She closed the drawer and set
the pile in her hands into the suitcase. Then she
shut the suitcase and set it over by the door.
"See?"

He didn't argue. He hobbled over to the door
and pulled it open. Carolyn grabbed the suitcase
and brought it down to the truck. He watched her.
He couldn't even carry a suitcase. How could anyone believe that he had murdered a teenage girl?

Carolyn came back up the stairs.

"Get what you need," Thomas said, "And then
let's go."

"I have a few things to finish up. I will leave
here shortly."

"Then I will wait." Thomas followed her back
inside and closed the door. "I'm serious about not
wanting you here alone."

The phone rang. He crossed the room to answer
it while Carolyn went back into the kitchen.

He picked up the receiver. "Hello?" he said,
keeping his tone curt. He didn't know who would
be calling now. Anyone from reporters to Connie
to that hotshot attorney.

"Turn on the radio!" It was Jillian.

"What?" he said.

"Turn on the radio. Now. KLCC in Eugene. 89.7 FM. Hurry!"

Thomas set the phone down and crossed the room to the little radio beside the cot. He turned it on, flipped the dials, and finally tuned into a rich female voice.

". . . Stanton," it said. "Police still aren't willing to say what has caused the deaths on that particular stretch of Oregon beach. But off the record, more than one officer admits that there is something eerie going on. For National Public Radio, I'm Jillian Maxwell in Seavy Village, Oregon."

The announcer segued into a piece on the summer Olympics and Thomas turned the radio off. He went back to the phone. "How did you find time to do that?"

"One of the stations in town gave me some space. I phoned it in to NPR and they aired it almost right away." She sounded excited, happier than he had ever heard her.

"I missed most of it. What did you say?"

"Basic stuff. Mostly about the girl dying and the things you've suffered, with Heather's death and the gulls and stuff. I think you came off real well and I think they aired it because of the spooky angle."

"You sound pleased."

"Yeah," she said. "I can still do the radio work. I thought I had forgotten how. And they'll still take my stuff. I guess I can go back if I want to. I almost had myself convinced I couldn't."

He smiled. "That's good, Jillian." His voice sounded smooth, sounded as if he truly believed that. But she was happy and things were going well for her because a teenager died. He wondered why no one besides himself and the parents saw the girl's death as important. Even Tiger viewed it as a way to solve one of the area's biggest crimes, to promote himself higher in the local ranks.

"Jillian," he said, "I'm moving to the Shilo and closing up the house. You want to meet me at the hotel for dinner later?"

"The Shilo?—He says he's at the Shilo." The last sentence sounded as if she were speaking to someone in the same room. "Alicia is here."

"Bring her along."

"I wish I could," Jillian said. "But I still have a lot to do on this story. I want to talk with Carolyn, a few of the police officers, and the parents if I can. I have to fax everything to the *Oregonian* before midnight. So I have a lot to do."

"And you're not going to eat?"

"I'm going to grab a sandwich while I'm running from place to place, probably. Or maybe I'll wait until I'm actually writing things. I've got enough fudge to last me."

Thomas laughed. "All right," he said. "Can I see you tomorrow?"

"Probably," she said. "If nothing else, I'll have to interview you too."

Thomas chuckled again and hung up the phone. He walked over to the kitchen. Carolyn had placed some of the perishable food into a grocery sack. The rest she had stored into the freezer. She sa

Thomas watching her. "I can't let it all go to waste," she said.

He nodded. "You about ready?"

"No." She smiled. "But if I wait until I'm ready, we won't leave here until tomorrow."

"I don't see a lot to do, Carolyn."

"If you're going to leave a house empty, there's a lot to do. You want it clean. You want timers set so that lights click on and off as if someone's home. You want to check plug ins, wiring, everything, so nothing unexpected happens."

"I'm not leaving town, Carolyn, just leaving the house."

"All the same," she said. She picked up the grocery bag and tucked it under her arm. "But I guess it can wait. I want to bring a few things over to that poor family and I have a few other errands to run."

Thomas put his arm around her. "You're a good woman, Carolyn."

"Not really," she said. "I just do what needs to be done."

Which is more than the rest of us do, Thomas thought. He made his way to the door, pulling it open for her like he had done the last time. After she went through it, he followed, closing and locking the door behind him.

There. Closed, empty, and safe. No one else was going to die there if he could help it. Tomorrow, after he had talked with the attorney, he would go to the realty office and see if they had another house that interested him. If he found one, he would move all of his stuff there. Otherwise, he would place everything in storage and block off the house. Maybe he would sell it. Maybe it was time to give up this section of beach.

Carolyn was already in her car by the time Thomas climbed down the stairs. She started it and the engine roared. The muffler had gone. The blue smoke rose around the back like a giant dust cloud. He was half tempted to buy a new house just so that he could keep her on and maybe pay her a little more. Carolyn was more valuable than she realized. She deserved better than a ragged old Oldsmobile that puffed blue smoke.

She waved as she backed out of the driveway. He waved back. He waited until he couldn't see her anymore before walking to his truck.

The police line tape marred the view of the ocean. Edges of the waves rose and disappeared behind the yellow line. The wind was chill and damp. The sky was overcast and the entire feeling was oppressive. He remembered the feeling when he first bought the house, how it seemed like a gothic to him, something out of film noir, and he had liked that. The feeling remained, but he was nearing the end of the film where the corrupt world had proven to be even more corrupt than he had expected and the woman he loved had betrayed him. Only in this case, it wasn't a woman. It was his own memory. Tiger was convinced he hadn't killed Kari, as were Carolyn and Jillian. But he wasn't. Not anymore.

A man who looked like him had lured the little girl away.

And he didn't remember.

Just like he didn't remember his sister's death, or filming a movie in this very town years before.

He wiped some of the mist off of his face and climbed into the truck. Funny how quickly his feelings had changed. He didn't think he would miss this stretch of beach. He didn't even really want to be in Seavy Village anymore. Jillian's obvious delight at the radio story disturbed him, the lack of caring for the girl, like his lack of caring for Heather, disturbed him too. Seavy Village was a haven that wasn't a haven anymore. It was time to leave. Time to go back to Anthony Short and his cat Rumbles. The make-believe world that he was used to. Maybe it was good that the attorney was coming in the morning. Maybe she would make his escape easy, or easier than it would have been otherwise. Maybe tonight would be his last night in Seavy Village.

30

Thomas walked into the hotel room and immediately turned on the television set. Hotel rooms made him feel lonely, like a man without a home. He had lived in too many of them. Their barrenness reminded him of the fact that his life was not normal, that he didn't have a wife, two-point-five kids, a two-car garage, a mortgage, and a nine-to-five job.

The bellboy set Thomas's suitcase on the little suitcase rack. Thomas handed him five dollars and watched as the boy closed the door behind him. Fortunately, the hotel had given him a room on the first floor. Thomas hadn't thought to ask for a room with easy access and, it turned out, the Shilo was one of those hotels that didn't have handicapped access to its upper floors. The stairs were all built on the outside, running in ninety-degree twists along the parking lot. All three floors were stretched along an open balcony which provided a beautiful view of the ocean, but no elevators ran up to the floors, and the stairs were barely wide enough for Thomas and his crutches.

The curtains were open, revealing the long stretch of beach. Multicolored wind socks fluttered in the breeze, spinning blue, orange, yellow, and red. As the dusk grew, the kite shop that put the wind socks there would take them down and would wait until midmorning to put them back up again. On the beach two sets of couples roamed. One woman squatted on a rock, staring into a tide pool. Children chased each other along the water's edge and their mother watched from a safe distance. Thomas pulled the curtains closed and clicked on a lamp.

The room was done in tasteful browns and tans. Two beds filled the center and reading lamps were within easy reach of the pillow. Although the room wasn't as plush as he was used to, he would be comfortable here.

Canned laughter echoed off the television set and he focused on the program. The old *M*A*S*H* series. Alan Alda muttered something insane, followed by a terse comment from Wayne Rogers. The episode aired early in the show, back when it was still breaking ground and struggling to survive. He remembered watching them in those old days, envying the actors their regular work, and wishing that someday he could be on something as important, as monumental.

He never was.

Oh, Anthony Short was wonderful, steady work, and he was popular. Jason on *Restless Heart* had been popular too. But popularity didn't equal longevity and film sometimes seemed even more ephemeral than theater.

He was ready to go back. He wanted out of this tiny little village with its macabre reminders of gruesome deaths. He would tell that to Connie when he spoke with her in the morning. And then he would have the attorney do everything in her power to help him leave.

He lay down on the bed. His entire body ached and his leg throbbed. When he got back to Los Angeles, he would see a doctor about the cast and the way the leg was healing. Then maybe he would start a weight lifting program or something to get himself back in shape. He was tired of being twenty pounds overweight, tired of being inactive, tired in general.

A figure in a cloak rose before his eyes. He willed it away and instead watched as it ran along the beach. The girl had told the police that the figure in the cloak had looked just like him.

He rolled over. An old dial phone sat beside the bed, the phone book underneath the phone's base. He pulled out the book, and looked through it, starting with the L's. When he saw Hargrave Lester's number, he stopped.

Of course, he had been looking for the old man's phone number, or why would he have looked in the first place? The old man didn't like him—true enough—but he had also said that there were things Thomas needed to know. Thomas hadn't been ready to hear them the afternoon he saw Hargrave.

He was ready to listen now.

Thomas eased himself off the bed, turned up the volume on the television set, grabbed his room key, and went out the door. The truck was parked right across from the room. Thomas made his way across the parking lot. It was full of out-of-state cars, most with California plates, although a few were from Idaho and Washington. Children ran, screaming, down the steps from the third-floor balcony. Thomas sighed. The hotel wouldn't be as quiet or as private as he would have liked.

He got into the truck, backed up, and drove out of the hotel's parking lot onto a road that ran parallel with the beach. Unless he was completely wrong, the back road would take him to Hargrave's. Thomas drove until he saw the windblown trees, then he turned left and followed the road to Hargrave's driveway.

The dogs lay in the middle of the dirt. They got up reluctantly for the truck. Thomas pulled in as close to the garage as he could. He got out of the truck just as the curtain in the main window swung back into place. Hargrave knew that he was here.

Thomas walked along the curved sidewalk to the front door. The door opened just as he stopped in front of it. Hargrave stepped out. He held a beer can in his left hand. "I don't have anything to say to you."

"That's not what you said when I left here the last time."

Hargrave shrugged. "That was before the kid died."

Hargrave's tone carried blame with it. Thomas let the emotion ride over him and then said, "Let me buy you dinner. I have a few questions to ask."

Hargrave stared at Thomas. The old man's eyes were watery blue. "You don't like me," the old man said.

"You don't like me either, but something's happening here. I feel like I have the pieces, but not the shape of the puzzle. And you said you knew more than you were telling me."

"I'm beginning to like you better and better," Hargrave said. "You're showing more backbone than I would have expected."

He stepped away from the door. Thomas walked inside. The smell of dogs, old books, and stale beer rose to greet him. "I got a pizza ordered. Glad I asked for a large."

"I guess," Thomas said. He frowned. The old man was having pizza? "I was thinking of taking you to a nice restaurant somewhere in town."

"If you're having dinner with me," Hargrave said, "we're having pizza. But you can pay for it."

Thomas grinned. "I'll buy."

He hoped he had brought enough cash to cover it all.

"I have beer in the fridge," Hargrave said.

Thomas was about to decline, but then he reconsidered. He hadn't had beer in months. "Sounds good," he said. He picked his way across a floor littered with newspapers, magazines, and overgrown plants.

The kitchen was tiny and smelled faintly of rotting food. The counters were cluttered with dirty dishes. Water-filled pans sat in the sink and the cupboard doors stood open. Thomas opened the refrigerator. Bottles lay on their sides. Half-eaten packages of meat stood open. In the clear vegetable bin, he could see something growing along the sides. He grabbed a beer off the six-pack toward the front, glad that Jillian had brought the beer fresh, even though beer didn't spoil.

"Find it?" Hargrave called.

"Yeah," Thomas said. He came back out into the living room. Hargrave was clearing the coffee table, dumping the books and magazines onto the floor beside the couch.

"For the pizza," Hargrave said.

Thomas nodded. He pushed aside a copy of Joyce's *Ulysses*, Hemingway's *The Snows of Kilimanjaro*, and Harold Robbins's *The Carpetbaggers*, and then sat down. "You know all about the murder."

"Yup," Hargrave said. He perched on the arm of his usual armchair and kept glancing out the grimy window for the pizza delivery truck. "And it doesn't surprise me any either."

Again the slight blame to the words. Thomas wondered if coming here was a good idea.

"I moved over to the Shilo tonight," Thomas said. "I'm going to figure out what to do with my stuff and the house tomorrow."

The doorbell rang and Thomas jumped. Hargrave got to his feet and extended his hand for some money. "Just a second!" he called.

Thomas pushed himself up and pried his wallet out of his back pocket. He handed Hargrave a twenty, hoping that would be enough. The old man pulled the door open and directed the delivery boy inside. The boy surveyed the room with a look of startlement. His eyes grew even wider when he saw Thomas.

Hargrave snatched the pizza out of the boy's hands and set it on the coffee table. Then he put the twenty in the boy's hand and propelled the boy to the door. "Keep it," Hargrave said and slammed the door closed. He turned back to Thomas. "You always have that effect on people?"

"No," Thomas said, pulling open the hot cardboard. "But I suspect that you do."

Hargrave laughed, grabbed a napkin, and took out a large piece of pizza. The pizza was decorated with everything from pineapples to anchovies. Thomas looked at it and tried not to grimace. He made himself reach in and take a piece.

There were so many taste sensations that Thomas wasn't sure what he was eating. The bottom layer tasted like pizza and pizza crust, with the thick, spicy tomato sauce and an underlying flavor of cheese. On top though, his mouth found hot sausage, Canadian bacon, green peppers, and onions—and those were the flavors he could identify.

He wiped his mouth with a napkin. "I talked with the detective on the case today. He told me something that I wanted to bounce off of you."

Hargrave reached for his second piece. "Yeah?"

"He said that one of the girls on the porch saw who Kari went off with."

Hargrave set his piece of pizza down and wiped his fingers on the nearest napkin. His expression had grown serious. "Who?"

"A figure in a black cloak who looked exactly like me."

Hargrave leaned back, then looked away. He ran a hand through his thinning gray hair. His fingers were shaking. "Black cloak."

Thomas nodded. "I saw someone in a black cloak the night Heather disappeared."

"I know." Hargrave took a deep breath as if to steady himself, then grabbed another piece of pizza, leaving his second half-eaten on his napkin. "Jillian doesn't know about this, does she?"

Thomas couldn't read Hargrave's mood. "Why? Are you thinking I did it too?"

"Don't be ridiculous," Hargrave said through pizza. " 'Too'? The cops think you did it? With that cast?"

"They don't know. I'm bringing in an attorney tomorrow to make sure they give up the idea, though."

"The benefits of wealth." Hargrave finished his third piece and reached for a fourth. "It makes a lot of sense, though."

"That I did it?"

"That they would suspect you. Hell, I've suspected you for a long time."

Thomas took another piece. The pizza was growing cold. "You saw someone who looks like me mutilate that bird."

"I saw you mutilate a bird."

"And I was wearing a cape?"

Hargrave grabbed a napkin and wiped off his tomato-stained fingers. "What are you getting at?"

Thomas set his piece of pizza down. Frustration made his throat tight. "Was I wearing a cape?"

"I already told you that you were."

Thomas let his breath out slowly.

"What are you thinking?" Hargrave threw the napkin in the top of the pizza box.

Thomas looked at the old man, really looked at him. His eyes were small, his skin lined and age-marked, his hair receding. He didn't look wise. He didn't look the keeper of any great secrets. He just looked like an old man who told stories to keep the loneliness at bay. "What were you going to tell me the other day?"

Hargrave slurped his beer and leaned against the couch. He seemed to be measuring Thomas just as Thomas was measuring him. "I was going to tell you that something changed during that filming. In the beginning, you were like a great caged tiger, always pacing, always moving, never happy, growling at everyone. And then, just before that bird died, the energy left you, even though you kept shoving that crap up your nose. And I remember reading that you collapsed just after the filming, and the news didn't surprise me none."

"I was doing too much junk," Thomas said. "I'm clean now." Except for the beer he held in his hand. Except for the pain pills he tried to ignore in his cabinet. He was cleaned off the coke. He no longer smoked pot. He didn't mix his drugs.

"No," Hargrave said. "It was more than that. It was as if you set the tiger free. I see no evidence of it, even now. The last time I saw that restless energy was the night you mutilated that bird."

Thomas felt rooted to his chair. He could barely remember those days leading up to the collapse. And when he had awakened in the clinic, he'd felt diminished, as if he had lost something. The doctors said the feeling of loss was normal—he was losing his crutch—but it never felt normal. It always felt as if he had lost a part of himself. He shook the feeling away and stood up. "You've been a lot of help."

Hargrave watched him from the floor. "You don't look like I helped you."

"I still don't know the shape of the puzzle," Thomas said. "But the pieces are clearer."

"You're scared."

"Damn straight I'm scared," Thomas said. "There's a lot I don't remember. Then you come up with this bird thing. And then there's the fact that the girl died while I was asleep, like Heather."

"You didn't kill Lisa Wilson."

Thomas looked at Hargrave for a moment, before the name sunk in. Lisa Wilson. The woman who had died in his house. The one whose murder had spooked the realtor.

"And you didn't kill that little girl who died before her."

Thomas leaned on a crutch. "I thought you didn't like me."

"I don't want you involved with Jillian. She doesn't need someone like you. She needs someone who'll care about her, help her become the best person she can be. She doesn't need a selfish, egotistical man like you."

Thomas let himself sink back into the chair. "But you don't think I killed anyone."

"You do." Hargrave was staring at him. "You think you killed them."

"I don't know," Thomas said, grabbing for his beer. "It worries me that I can't remember."

31

Pounding, fierce pounding on the door. Thomas's mouth tasted like cotton. He groaned and tried to roll over but his cast got in the way.

The pounding continued. It was uneven, ragged, not like a shutter banging, but like someone was beating on something. His dad, beating on his sister. Thomas's head throbbed. He wished the sound would go away.

Outside, the roar of the ocean blended with the pounding. Ocean. Pounding. Someone was being beaten to death. Heather was being beaten to death downstairs.

Thomas sat up. He was in a hotel room. The television sat like a large ghost over in the corner, the bed next to him was empty, and in the thin darkness, he could see his own movements reflected in the mirror above the dresser.

The pounding hadn't stopped. Someone was at his door. "What?" he yelled. He had a headache the size of Los Angeles. How many beers had he had with Hargrave? Four? Five? He hadn't left until nearly midnight when the old man staggered to bed. Thomas didn't remember the drive home.

"Open the goddamn door." Alicia. He sighed. He had to talk to the little bitch, but not this morning, not when he was feeling like this.

"Can't it wait?"

"No. Open the goddamn door."

"Give me a second." Thomas reached for his robe. He swung his legs out of bed, put on the robe, grabbed his crutches, and went to the door. His leg ached almost as bad as his head. He pulled the door open. Thick, dazzling sunshine burst into the room.

"What happened to you?"

"Four beers too many." He squinted at her. Her hair was tousled, her clothing looked as if it had been slept in, and deep, dark circles ran under her eyes. "What do you want?"

"I came to see Jillian."

"Jillian is not here."

"Bullshit." Alicia pushed past him and into the room. Thomas left the door open, but watched her.

His clothes were strewn all over the floor in the order that he had taken them off. He had been more than tipsy last night. He had been drunk. He hadn't had alcohol hit him that hard in years. But then he hadn't had much to drink in years.

Alicia scanned the bedroom, then went into the little alcove leading into the bathroom. She pushed open the bathroom door. "Where is she?"

Thomas shrugged. "I haven't talked to her today."

"She didn't come home last night."

Thomas went back to bed and lay down. The spot he had left was still warm. Laying down didn't help the queasy feeling at the base of his stomach. "She's a big girl. She can stay out all night if she wants."

"She's never done that before."

"But you have." Thomas put an arm over his eyes to shut out the light. "Go away, all right, Alicia?"

"I want to know where Jillian is."

He sighed and propped himself up on one elbow. "Why the hell are you so worried? She was working on a story last night. She said she had a midnight deadline. Maybe she found something and kept working through the night."

"That's not like her," Alicia said. "She would have called."

Finally the worry in the girl's voice reached him. "You haven't heard from Jillian since when?"

"Since that story was on *All Things Considered* last night. Since she talked to you." The "you" was bitter and Thomas remembered why he had wanted to talk with Alicia.

"I don't see why that's cause to worry," he said.

"She hasn't been at the newspaper office. Her car isn't anywhere that I can find around town. Jillian doesn't just disappear. She calls, she's real careful of me. She lets me know what's going on."

"That's more than you do for her." Thomas sat up. He had to take some antacid. "You really don't see anyone past yourself, do you, Alicia? Jillian forgets to call you once and you assume it's a major emergency. You don't think about how she'll feel when you're gone all night. Or what she would think if I told her about the notes you sent me."

Alicia froze. "Notes?"

"Don't play stupid," Thomas said. He got off the bed and went to his suitcase. There, in the little side pouch, was a packet of antacid and a box of aspirin. He wondered how long it had been in there, and then decided that he didn't care. "The girls sitting on my porch that last time saw you. Hell, I heard you talking with them. I should have figured it out from the start. You're really jealous of the time I spend with Jillian, aren't you?"

"She's in love with you."

"Are you saying that I'm not in love with her?"

Alicia dug her hands deep into the pocket of her jacket. "I'm saying that you're going to hurt her."

"No." Thomas took out one antacid and clutched it in the palm of his hand. "You're afraid that she's going to hurt you. Something happens with me and little Alicia is out of the picture, right?"

"No," Alicia said, but her chin was trembling. The light from the door fell on her, making her look sallow and tired. "Jillian loves me."

"Yes, Jillian loves you. She loves you more than you realize. Enough to open her home to you, enough to care for you, enough to try to get help for you. She's giving up a lot just for you and she's worrying enough to get an ulcer, but you don't really care about her. Jillian is just a safe place for you to be. You never see her as another person. If I spend time with Jillian, that takes her away from you. If I fall in love with Jillian, there's a chance that I'll take her back to L.A. with me. And then what happens to Alicia? You automatically assume that you would get left behind."

"Wouldn't I?" She took a step closer to him and he could see how thin she was. Her skin stretched over her cheekbones, carving out the hollows into her teeth. "You hate me."

"You never tried to be likeable. Why should I care about someone who insults me all the time? The first words you said to me were rude and you haven't gotten any better."

"See?" Her voice broke over the word. "You would leave me behind."

"No," he said softly. "I wouldn't. In case you hadn't noticed, I've been doing my best to be nice to you."

A tear ran down Alicia's cheek. The teardrop caught and reflected the light as it traced its way to her chin. But she didn't move. Her stare was still defiant, her lips pursed tightly together. Thomas found himself admiring her determination.

"Let me take this antacid and then we'll talk," he said. "Turn on a light and close the door."

He went into the bathroom. Behind him, he heard a light click on. He looked in the bathroom mirror. His skin was pasty and his eyes bloodshot. He looked as bad as he felt. He took the antacid and dry-swallowed an aspirin, then he threw on a pair of blue jeans and a sweatshirt and came back out into the main room.

Alicia was sitting on a chair near the window. She had pulled back the curtains, letting more light into the room. The ocean was wide and blue, with large whitecapped waves rolling in. A half dozen people were playing on the beach.

Thomas ran his hand through his hair. It felt matted and clumped. He took a deep breath. His stomach was settling down, but he needed some food. "I'm calling room service," he said. "You want anything?"

Alicia shook her head.

Thomas dialed, ordered some toast and weak tea, and hung up. Alicia had drawn her knees to her chest and was staring out the window. He went to the chair across from her, sat down, and stretched out his legs. An itch was building inside his cast. He rubbed the hard plaster top. "My life is a fairy tale," he said. Alicia swung her head around and looked at him. She rested her chin on her knees, keeping her expression impassive. "I go in front of cameras, do a glamorous job, and get paid a lot of money for it. Most people admire me, some idolize me. I have it made, right?"

She didn't say anything, just watched him with those cold, gray eyes.

"When I was twelve," he said, "my father was taken out of our home for molesting my sister. He was doing some pretty awful things to get removed because they didn't normally do that in the early 1960s. They sent me and my sister to a foster home. One day, he showed up—and beat her to death. I called the cops, but didn't do anything else. The state put him in jail, and kept me away from my mom until I was eighteen."

Thomas rubbed a hand over his face. His skin

felt oily. The words were no easier to say now than they had been before. The difference was that the memory was coming back. The words felt like the truth. "I moved back in with her when I was eighteen. Then we had a fight and I left. I never came back, not even when I heard that she was dying of cancer. I was too busy, focusing on my career, on school, on myself."

"Am I supposed to care?" Alicia asked.

"No," Thomas said. A knock sounded on the door. He got up and opened it. The room service waiter came in, set the tray on the table in front of Alicia, and handed Thomas the bill. Thomas added a tip and signed the paper, sending the boy away. Thomas sat back down, poured himself some tea, and took a sip. The liquid tasted good against his parched throat.

"If I'm not supposed to care," Alicia said, "then why did you tell me?"

"Because I thought maybe you would understand." He took a bit of toast. The butter was thick on the surface and dripped onto his fingers.

"Understand what?" Alicia sounded annoyed.

"That we're very similar. I'm just older. That's why I recognize you—and why you probably understand me better than Jillian does. We can call a truce for as long as I'm here, as long as I'm with Jillian, or we can keep fighting and ripping each other apart."

He ate a few more bites of the toast and pushed the plate aside. Then he took another sip of tea.

"Nobody got murdered in my family," Alicia said.

The words sent a sharp pain through Thomas. "No," he said. "But someone's doing a damn fine job of committing suicide."

Alicia flushed. She ripped off a piece of toast, and played with it. "How long are you going to be with Jillian?"

"I don't know," Thomas said.

"So you are going to hurt her."

Thomas set the teacup down and looked at the girl across from him. Her hair had fallen across her face. "Probably," he said. "That's part of the risk of loving someone."

Alicia stood up. "I want to find Jillian. I don't care about all of this shit."

Thomas sighed. "I don't think Jillian is missing. I think she probably fell asleep after she finished last night and will call you when she wakes up. You're probably better off at home, waiting for her call."

"I can't sit around there," Alicia said. "I tried tracking her down. I went to the newspaper office, but no one had seen her. She hasn't been to the radio station since yesterday afternoon. I don't know what she had planned last night—"

"She went to see my housekeeper, Carolyn, and then she was going to file her story."

"Maybe Carolyn knows where she is," Alicia said.

Thomas sighed. The least he could do was call since Alicia was so worried. After that, he would take Alicia home. They would probably find Jillian asleep on the couch.

He moved over to the bed and dialed Carolyn's number. Her son Ken answered.

"Ken, this is Thomas Stanton. Is your mother there?"

"No, Mr. Stanton." Ken sounded confused. "I thought she was with you."

"I haven't seen her." Thomas's heart suddenly lurched. "She didn't go over to the house, did she?"

"Yeah. She and that reporter lady last night. When they didn't come back, I thought they decided to stay with you."

"I haven't been near the house," Thomas said. "I stayed at the Shilo last night."

Alicia had pulled up next to him. "What's going on?" she whispered.

He waved his hand to quiet her.

"The reporter lady wanted to see it again, so Mom took her over there. They left about nine o'clock. Mom wasn't real willing to go. She said you didn't want her to, but the lady said it would be okay with two of them. And they haven't come back. I thought they would, too, because that reporter drove. Mom left her car here. What's going on, Mr. Stanton?"

"I don't know," Thomas said. His breath was catching in his throat. "But I think I'll go home and see."

"You want me to meet you there?"

"No," Thomas said. "I'll call you. You stick by the phone in case your mom calls or comes in or something."

"What do you think has happened?" Ken asked.

"Probably nothing," Thomas said. "I'll call you soon." He hung up.

Alicia's eyes had grown wide in her face. "Something's happened."

He couldn't lie to her. The panic filling his body was palpable. "Jillian and Carolyn went over to the house and they haven't come back."

"Great." Alicia said. "And I've been sitting here watching you eat breakfast."

Thomas didn't say anything. He felt just as appalled at his own delay as she was. He put a shoe on his good foot and grabbed his crutches. "Come on," he said. "I'm taking you home and then I'm going down to the house."

"I'm not going to wait by the goddamn phone," Alicia said. "I'm going with you."

Thomas looked at her. Her chin jutted forward in determination. "A girl was murdered there yesterday, Alicia."

He left the rest of the sentence unspoken, but Alicia understood it. Tears lined the rims of her eyes, but none trailed down her cheeks. "I know," she said. "That's why I don't want to stay home."

"It would be better if you did."

"Better for who? You? I'd feel trapped and useless. I want to go with you."

"No." Thomas opened the door. Alicia led the way out, then stopped at the edge of the parking lot.

"If you don't let me," she said. "I'll find my own way there."

He stared at her. She would. She would walk or hitch a ride or something. And chances were she would end up there alone. Thomas's headache returned, strong and piercing. "All right," he said.

He got into the truck. Alicia climbed in the other side. She put her elbow on the armrest and propped her chin on her fist, ignoring him. Her other hand was clenched on her lap. The knuckles were turning white.

Thomas's breakfast turned over and over in his stomach. What could Jillian have been thinking of? She knew about that beach, how dangerous it was. She shouldn't have gone. But then, she did go with Carolyn. Perhaps with two, they would be all right. Besides, he had been with Hargrave last night, getting drunk.

But he didn't remember the drive home . . .

Thomas didn't want to think about it.

He pulled out of the parking lot, his tires squealing against the pavement. He drove up the windy, curvy road to 101. He couldn't remember the back route to the house and he didn't want to risk getting lost.

The traffic on the highway was thick. Too thick. Jesus. For once, couldn't the traffic thin? It was an emergency. He'd seen ambulances stuck in this mess. What happened if someone died because of the traffic. If Jillian died . . . ?

Thomas couldn't see any breaks at all. He waited for maybe a minute, then hit his horn and turned out in front of a BMW. The BMW honked at him, but Thomas ignored it. Alicia glanced at him, her face even paler than before.

"I didn't think you drove all those stunts yourself," she said.

"I didn't," Thomas replied. But he felt the need to drive them now. He passed three cars on the shoulder, sending gravel flying. Then, as they rounded a curve, the shoulder ended. He slid back in front of a Ford Pinto. The Pinto's brakes squealed. Thomas kept driving. Alicia reached behind her, grabbed her seat belt, and clicked it on. She clamped both hands in her lap and stared straight ahead.

The traffic hovered around fifty-five. Thomas rode the bumper of the car in front of him, turning toward the right side of the road every time he thought he saw another shoulder beginning. But nothing was long enough for him. Too many curves, too many trees jutting out. He would overturn the truck and where would that get Jillian?

Finally the road to his house appeared. He turned on it and gunned the truck forward. Sure enough, Jillian's car sat in his driveway. Tension danced in Thomas's stomach.

"She's here," Alicia said, but there was no joy in her voice. Only a reflection of the tension that Thomas felt.

Thomas's hands had turned cold. He pulled up beside Jillian's car and shut off the truck. Alicia unclicked her seat belt, but he grabbed her hand. Her palms were clammy.

"Let me," he said.

He got out, grabbed his crutches, and made his way slowly across the driveway. The first spot of blood appeared upon the gravel. The blood stain grew, nearly covering the lower step, trailing up the porch as if someone had been dragged.

Thomas swallowed. The front door stood ajar. He mounted the stairs, carefully avoiding the blood, and pushed the door open with his crutch.

The house was a wreck. Furniture overturned and smashed. Flowers strewn across the floor. Dishes broken. The curtains hung at strange angles and it appeared as if the large picture window had shattered. He stepped inside. The place smelled of iron, rust, violence, and fear. Little shivers were running along his arms. One of his movie posters tilted crazily and the other lay facedown on the floor.

Blood covered everything—the floor, the couch, the table. Thomas felt his crutches slip beneath him as he walked.

"Jesus."

He turned. Alicia had followed him inside. Her mouth was slightly open and she clung to the doorway.

"I thought I told you to wait."

"I couldn't," she said. Her voice sounded hollow. "Do you see her?"

Thomas shook his head. He hadn't seen anyone so far. "Don't touch anything." The words came out of his mouth as if they had been scripted for him.

He stepped further into the living room. A foot stuck out from under the coffee table. He bent over, balancing his crutches precariously, his gaze following the foot upward to the tattered clothing, the shredded skin.

"Holy Christ," he whispered. "Jillian."

"You found Jillian?" Alicia's voice echoed strangely in that dilapidated house.

"I don't know." Thomas said. He kept staring at the leg, torn almost beyond recognition, blood matted against it, muscles showing, and, here and there, little spots of white. Through the corner of his eye, he saw Alicia step forward. "Stay there."

She stopped. He leaned further.

For a moment, he saw his sister, as his father had left her, broken on the living room floor, blood everywhere. The memory was as clear as the room.

He took a deep breath. He couldn't get lost in the memory now. He had to stay here.

The body was crouched in a modified fetal position, the head tucked between the arms as if to protect it. He recognized the wedding band on the left hand, the short square fingernails. Carolyn. His stomach heaved at the violence he saw before him and he had to fight to keep from being sick.

"It's not Jillian," he said.

"Then where the hell is she?" Alicia's voice was flat, even, although her words were charged. It was as if her emotional side had been shut off, much as Thomas felt. He knew that if he allowed himself to feel anything, he would run, screaming, from the house.

The phone rang. He straightened quickly and nearly fell over. He put a crutch behind himself to regain his balance and the crutch slipped in blood. For a single moment, he slid backward, then Alicia put a hand under him and kept him from falling She kept her hand on his arm after he had his balance back. He looked at her. She was staring at Carolyn.

The phone rang again. It had to be his attorney.

"We have to find Jilly," Alicia said.

Thomas nodded. He suspected that they would find Jillian in much the same situation, probably upstairs or in the kitchen. He took a deep breath. "Let's look," he said.

The phone's ring seemed alien in the bloody house. He glanced at the table. The phone still sat there, untouched except for a few spots of blood along the receiver. He couldn't bring himself to answer it. Instead, he turned around and headed for the kitchen.

The blood stopped in here, except for a red handprint on the refrigerator and another on the stove. The cupboards stood open and everything on the counter had been swept to the floor. It looked as if someone had been trying to get away or had been dragged and had been holding on to things in order to break free. Thomas pushed at a pan with his crutch and then saw the lighthouse mug. It lay on top of the mess as if it had been carefully placed there. He remembered seeing it in Heather's hands so many years ago, shortly after he had first bought it. It had survived her and now, Carolyn.

Jesus, Carolyn. He had known that she was in trouble ever since she had touched those birds. But Jillian. Jillian was safe, wasn't she? She hadn't done anything wrong.

Except to come back here last night with Carolyn. He couldn't blame them. He would have come too, thinking that two of them were enough. Here he was with Alicia. But it was broad daylight. And that made a difference, didn't it?

"Alicia?"

"Yeah?" Her voice sounded muffled, but it relieved him to hear it. He left the kitchen. She came back from the bathroom. "Find anything?" she asked.

He shook his head. "Let's keep close, okay?"

"Yeah." She stopped next to the stairs and looked up. "Except one of us has to look up there." She glanced at Thomas's leg. "I'll go if you stay right here."

"I won't move," he said.

The blood on the stairs seemed to run only to the first landing. Alicia walked up the sides near the banister, but Thomas could see the prints her tennis shoes left. The stairs creaked beneath her slight weight and as she disappeared from sight, he listened to each creak as it marked her progress. Then he heard a whistle, ever so slight, as if she were exhaling.

"What?"

"Nothing's been touched up here for a long time," Alicia called down. "But through the window, it looks as if something has been dragged across the grass."

Thomas felt the nausea return. He remembered the cloaked figure running across the beach in the moonlight, the banging of the shutters, and walking down those creaking stairs himself to find Heather's sheets crumpled at the edge of the couch. "Come down, then," he said.

The creaking grew closer. Alicia rounded the corner. The bottom part of her jeans were streaked with blood and she kept rubbing her hands together.

"We have to check the basement too," Thomas said.

"But what about the grass?"

"Next." He led her to the basement door. It was shut. There was no blood on the floor nearby. He opened the door and clicked on the light. A damp, musty odor eased up from below.

From the top of the stairs, the basement looked empty and untouched. Alicia walked down five steps, clinging to the banister with both hands as she walked. She leaned over the banister and brushed at a cobweb with her right hand. "I can't see anything," she said.

The phone rang again. The shrill sound echoed in the house, sounding almost like a scream. Thomas's heart was pounding too fast. "Okay," he said. "Come on up."

Alicia ran up the stairs and stopped beside him as the phone rang again. "You going to get that?"

"No," he said. He couldn't imagine himself making polite conversation with a woman he had never met while Carolyn's body was inches away from his feet. "But I think I will use the phone."

He had to call the police. And then he was going to follow that trail in the grass. He didn't care how much it hurt his leg. They had already wasted too much time—him for not listening to Alicia and Alicia for waiting until midmorning to get him. His brain felt fuzzy and his nerves too tight. His headache was still there, gnawing at the back of his skull.

He made his way back into the living room, stepping over things and testing his balance before moving too far forward. When he reached the phone, he unbuttoned the cuff of his shirt, slid his hand inside it, and grabbed the receiver. He heard a dial tone. The person who had been on the other end was gone. He didn't want to touch his fingers to the blood. He pretended his forefinger was a pencil and pushed 911.

"Nine-one-one, may I help you?" The female voice on the other end was dispassionate and unconcerned. Thomas almost felt as if he were calling a doctor's office. The entire morning was taking on an air of unreality. He almost laughed at the banality of it all.

"Nine-one-one. Is there someone there?"

"Yes." His voice squeaked out. Funny that it could work with Alicia and not operate on the phone. But he didn't know what to say. It all sounded so melodramatic, so trite, and yet it was there, smeared in front of him in blood dried brown. "There's been a murder."

Alicia was standing by the kitchen door, her hands pressed against her stomach. Thomas knew how she felt. He felt as if he were floating.

"Where, sir?" He could tell from the edge in the voice on the other end that she had asked the question twice.

He gave her the address. "It's a mess," he said. "And Jillian is missing."

"Jillian?"

"Jillian Maxwell. The reporter. She was here too. Her car is still here, but she's gone. We've looked everywhere."

"We?"

"Her sister Alicia and I. Please send the police out here and maybe an ambulance. We're going down on the beach to look for Jillian."

He hung up the phone and suddenly couldn't remember most of the conversation. Alicia was staring at the floor. "Did I give them the address?" he asked.

"Yeah." She continued to stare in front of her. Thomas came back toward the kitchen, carefully averting his gaze from Carolyn's body. Then he saw what Alicia was staring at. Jillian's tape recorder lay on top of some broken glass. The tape deck was open and smashed, the cassette beside it, with the tape pulled out. The microphone was only a few feet away, its cord gone.

Thomas swallowed heavily. As if the car weren't proof enough that Jillian had been here. He reached across his crutch and grabbed Alicia's arm and shook her a little. Her eyes were glassy and the pupils wide. She moved as if she were under water. He followed her onto the porch.

The sunshine looked trivial and fake. It shone off the roof of the cars, almost dazzling him. The intense brightness had the quality of television lights, illuminating everything with a glow that obscured rather than clarified.

"We haven't checked the porch," Alicia said.

It took the words a moment to sink in, as if Thomas were in the middle of a dream. He had to wake up. If Jillian was alive somewhere, he had to have energy and clarity to find her. "I'll look this time," he said.

He walked along the length of the porch, past the place where he had found the gull bodies, past the place that the sandpiper bodies had been stored. On the part of the porch overlooking the ocean, he stopped. The grass had been flattened as if something were dragged, long enough ago, however, so that most of the blades were springing back. The tide had already come in once and obscured all but the highest prints on the beach.

None of this looked familiar. He hadn't done this. He couldn't have done this.

He would have remembered.

He continued walking, his crutches and his feet beating out a strange rhythm against the wood. He noted that the glass on the picture window had been broken outward, but other than the stairs leading up from the driveway, he saw no more blood.

"She's not here," he said when he reached Alicia.

She took a deep breath and glanced at the grass. "Okay," she said.

Then he realized that she meant to go alone. "I'm coming with you," he said.

She snorted, sounding, for a moment, like the old Alicia. "It's a fucking beach."

"I don't care," he said. "You're not going by yourself and I don't want to wait for the cops any more than you do."

"You may as well leave them here then," sh

said, referring to the crutches. "They'll be damn near useless in sand."

"But they're the only weapons we have."

She looked up at him, surprise registering on her too-thin features. He had finally gotten through her shock and dreamlike reaction. "Oh, Christ, Thomas, maybe we should wait."

"I can't," he said. Not after seeing Carolyn. Not after seeing all that blood and the destroyed tape recorder. "Come on."

He went down the stairs, taking extra care not to slip. When he reached the gravel, he followed the drops of blood to the grass. At the edge of the grass, the blood stopped. Alicia was hugging close to his side.

"It doesn't look as if anyone was bleeding," he said, careful not to refer to Jillian. "It looks more like the blood was dripping off something else."

The knife maybe. Had he held it to her back as he led her across the driveway? No, he had dragged her. That was clear from the grass. So she was unconscious, but not bleeding. He had wanted her alive at least for a while. That was a good sign.

Thomas stepped onto the grass. It was marshy, which meant that the trail could have been older than he had originally thought. He kept staring at the blades, hoping to find something, anything that would lead him to Jillian. But so far, there was nothing except balding grass and mud.

He walked to the sand, the sand that the ocean hadn't touched in ages, and there he stopped. There, he saw occasional clear footprints, followed by another, larger print. Someone had most certainly been dragged. He could see the flat mark of the body itself, grooved by the imprints of two heels. On each side of the large print were eight thin trails, probably left by fingers brushing against the sand.

Alicia jumped beside the print, careful not to mar it. "Let's go," she said.

Thomas climbed down carefully. His crutches sank in the sand and his cast felt unwieldy. This was going to be more difficult than he had thought. It took most of the strength in his arms to pull him forward.

Alicia walked on ahead a little ways. The prints ended at the waterline in front of a large rock. She walked out in front of it and stood in the damp sand. "It continues on the other side," she said.

Thomas followed her lead. Farther down the beach, the ocean pounded against the sand. Misty drops bit into his skin. What good could he do if they did stumble on Jillian? Club the cloaked figure with his crutch? He would be so winded and he was moving so awkwardly that the cloaked figure could carry both Jillian and Alicia off before Thomas could do anything.

"Aren't there sea caves that way?" Thomas asked.

Alicia looked at him. "Not really. They're just called sea caves. They're more like jutted-out openings in the rocks."

"That's where they found Heather," Thomas said.

"Jillian couldn't have been there during high tide," Alicia said. "It would have killed her. The way the waves come in, smashing against all that rock.''

It would have killed her. If she wasn't dead already. Thomas trudged to the wet sand and was surprised to find that it was easier to maneuver on.

The breeze off the ocean ruffled his hair. The water rushed against the sand, creeping up near his feet almost as if it were an alive thing. The beach was silent. No gulls flew overhead, no sandpipers ran with the waves. He gazed down near his feet and didn't even see any evidence of creatures living in the sand. On the other side of the rock, a dead fish lay, its insides torn away. He turned his face, the nausea rising again. Poor Carolyn. He had really grown to care about her. And to die that way, bleeding everywhere, almost no skin left. What had happened in that house? How had Jillian survived? And why couldn't both women have worked to save each other?

His shoulders ached. He moved the crutches forward, felt them sink, and then swung his feet forward, balancing on his legs as he pried the crutches free. Alicia wanted to move faster, he could tell, but she said nothing. She never walked more than a foot or two ahead of him.

He had never seen this part of the beach. Rocks hugged the sand toward the east, the ocean framed it on the west. If the tides came up too high, he and Alicia would be trapped against a mountain of rock. They weren't following any path now, except for an occasional print in a patch of dry sand. Up ahead, the beach sloped upward, becoming rocklike.

"The sea caves are over there," Alicia said, pointing in front of them. Thomas squinted. He thought he could see some openings in the rock. Then he saw a fountain of water rise in the air like a geyser.

"What's that?" he asked.

Alicia took a deep breath. "That's part of the sea caves too. It's like Depoe Bay. The rock has holes through it that the sea forces its way through. It builds up pressure and sends water flying. We're safe at the low tide if we don't go down to the main area, but during high tide, this whole part of the beach is flooded and the waves do their pressure number on the rocks over there."

Thomas nodded. He understood now what Alicia meant by Jillian being unable to survive during high tide. Suddenly he wondered if they would find Jillian at all or if, like Heather, she would disappear for years.

His throat was dry. The ache had crept down into the muscles of his back. He had been stupid not to keep in shape. Then, at least, he could have used some built-up strength and endurance to push forward. He was feeling winded and frightened. Alicia looked determined. The wind was blowing her hair too and occasionally she would reach up and move a strand that had caught against her lips. Her arms were so thin, though, he could see the bones, and her skin appeared almost translucent.

His crutches made little squishing sounds in the sand. He concentrated on the sound; it helped him to move forward. The rocks were farther away than they seemed. The sky and ocean created an optical illusion of nearness. Either that or this was a dream and the beach kept stretching forward, growing longer with every step that he took.

"Jesus," Alicia said. She pointed. Up on top of the rocks, a figure stood, a black cape billowing out behind him. He was looking away from them, his hands clasped behind his back. Thomas looked for a place to crouch down, so that they wouldn't be seen, but he could find nothing. The rock wall to their left was sheer—most of the juts and fallen rocks were in front of them. Alicia moved as close to the wall as she could, but kept staring at the cloaked man. "I don't see Jillian," she said.

"She's got to be there," Thomas whispered back. He didn't know how well voices carried. He doubted that they could be heard over the roar of the ocean.

Almost as if he heard Thomas's thoughts, the cloaked figure turned in their direction. Sunlight fell across the figure's face, and Thomas was looking at a reflection. Only better. The Thomas Stanton that the makeup people and the ad people, with their paints and airbrushes, created to heighten women's fantasies. It was as if the cloaked figure were the real Thomas Stanton—the one he had worked for decades to create—and Thomas himself the imposter.

"Christ," Alicia said, her voice trembling. The cloaked Thomas looked away. Thomas could feel relief running through his limbs, making them rubbery. The cloaked Thomas hadn't seen them after all.

The cloaked Thomas turned around and headed back toward the rock wall. He appeared to go inside of it, but Thomas realized he must have entered a sea cave. "At least we know where Jillian is," he said.

"Yeah." Alicia had grabbed his arm. Her fingers felt like ice. "Th-they weren't kidding, when they said he looked like you."

Thomas glanced at her. Her face had grown even paler. He frowned.

"Who is he, Thomas?"

Thomas shook his head. His heart was pounding against his chest. "I don't know," he said. But that wasn't true. He did know, on some subconscious level. The shock of recognition had gone deeper than that of seeing his own face on someone else.

He swallowed. His mouth tasted of sand. He didn't have time to figure this out. He had to get to Jillian.

As if it would do any good. The cloaked Thomas had to be strong, to kill Carolyn that way.

The way his father had killed his sister.

Thomas closed his eyes, just for a moment. His breath was coming harshly now. Why would someone go to such lengths to imitate him? To destroy him? Even down to the repetition of the murder.

He opened his eyes again. Alicia was staring at him, her mouth a thin line. He could leave, let the police do the work. He glanced behind them. Their tracks seemed to go on for miles. He would have to force Alicia to turn back with him and then he would have to wait while the police made the same trek across the sand. He had made that mistake once before.

And his sister had died.

He had come this far. He would find Jillian and hope that, when he needed them, the cops would play cavalry and arrive.

The beach had sloped upward. Thomas could feel it in the additional strain on his arms and back. He kept moving, pulling. Jillian had to be alive. Somehow they would have to help her.

Off in the distance, he thought he heard sirens. He listened closely, but the roar of the ocean drowned out most of the sound. The sirens could be just wishful thinking. He and Alicia had walked so far down the beach that they probably wouldn't know when the police arrived at the house. Thomas prayed that Tiger looked at everything with clear vision and saw the drag marks across the grass, the prints in the sand, and Thomas's crutch prints off to the side. That should lead the police right to them.

The sand was growing harder, firmer. Thomas looked down. The sand had actually blown over the rocky surface. They were on the last incline toward the top of the rock barrier. Thomas's crutches slipped in the sand. He shivered a little. More treachery. The rocks up ahead had cracks and crevices large enough to catch the bottom of his crutch and send him plunging forward. In a brief instance of memory, he felt himself sliding down the rock face in Depoe Bay, arms and legs thrashing, trying to reach anything to break his fall. His heart was pounding harder. He couldn't fall again. Anything but that.

Alicia's grip tightened on his arm. "What are we going to do?" she asked.

Thomas looked at her. She expected him to have a plan. Christ. People wrote his scripts for him. He had never had to think for himself before. Harrison Ford had never made up the escapes in the Indiana Jones movies any more than Richard Dean Anderson made up the wacky solutions to the McGyver series. Thomas wasn't Anthony Short. It was amazing he had been able to track Jillian this far. "We have to find her," he said as if that were an answer. It was important at this point that Alicia believe they could save Jillian. Any fear would destroy them both.

They reached the top of the rock face and Thomas found himself looking down onto another, lower beach. It was about as far down as the fall he had survived in Depoe Bay. He shuddered, feeling fragile and precarious on the rock face.

They had been climbing steadily on a sloping incline for some ways. The beach ahead of and below him was probably at the same level as the beach in front of his house. Only the beach below was different.

It too was a sheltered beach. Rocks protected it from all human contact. A large mountainous rock grew to the west and straight across from Thomas, albeit a few miles away, jutted down into the sea. Along the ocean, more rocks rose, making entry into this little cove impossible for ships of any size. The only way to the beach was the way they had

just come, and even that was treacherous when
the tide came rolling in. An agile person, like Alicia, could climb to the beach below, but the
chances of getting out were slim. As Thomas
watched, waves rolled in, large waves covered
with foaming white power. They squeezed through
two huge rocks sitting like guardians at the mouth
of a forked hole growing into the rocks. He could
see the water weave its way through and suddenly,
it spouted out from three different openings high
upon the beach. Foam floated through the air like
snow and Thomas had to wipe some of it from his
face. The water boomed as it hit. Thomas suddenly
felt very small, very weak, and very naked.

He looked over in the direction that the cloaked
Thomas had disappeared. The rocks were dry, but
had large tide pools in them, proving that the water did travel this high at certain times. In the rock
wall, three openings showed themselves. Jillian
had to be up there. He took a deep breath. He had
come this far. If he stayed away from the edge, he
would be all right.

"Come on," he said.

The path to the caves was a good three or four
feet above where he and Alicia were standing now.
Alicia climbed the rocks easily, ignoring what appeared to be a man-made staircase circling up the
rock. Thomas took a deep breath and pushed himself forward. His left crutch slipped and fell into a
tide pool, splashing water all over him. He almost
screamed, thinking he was closer to the edge than
he was. His cast hit the rock and sent a shivering
pain through him.

He pulled the crutch out of the tide pool and started up the stairs. As he walked he realized that they weren't man-made at all, but merely part of the rock formation. The flat stones wiggled beneath his weight. He had to force himself to concentrate on the path in front of him. All he could think of was falling. In his imagination, he saw himself tumbling, tumbling, the rocks sliding with him as he curled himself up into a ball to avoid impact. Only this time he wouldn't be able to curl. His leg would jut forward and hit the rocks first. Alicia waited at the top, her hand out to help him, as if she could prevent his fall.

Finally he stood beside her. His leg ached and he wondered if he had done something to injure it further. He looked down and saw a thin crack running up the side of the cast.

The water boomed below as it hit against the rocks. Spray doused him, cooling him after his long trek upward. A movement from the sea cave caught his eye. The cloaked Thomas emerged and placed his hands on his hips. He was facing them; the cape blowing behind him, like it had behind Thomas on the Short set. A smile curved the cloaked Thomas's lips. He almost seemed to be beckoning them.

"Jesus," Alicia said. "There's Jilly."

Thomas looked, then finally saw her, sprawled in front of the sea cave. Dried blood streaked the side of her face and matted half of her hair. The wind blew her ripped shirt back against her body. Her jeans were shredded and covered with sand. Her white tennis shoes were caked and nearly brown. Her hands were covered with blood and then he realized that she must have lost most of her nails when she was dragged across the sand.

She was dead. They were too late, and she was dead.

"Jillian!" Alicia started to run forward, but Thomas grabbed her. His right crutch slipped from his armpit and clattered down the rock. She spun around, nearly making him lose his balance. He braced the other crutch and tried to hang onto her, but she shook him free.

She ran across the rocks. The cloaked Thomas moved back, away from Jillian. For a brief moment, Thomas thought that Alicia would be able to reach Jillian, when the cloaked Thomas pulled out a very long, very thin knife.

The blade reflected the sunlight. Thomas pushed himself forward, leaning awkwardly on his remaining crutch. Alicia had stopped. She was panting and she held out her hands.

"Come on, Jilly. Let's get out of here."

Jillian didn't move. She had only been brought up here as bait. Bait to lure Thomas, not Alicia. And Alicia was going to die.

"Alicia!" he called, to get her away from there. She turned and in that instance, the other Thomas grabbed her and pinned her hands behind her back. He moved her in front of Jillian. Thomas suddenly had a horrible feeling in the pit of his belly. It was just like his sister.

He pushed forward. Alicia struggled in the other Thomas's grasp. She kicked, and ducked and swung, all the time avoiding the knife. Beside them, Jillian's head came up once, then went right back down.

She was alive after all. She was alive. The thought gave him an extra burst of adrenaline. The other Thomas swung the knife and caught Alicia in the arm. She screamed and pulled away as Thomas stopped before his duplicate, braced himself, and swung his crutch like a club at the other Thomas's head. The crutch hit and shattered, sending splinters through Thomas's hand. Alicia used that moment to break away. The knife clattered against the rock. Thomas fell forward and grabbed it, feeling a stinging pain as his leg collided with the rock.

Thomas rolled in the direction of his twin. The other man kicked Thomas in the stomach and all the air left him. He was tired and the pain in his body was growing critical. As the cloaked man got closer, Thomas felt more and more energy leave him. The other Thomas was sapping his strength. Thomas looked up and saw himself—a part of himself he had lost on this beach the night he had come here with Suzette. The demon, Hargrave had called it. The tiger. The rage that had built inside him since he was a very small boy.

Alicia held her arm and rammed into the cloaked Thomas, making him lose his balance. At that moment, Jillian reached up and grabbed his foot. He stumbled.

Thomas could have attacked the other man then, but he didn't know how. If what he felt was true, then the other Thomas wasn't real—

Or was he? Was he as real as Thomas himself?

The cloaked man regained his balance. Thomas pushed himself to his feet, then realized he was at a disadvantage. The other man shared Thomas's physical skills—was probably stronger than Thomas right now.

The cloaked Thomas grabbed his shoulder as Alicia stood up. Thomas could feel the energy drain tingle through him, but he watched Alicia. She was about to ram the man again, but Thomas shook his head.

"Run!" he yelled. "Get help!"

Alicia turned and ran along the rock, passing Thomas closely. He could hear the breath whistling through her teeth, knew the kind of pain she was feeling. She glanced back once at Jillian, but Jillian raised a hand and waved her onward.

Thomas could barely breathe. He looked up into his own face, contorted by rage. Thomas held the knife, but the other Thomas held the anger. The power. He brought the knife up, but couldn't find the ability to plunge it into the other's body. The other Thomas smiled.

"You have no hope," he said in a voice made familiar by a thousand videotaped viewings.

Thomas felt drained. He could almost lean forward against the cloaked Thomas, but he didn't dare. Through the corner of his eye, he could see Alicia running down the beach, still clutching her arm to her stomach. Far away, he could see other movement—people winding around the rock.

The wind increased. It buffeted Thomas and he would have fallen if the other Thomas hadn't hung on. They stood there, staring at each other like long-lost lovers, neither complete without the other.

But Thomas was complete. He had felt complete. He was making up a fantasy to cope with the madness he faced, and this creature before him was a demented fan, trying to destroy everything Thomas had.

Either way, Thomas had created him. Either way, Thomas had unleashed this horror on the people he loved.

He wrenched his arms free, losing his grip on the knife, and stepped backward at the same time, dragging his bad leg with him. His balance was precarious. His arms swung like propellers, but he managed to right himself. The knife bounced against the rock, and with a twist fell to the beach below. Thomas watched it. He could have fallen like that.

The cloaked Thomas lunged for him. Thomas took another step backward and tripped over Jillian. And then he was falling, the nightmare loss of control sending all his muscles into hard spasms—the vertigo, the wrongness of it stretching out into forever. He landed on his back, feeling the air leave him with a painful squeezing against his lungs. He flung his arms out to find something to push himself up against and found himself clutching air. He turned and saw the beach below, the water pounding into the crevice. His back rested on the ground, but his shoulders were over the beach. He tried to push himself forward, but his double stood in the way. He offered Thomas his hand.

Thomas stared at the offered hand, unable to respond. This man was trying to save him. This man who had killed Carolyn. Who had nearly killed Jillian.

Who had killed Heather.

And all, somehow, because of him.

"Why do you want to save me?" Thomas asked.

"We're a pair," the other Thomas answered. "We can't survive without each other."

Thomas glanced out to sea, saw the waves gathering in one large mountain with rolling hills following. He needed strength. He willed it from his tired muscles. In his mind's eye, he could see Heather, matchstick-thin, sitting on his porch.

We can't survive without each other.

Through the legs of his twin, Jillian was watching him, her beautiful face covered with blood.

"You don't like that idea," the other Thomas said.

Thomas swallowed his fear back. He had to move quickly, before his need to survive took over. He took the other Thomas's hand, and pulled him down on top of his own body. Where their skins touched, Thomas felt an electricity. And then he understood. The other Thomas wanted all that was left of him.

Thomas grabbed his other half, and together they rolled over the precipice. The fall was an eternity, man clinging to man, fear passing between them like a current. Wind whistled past Thomas's face. He tried to turn, so that the other Thomas would take most of the fall, but as the ground loomed closer, he found his arms were empty.

His body felt heavier.

And the sense of something missing was gone.

Memories choked him:

His hands shredding Carolyn's skin—

Hating himself for the way he treated Heather. Hitting her on the set, his body splitting in two, until he watched himself slapping her. He had been smiling. He tried to stop himself, but his second self ran away—

And Heather, Heather on the beach, hours before he killed her, screaming "No! Please!" as he removed her clothes—

Foam flew up and flecked Thomas on the face. The cloak, empty now, tumbled past him and landed on the rocks. The ground rushed up toward him. The rocks were sharp, jagged. He couldn't be so lucky as to survive such a fall twice, and perhaps he shouldn't survive, with what he had inside him.

Behind him, he heard Jillian scream, "Thomas!"

He tucked his body into a ball and held his breath, praying that he would pass out before impact.

Then he remembered what he had learned in his first fall:

Balls bounce.

Thomas doesn't.

DISCOVER THE TRUE MEANING OF HORROR...